BY ANNE MCCAFFREY AND
ELIZABETH ANN SCARBOROUGH

Powers That Be
Power Lines
Power Play
Changelings
Maelstrom

MÆLSTROM

MÆLSTROM

BOOK TWO *of*
THE TWINS OF PETAYBEE

ANNE
McCAFFREY

ELIZABETH ANN
SCARBOROUGH

BALLANTINE BOOKS

NEW YORK

Copyright © 2006 by Anne McCaffrey and Elizabeth Ann Scarborough

Published in the United States by Del Rey Books, an imprint of The Random House Publishing Group, a division of Random House, Inc., New York.

DEL REY is a registered trademark and the Del Rey colophon is a trademark of Random House, Inc.

ISBN 978-0-345-47004-1

Printed in the United States of America on acid-free paper

www.delreybooks.com

2 4 6 8 9 7 5 3 1

First Edition

Book design by Simon M. Sullivan

THIS BOOK IS DEDICATED TO
DR. TONY AND JEANNETTE ROGSTADT, PHYSICIAN, VET TECH,
AND RESCUER OF MANY CRITTERS DOMESTIC AND WILD.

The authors would like to acknowledge the advice
and support of their editor, Shelly Shapiro.

MÆLSTROM

CHAPTER 1

WAVING GOOD-BYE TO their parents and friends, their beloved river and forests, to their home world, Petaybee, Murel and Ronan Shongili strapped themselves in for another launch into space.

So soon! It seemed they'd only arrived home and now it was time to go again.

It'll be great fun, sure it will, Ronan assured his twin sister in thought-talk. *We'll see new places, meet new people, make new friends—*

I'd have liked a bit more time with the old places and old friends nevertheless, Murel complained. *But here we are again. It feels as if we never left.* She looked around the lounge of the *Piaf,* a luxury liner much larger and more sophisticated than Kilcoole, the tiny village that was home. The lounge alone was as long as Kilcoole's main street and could have held eight of the village's largest building, the latchkay lodge, inside.

Except for that, Ronan said, with a meaningful nod at the one big difference in the lounge since their last trip.

Since they'd traveled from school back to Petaybee less than three short months before, the small saltwater tank had been replaced by an enormous one that dominated the lounge and dwarfed its occupants. Now the tank held a single Honu, the sentient sea turtle that was the sacred totem animal of their friend Ke-ola. The tank looked vast and empty despite the energetic game of tag between the Honu and Sky, the twins' river otter friend. On the return journey, if all went well, the tank would hold many more—and even larger—Honus traveling with their people to what would become their new Petaybean home.

During takeoff, the ship's owner, Marmion de Revers Algemeine, and Captain Johnny Green, its commander, remained on the bridge. Marmion's friendship had helped their family, their village, and their planet countless times over the years. The twins had known her all of their lives, and by now she knew their most important secret, as well as their father's. Many people on Kilcoole knew but very few outsiders. Johnny was not an outsider, since he'd been born on Petaybee. When the time had come for him to leave the Company Corps, he had chosen service with Marmie over life on Petaybee, but he was Petaybean all the same.

Ronan, Murel, and Ke-ola watched the liftoff from the lounge's viewport and the bank of screens that flanked it. Ke-ola was the reason for their current journey—and the reason Ronan and Murel were using thought-talk. They didn't want him to overhear their complaints and get the idea that they hadn't wanted to come.

The actual sight of Petaybee receding to a cold white and gray ball seemed no more real than its image on the screens. The cabin's pressure and gravity were so well maintained that the ship might have still been on the ground. They could not hear or smell or taste the passage, or feel it in the wind that was not there. They felt no sensation of lifting or moving.

The water in the tank didn't so much as slosh, but the Honu and Sky swam to the side to watch the departure. Then Sky tagged the Honu's shell and they began their game afresh.

The twins and Sky had become swimming friends before they were sent away to Marmie's space-station school. When they returned, Sky was waiting to help them find their missing father, even though Da had been lost at sea where river otters didn't ordinarily go. For their sake, the otter had even allowed himself to be transported in a helicopter, which was how he, as the first and only otter of any kind to inhabit Petaybee's skies, however briefly, had earned his name: Sky, the sky otter. Murel hoped that now that the little fellow was going into space he wouldn't want to change his name to Space. She'd just got used to calling him Sky.

As soon as the ship was free of Petaybee's gravity, the twins and Ke-ola unstrapped and raced to the tank to swim with the Honu and Sky. Ke-ola climbed the ladder to the top of the tank. The ladder had a staging platform on the top and was situated right beside the wide waterslide that ended in a shallow pool from which the water was recirculated into the tank. Sky and otter-kind in general loved to slide. Also, when it came time to remove the Honu from the pool, the slide would allow the tortoise to descend to the smaller pool without injury.

Murel clambered up the ladder behind Ke-ola and pulled off her clothes so that she wore only the harness holding the tiny bag containing her dry suit. A passing crew member would have seen a brief flash of white skin and dark hair before she dived into the water. Instantly she transformed into a silver-brown seal and streaked through the water after Ke-ola, Sky, and the Honu. A moment later they were joined by Ronan, also in seal form.

The water was saline to suit the Honu, but it didn't smell or taste quite right to the twins. No fish, for one thing. Still, it felt wonderful to be wet again. They dived, surfaced, splashed, tackled, were tackled, escaped, and dived again until Sky suddenly said, "River seals, look!"

He swam to the front of the tank where Marmie stood. She was saying something as she looked up toward the top of the tank.

Ke-ola, who had to go up for air more frequently than the others, was on the surface. He dived again, touched each of the twins, and pointed toward the top of the tank. Then with a pump of his arms and a thrust from his muscular brown legs, he shot upward.

Sky streaked past everyone and flung himself through the opening at the top of the tank that formed the lip of the waterslide. *Hah!* he cried. *Otters first!*

Ke-ola surfaced almost at once, followed by the twins. At the bottom of the slide they jumped onto the wet deck and shook themselves dry until they resumed human shape. A privacy screen installed beside the pool provided cover for them to pull their dry suit packets from the harnesses on their backs and pop into the suits before joining anyone else who happened to be in the lounge.

When they came out, Ke-ola and Marmie were sitting in bright cushioned chairs, sipping from tall drinks on the table between them. Sky sat on another chair, grooming his coat. A pot and four cups for tea sat on the table, along with a plate of chocolate biscuits. When Murel picked one up, she found it was just-baked warm.

Marmie smiled as they approached and took the other two chairs. "Ah, *mes petits,* I am sorry to interrupt your play, but we need to talk."

"Certainly, Marmie," Ronan said, sitting erect and using his best manners. Marmie had changed out of the white, fur-trimmed snowsuit she'd worn on Petaybee into a long skirt made of many colored patches of smooth and textured fabric that looked as soft as the coat of one of Clodagh's cats. With it she wore a long-sleeved turtleneck the color of the deepest part of the river on a sunny day. The fabric shimmered from midnight blue to steel gray with flashes of silver and cobalt. Around the high collar was a copper torc in the shape of a clamshell. Now and then Sky looked up from his preening to peer at the neckpiece.

"What's the matter?" Murel asked.

"Oh, nothing! But some of your fellow Petaybeans had questions about why you, mere children, only recently returned from school, were chosen for this mission instead of adults still able to travel. Do you two also have such questions? Or any others?"

"It's okay, Marmie," Ronan said, with a quick glance at Ke-ola, who seemed more interested in selecting a biscuit.

"Well, actually . . ." Murel said, hesitating. She didn't want to appear reluctant to help, but after all, Marmie was giving them the opportunity to speak up. Who knew when another chance would come? "I do wonder about one or two things."

"Yes?" Marmie asked, cocking her head and leaning forward slightly, her light exotic perfume flavoring the recycled air of the lounge as if a few flowers had blossomed there.

"I don't think I know why exactly you *need* us to come. Ke-ola can tell his people about Petaybee and that it wants them to come and live there. They'll believe him before they'd believe us, surely."

"Yes, *chérie*, but Ke-ola is not yet considered a Petaybean. It was very difficult to convince the Federation that Petaybee is not only a sentient planet but that people who live there for any length of time acquire a symbiotic relationship to the world. People died—"

"Laverne!" Ronan said. "Liam's mum. The Corps arrested her and she died when they took her offplanet for questioning. Bunny and Diego have a really sad song about it they sing at latchkays sometime."

"Yes, and your mother and father fought very hard to convince the company that removing your people from Petaybee and taking them elsewhere would be fatal to them. Ultimately they and other scientists were able to provide enough scientific evidence that the Federation recognized officially what you grew up knowing about Petaybee. The board feels that only people native to the planet have a unique interest in fulfilling Petaybee's wishes."

"And they—the Federation—think that if we are symbiotic with Petaybee, we won't want to do anything that goes against what

Petaybee needs because it's what we need too, is that right?" Murel asked. "Because it isn't really about wishes, you know, Marmie. Clodagh says we don't always understand why Petaybee requires what it requires, but it doesn't ask much of us, so when it does, we should pay attention."

"Clodagh and the Federation Council are in accord regarding that understanding," Marmie said, "though of course the council has no idea just how profound your particular link with your planet is."

"That's just it. They don't know how different we are. I was wondering why Johnny couldn't represent Petaybee. He's a native and knows all about it too. Besides, he's the captain of a spaceship and people look up to him. They'd believe him and Ke-ola before they'd believe us."

"He was born on Petaybee, it's true, but he has not resided there for long enough periods since leaving to undergo the adaptation that makes other adults *un*able to leave."

"So any adult who is Petaybean enough to represent the planet isn't able to leave, and anyone who is able to leave isn't considered to be under Petaybee's influence enough to have its best interests at heart?" Ronan asked. With a snort he added, "Does that ever sound like the PTBs!"

Marmie shook a scolding finger at him but her eyes sparkled with amusement. "Now now, Ronan, not all of the powers that be, as your people call them, are unreasonable. I, for instance, am considered powerful in many circles."

"Not you, Marmie! I mean, we know you're powerful and everything but you're our friend!" he protested.

"Oh yes," Murel agreed, "You're completely different! You could be a Petaybean if you wanted to!"

"*Merci, chérie.* Unfortunately, in this situation, if I were to presume to represent Petaybee, others would accuse me of promoting my own interests when interpreting Petaybee's. They would say I was taking an unfair business advantage over my competitors. Since Johnny works for me, that is another reason why he cannot represent Petaybee."

"It doesn't seem fair," Murel said.

"Perhaps not but it is as fair as the council could make it. *Vraiment,* I fear you have me to blame. I insisted that in certain matters the planet be personally represented by a native or natives. As the oldest native-born people still able to leave the planet, you are uniquely qualified."

"I wonder what they'd say if they knew how unique we really are," Murel mused.

"With caution and luck we will never find out," Marmie said. "Your parents and I foresaw that you might one day be called upon for this kind of mission. As you recall, that was one of our reasons for bringing you to Versailles Station to study."

"This is my fault, isn't it?" Ke-ola asked. "You having to come to invite my relatives?"

"No, no, Ke-ola, we don't mind, honest," Murel said. "We *want* your people to come, don't we, Ro? Ever since you told us about them and what's happened to them."

"'Course we do," Ronan said. "And what if we don't get to be home as much as we'd like for a while? Like Marmie said, it's only going to be a very short time that we can do this for Petaybee. Pretty soon we'll be too old too."

"And nobody put a laser to our heads, Ke-ola," Murel said. "We *could* go home and go swimming and have fun all the time, but then if something happened to Petaybee because we had wussed out when it needed us to speak for it, it's like Marmie and the Federation figure. Anything bad that happens to Petaybee would happen to *us* too. So doing this is an honor, really. Not one that anybody else could be chosen for, apparently, but an honor all the same."

"That's right," Ronan said. The two of them nodded to Ke-ola and then stared at Marmie, presenting a united front.

She gave the table a satisfied little slap with her fingers and sat back. "*Bon!* Then we are in accord?"

"Yes, ma'am," the twins said together.

MARMION WALKED OUT of the lounge. She was satisfied, on the one hand, that the children understood as much as possible beforehand what was needed from them and why. On the other hand, it was sad, so sad, to have to ask them to grow up so soon. They had been adorable babies, adorable seal pups, so lively and playful, bright and full of mischief. But she had not known for sure that they possessed the intelligence and resourcefulness needed until she saw for herself how well they did in the space station school, both academically and, after an adjustment period, socially. Their handling of the situation between their science teacher and the Honu had clinched the matter for her. Their actions once they returned to Petaybee had further reassured her and their parents.

Now no one could say she had not been frank with them—the conversation had been recorded, of course. The children had the facts, and they understood and felt they were up to the task—the many tasks, she feared—that would be required of them.

Oh well, at least they had had some childhood to enjoy. In other places, on other worlds, children were worked to death before they reached puberty, and nobody found it remarkable, much less lamentable, that they had to do so. It was simply how life was in those places.

Melancholy slowed Marmion's footsteps and she retired to her own cabin. She turned the cabin lights low and set the color therapy and aroma therapy settings, put on dreamy music, and lay down upon her soft bed, which massaged her back with soothing vibrations. It had been a long journey with very little time to recuperate on Petaybee. She had been negotiating very hard to acquire the slenderest thread of permission to relocate Ke-ola's people under any circumstances. Even that had not actually been through proper channels, and now she was exposing these children to danger, as she had once been exposed. The only difference was that in her case there was no good reason that she had to endure what she did, and certainly no one to explain the reason to her had there been one. But the twins were much better protected. On Petaybee they had the wisdom and good sense of their parents and Clodagh and most of the village where they'd grown up. And offplanet they would have her, always, and all that she was able to command.

WHEN MARMIE LEFT, Murel said aloud, "Well. It's nothing we didn't know already, I suppose, but I guess it's official now, isn't it?"

"I'm glad she told us what was going on and we were asked—sort of—instead of like the last time when Petaybee wouldn't let us in the communion cave. I asked Clodagh about that while you were off helping Bunny sew clothes for her baby. Clodagh said it was just Petaybee's way of telling us we didn't belong at home right then— that we were supposed to go."

"Hmph," Murel said. "I wish it had just had Marmie tell us to begin with. I liked her way better."

Ke-ola looked from one of them to the other, raising his eyebrows in bewilderment.

Murel explained: "Before we came to the space station, the last day we spent at home was our birthday, and there was a night chant after our birthday latchkay. Petaybee wouldn't let us into the communion cave."

"It wouldn't?" Ke-ola asked. "Why not?"

"We thought it was mad at us because we'd got into a little trouble with some wolves the day before, when we met Sky for the first time," Ronan answered. "I'm just glad to know now that we were wrong."

"But how did it keep you out?" Ke-ola asked.

Murel found a lump rising in her throat all over again as she told him how they had been unable to follow their family and friends into the cave. The communion cave was the best part of the night chants, better than the food at the latchkay. It was where Petaybee shared its presence with its inhabitants and they opened their minds and hearts to their world.

Ke-ola nodded. He had experienced the cave and it had welcomed him too; it had given him that sense of belonging that Murel and Ronan had taken for granted before it was denied to them.

"We don't know how it did it, exactly. We just couldn't pass beyond a certain point."

"Like a force field?" Ke-ola asked.

"Sort of. Yes, I guess so."

"Wow, that was pretty cold. You guys must have been plenty upset."

"We were," Ronan said, "and when everybody else came out, Marmie and our parents told us we were supposed to go visit her on her space station to go to school. It was all part of this, but they didn't tell us that then."

"Well, they did, actually," Murel amended, trying to be fair. "But I guess maybe we were too young to understand. We didn't believe them. We thought they were making excuses and we were being sent away because we'd been a handful. Again."

"But that wasn't it at all," Ronan explained. "It was the beginning of getting us ready for what Marmie was talking about. We've got a real mission, like she said. We're essential, we are."

Murel smiled, glad that Ronan was pleased. For her own part, she had been looking forward to another lovely cold winter undulating her gray-brown seal's body beneath the clouds of river ice. Even with the crisis with Da missing and the volcano erupting, she had enjoyed the chance to swim freely in seal form and explore the previously unknown sea. Still, Ro was right. Being chosen like this was an honor. She should be—was—proud, but she was also wishing it was over and they were returning with everything accomplished, waving at the grateful populace and so forth before running to the river and diving in without so much as a "last one in is a rotten fish."

Later, they shared dreams as they sometimes did. They swam urgently down empty corridors toward a place they absolutely had to find before they—or maybe it was the place—ran out of air. The problem was, they had no idea where the place was or what it looked like. When they tried to search, they were caught in a dizzying galactic spin of anonymous stars. Then the stars turned into the lights on an instrument panel that extended as far as they could see. If they pushed the wrong button, they would die. If they pressed the right one, they would reach the place they'd been seeking. But which one was which? How would they know?

The thoughts they shared when they woke up were almost as confused, the dreams half forgotten, but the anxiety they'd produced remained.

Johnny was in the lounge when they arrived that morning. Ke-ola was talking to him, and the twins knew he'd been talking about them by the way both he and Johnny looked up at them with carefully blank expressions.

"So," Johnny asked, "how did you sleep?"

CHAPTER 2

THE TWINS TOLD Johnny and Ke-ola as much about their dreams as they could remember, but it wasn't a lot.

"You knew about them, though, didn't you?" Ronan asked Ke-ola.

"The Honu picked up that you were not having a good sleep," Ke-ola admitted.

"Hmph," Murel said, her irritation magnified by the fitful sleep. "Honus should mind their own business sometimes. It's not nice peeking into other people's dreams."

"He didn't. All he said was that you were having bad dreams."

"I'm not a bit surprised myself," Johnny said, "after your conversation with Marmie yesterday."

"And how did *you* know about *that*?" Murel demanded. "Isn't anything private around here?"

"Shush," he said soothingly. "I know because we both talked it over with your parents and Clodagh before ever she spoke a word to you on the matter. It's a great deal to lay on the shoulders of young ones. As for the corridors and stars and strange instruments in your dream, I'm no psychic but do you know what I think?"

They shook their heads.

"Well, I've not a clue about the corridors but I do know about stars and instruments, so what do you say to spending less time in the lounge and more on the bridge so I can teach you—"

"You'll teach us to fly the *Piaf*?" Ronan asked, going from depressed and disheartened to euphoric and elated at warp speed.

"As much as I can, though she's a very complex ship, is the *Piaf*," he replied. "But I can help you learn what many of the instruments are for and teach you to fly shuttles and flitters and such. And the ship's computers are good for more than fairy stories and games, you know. In your dream, so you said, you didn't know where you were going or how to recognize it. The universe, of course, is vast and it's impossible to know everything about everything. But we do know a few worlds fairly well and have collected information on others you might find enlightening. Perhaps if you learn more about your destination and what we'll be passing on the way, you'll feel better able for your task."

"So," Murel said. "More school, eh?"

"It'd be *flying*, Mur," her brother said.

"I'd not say school," Johnny told her, "but educational yes. The professional emissaries and ambassadors would call it fieldwork, I believe. And that's different altogether."

She sighed, as if accepting his suggestion reluctantly, because her mood was still dark. In truth, she felt a bubble of excitement rising inside of her. This wouldn't just be study for its own sake. This would be learning things they actually needed to know. "It will pass the time, if nothing else. Swimming in the tank is better than not swimming at all, but it's not nearly as good as swimming in the river or sea at home."

Ke-ola asked, "Can I come too?"

"You can," Johnny said, heartily clapping him on the back. "Come along, all of you."

They accompanied Johnny to the bridge, where he introduced them to each of the crew members by name, listing the person's credentials. The instrument panels surrounding the bridge were almost as intimidating as the gigantic one in their dreams, but Ro was looking at it hungrily now, and Murel could tell he was already trying to guess what each one did. Johnny sat in the command chair and asked the navigator and first officer, Commander Adrienne Robineau, to relinquish her seat beside him, and beckoned Ronan to take her place.

"Commander Robineau, would you be good enough to show Murel and Ke-ola the path our journey will be taking?" he suggested, and to Murel he added, "Next shift you and your brother will change places, but I can't be having you kids replacing more than one of my crew at a time until you've had a few more lessons."

When the commander was seated at the navigator's duty station with Murel on her right and Ke-ola on her left, Murel was pleased to see that her first lesson involved just as many instruments on the panel and stars in the cosmos as Ronan's. The viewport spread from just above the top of the panel and curved high overhead on the ship's bow. The navigation charts were available on an array of screens and scanners encompassing the shallow U-shaped panel that sloped up an arm's reach from Commander Robineau on all sides.

She showed them how the screens reflected the individual stars, planets, and formations that were reference points for each immediate stage of the journey. As these points were encountered and bypassed, the screens shifted to the next set of reference points.

"Where's our world—Halau?" Ke-ola asked.

"We're too far for it to show up yet. It should be on this screen," she pointed to the one indicating the farthest set of reference points, "in four standard days hence. Meanwhile, let us begin with the closest reference points on the screen, and as they show up in the viewport, I'll help you identify them by site and we'll learn the factors you use to determine which one you are seeing, okay?"

"I thought navigation involved a lot of higher mathematics," Ke-ola said.

"It does, in the creation of these programs and cues, and if you ever go into the Corps Academy, you'll be introduced to that process to see if you've an aptitude for it and to learn some basics in case of equipment malfunction. But on a day-to-day operating level, the calculations are already embedded in the program and the computer plots them in the required combinations. We use what it shows us on the screens. This, for instance, is Kayenta, another of the border worlds terraformed by Intergal. Most of what we'll be encountering on this journey are such worlds, all, like Petaybee, here on the outer rim of charted space."

Once that lesson was done, Ronan came to work with Commander Robineau while Ke-ola was sent to the engine room and Johnny introduced Murel to the *Piaf*'s sophisticated systems.

She had expected the information would be so technical and complicated that she'd be too swamped with details to sort them into anything she could actually use. However, although it wasn't easy and there was a lot to learn, processing this information was no more difficult than learning the rivers and streams of Petaybee and relearning them as the seasons changed. Ice and eddies, new channels and shifting currents, fish and floods, constantly altered. When they were in seal form, the twins learned the changes in their habitat without having to think about them. Learning the star charts and the ship's instruments required more concentration and asking a lot of questions, but Johnny and Adrienne—as she told them they could call her—were both patient.

The engineer, Cadwallader Brown, was different. He got on well with Ke-ola and Ronan, apparently, and they seemed to enjoy their lessons with him. However, he had no time for Murel's aversion to the noises and smells of the engine section and her trepidation at touching any of the enormous and dangerous-looking equipment. He rolled his dark eyes in exasperation and his explanations were delivered in a curt and cutting tone.

Murel was delighted when she was told to move on to the hydroponics garden for instruction in intergalactic biocultural ecology by the erudite gardener, Midori Eisenbeis. Midori had taught at the academy, but said she found actually traveling far more rewarding. Murel was happy to spend the rest of her assigned watch helping Midori plant and prune, graft and cull, fertilize and water miniature ecosystems essential to many different peoples across the universe.

The tropical one was the most beautiful to Murel, who had never seen flowers so large or in such profusion, on such huge trees and bushes. Petaybean flowers bloomed large and bright during the brief growing season because they received sunlight all day and all night for almost three standard months. But the tropical flowers came in colors Murel had never seen on a growing thing. Midori smiled.

"I've enlarged this section a bit since I researched the original environment occupied by the people now living on Halau. When your planet's new zone is ready for settlement, we may be able to transplant some of these there."

"That would be amazing," Murel said.

At the end of their watch the twins and Ke-ola swam and played with Sky and, in a more sedate fashion, with the Honu, and afterward fell asleep without any dreams at all.

WHEN THEIR INSTRUCTORS were too busy to give them lessons, the *Piaf*'s cadets were encouraged to learn as much as they could about the worlds among which they currently traveled.

At the end of the day's second watch, while Ronan was in the engine room and Ke-ola with Johnny, Murel found the file for Halau.

A landscape like a rolling green sea with giant bubbles rising to the top appeared on the screen. As the camera zoomed closer, she could see that the bubbles were interconnected. The views switched to the interiors of the bubbles, quick shots of pools, gardens, beautifully furnished homey interiors, and lounge areas flashed across the screen.

A melodious female voice said, "Aloha! Intergalactic Enterprises welcomes you to view the latest modern settlement on one of its reclaimed worlds, Halau. The world's new name is taken from the native Kanaka tongue of its new tenants and means *school,* a designation highly appropriate for a place that has many intriguing lessons to teach those lucky enough to live here. Halau has been especially micro-terraformed to meet the requirements and taste of its lucky new tenants. Every possible amenity and convenience has been provided to make this world a happy home for its new inhabitants."

The voice went on to describe the climate-controlled environs, thirteen indoor swimming pools—including three saline ones for the cultural "pets" of the proposed inhabitants—the gardens, the woven grass and wood furnishings of the homes, and the equipment in the workshops where residents could produce handicrafts for sale to other worlds. Flowers like the ones Midori was growing bloomed everywhere within the bubbles. Finally, she described the small but efficient space port, capable of docking two large vessels simultaneously.

It was very pretty and pleasant looking and didn't seem nearly as bad as Ke-ola had described it.

The hatch to the research compartment hissed and Ke-ola said, "Whatcha doing, Murel?"

"Admiring your home planet. This looks pretty posh, Ke-ola. Are you sure your people will even want to leave to come to somewhere as cold as Petaybee? There's no telling how long it will take for the volcano to build a new island home for them and settle down enough for them to live there. From the looks of this, they don't have it so bad where they are."

"Huh. You think I was kidding around when I told you how bad it is?" he asked, offended.

"No, I know you think it's bad, but here are all these thirteen swimming pools and three saline ones and the gorgeous lounges and living areas, the space port and workshops—"

"That's all sim, Murel, can't you tell?"

"Well, no . . ." she said, staring at the screen more intently. "I can't, actually. You mean none of those amenities and conveniences she describes are there?"

"You'll see soon enough. But this thing you're watching? We play it once in a while on Halau and have a good laugh. Bitter, but good. The bubble networks aren't nearly as extensive as they look. We had to plant the gardens ourselves, and there were only a couple of pools, one salt and one fresh, but no way to maintain them. There were holes mapped out for others but our water allotment from Intergal wasn't enough to have water to live with and pools too. We did find another source eventually but it's got a few drawbacks. The furnishings were cheap, and they broke almost at once because the gravity is heavy enough that not even the pressurized bubbles are enough to keep us from trashing things. Including, I'm afraid, each other. Making handicrafts and babies doesn't keep people involved enough to keep them out of trouble. Aunt Kimmie Sue did the cultural classes to try to hold us together, but a lot of people couldn't believe that we could have ever had something as good as she described. The company makes sure that the only way out for us is the worker resource program they organized for their subsidiaries, or enlisting in the Corps."

"Well, I'm sorry I believed the lies, then." She shook her head, trying to reconcile what he was describing with the glowing images on the screen. "I'm glad we can offer you and yours a home."

Ke-ola nodded, but he looked worried.

CHAPTER 3

THE TWINS AND Ke-ola were on the bridge watching as the *Piaf*
approached Halau. It was a large planet, orbited by two
moons and an asteroid belt. As Ke-ola had intimated, it didn't look
like the pretty pictures on Intergal's vid clip. Its surface was as
pocked and colorless as someone in the last stages of a contagious
illness.

It didn't look like a place anyone would want to visit, much less
live. Nevertheless, the *Piaf* was not the only ship in the vicinity. In
the huge viewport, plainly visible between them and the asteroid
belt that partially obscured the pitted planet, another ship hung in
space.

The comscreen lit and suddenly another bridge with another life-
size crew was looming above the deck of the *Piaf*'s bridge. A woman
with dark, almond-shaped eyes and strawberry blond hair bobbed
asymmetrically across her forehead and down one cheek to just
below her ears was looking straight at them. She wore a uniform
similar to the one that hung in a bag in Mum's wardrobe. Company

Corps. Of course, she was only a lieutenant, and Mum had been a colonel by the time she quit for good.

"This is the Intergalactic Enterprises Company Corps carrier *George Armstrong Custer*," the woman announced. "You have entered restricted Intergalactic Enterprises airspace. Please identify your vessel."

The *Piaf* had a com officer too, Steve Guthe, who spoke twenty-seven languages and could sing in even more, but Johnny spoke up instead. "This is the passenger liner *Piaf,* flagship of Algemeine Intergalactic Enterprises. Captain John Green speaking, but Madame herself is aboard if there's a problem you and I can't sort out between us."

"No problem, sir, and nothing to sort out. Your ship must reverse course and leave this area immediately. Even under normal circumstances unauthorized vessels are not allowed to visit this world. And at the moment Halau is experiencing a condition-red emergency. We're standing by to be of assistance."

"I think you will find that as a senior council member of the Federation, Madame has clearance, as does this vessel, to visit just about anywhere in the known cosmos she wishes. Maybe if you fill us in on the emergency, we might be of assistance too. We're quite handy, you'll find, for civilians."

"No doubt, sir, but it's none of your concern, or Madame Algemeine's. Halau routinely experiences meteor storms. Such a storm is in progress at this time. We are standing by until our instruments indicate that it is safe to land and render aid to the inhabitants, if necessary."

"Where are the hits?" Ke-ola asked urgently. "What coordinates?"

The woman took in Ke-ola, who was peering over Johnny's head, with no sign of surprise. "I don't have that information at this time. From your appearance, I surmise that you may be a native of Halau, is that correct?"

"My people live there now, yes," Ke-ola said. "Can you tell me if the area around New Puna has been hit?"

"I'm sorry. I do not have access to that data at this time," the woman said.

"Perhaps you could obtain it, then," said Marmie, sweeping onto the bridge, dressed dramatically in a flowing scarlet robe with a tall black collar, trim in front and around the hem, and deep black cuffs folded back on a wide sleeve. She looked elegant, even regal, Murel thought. "My dear friend Ke-ola is naturally concerned for the welfare of his family."

Don't you love it when Marmie throws her weight around? Ronan asked telepathically. The twins had been able to speak to each other without words since they were small, and could communicate with nonhuman animals in that fashion as well. Usually the only other human they could talk to was their father, who was also a selkie, but sometimes people surprised them.

I love it that she's important enough to let us do things we wouldn't be able to without her help and that she's willing to do it, Murel answered a bit primly.

I wasn't being disrespectful, sis. I just think it's fun to see her sail in and take charge. She's awesome. Like a queen.

She is in a way, only of a company instead of a country. She's got presence, Adrienne says, and of course it's backed up with a lot of real power and money.

The com officer on the Company Corps ship was enough of a soldier to know superior firepower when she saw it. "Colonel Cally can better assist you with that information, ma'am."

"Then I'll thank you to fetch the officer in question," Marmie said, not in a snooty voice but as if she would be truly grateful to the com officer for doing her job. One thing the twins had noticed about Marmie was that she never bullied the "little people" unless they were acting like total idiots.

When a very official-looking man with an iron-gray crewcut and colonel's leaves on his uniform stepped up to the com screen, the corporal sat back, looking relieved.

"Madame Algemeine, I presume?"

Marmie nodded regally.

"Colonel Zachariah Cally at your service, ma'am. As my lieutenant has already informed you, this is restricted space and the best service I can render you is to advise you to return to the other pressing matters that no doubt compete for your attention and leave the current crisis to us. We are trained to deal with these things."

"Indeed?" Marmie asked. "As I explained to your corporal, one of the pressing matters to which you refer involves accompanying my young ward Ke-ola home to his family. If they are, as your officer indicated, in danger, then it is very much my business to do all that I can to make sure they come to no harm, as that would cause my ward considerable distress. Would it not, Ke-ola?"

"Oh, yes, Madame, I would be very much distressed. My brothers and sisters and aunties and uncles and cousins are all there—and the sacred Honu's family too. That is why I want to know where these meteors are landing. I am hoping they are not landing on my family."

"I'm sure Colonel Cally can understand your concern, Ke-ola, and mine. For of course we can surmise that since the company has sent a ship to aid the inhabitants, they must be in danger. It is a very large planet, and with very little, from the look of it, that could be harmed other than the people who have been settled there."

The colonel remained unruffled. "That's true, Madame Algemeine. We have feeds from the surface that indicate a large strike in the very midst of the largest settlement. And yes, I believe that's locally known as New Puna."

"Is that all? Have you had no communication from the inhabitants, no maydays or other requests for help?"

The colonel ran his tongue around his lips as if his mouth had suddenly gone dry. "Yes, we have. But right now, with the meteors still falling, it is far too dangerous to take a ship down there. While the situation is unstable, we would only be risking our people along with those below."

"I see. So no aid has been dispatched at all? No medical team or help in evacuating people to a safer location?"

"They have medical people of their own and we hope sense enough to leave the area while the sky is falling." His tone was snappish but he smiled, remembering to whom he was speaking.

"Yes, well," Marmie said, her accent more pronounced, drawled with a pursing of her mouth and a narrowing of her eyes that somehow conveyed that she was exercising great tolerance, "my ship has excellent shields and sensors for deflecting projectiles. I shall see to it at the next council meeting that we discuss having similar ones installed on the military vessels so you can take a more active role in this sort of emergency. If you would care to transfer some of your personnel to my vessel, we will be happy to give you safe transport to the planet's surface so you may carry out your mission with greater safety and so that Ke-ola's people will receive help as soon as possible."

Bright patches of red appeared on the colonel's close-shaven cheeks and traveled down his neck. "I'm afraid I cannot allow—"

"Mr. Guthe," she said to her own com officer, "do patch me through to the High Command so they can provide authorization for the colonel to make use of our resources."

The colonel turned away for a moment. Murel and Ronan were certain it was to get control of his temper. When he turned back to face them, he did seem to have regained a measure of composure.

"That won't be necessary, ma'am," he said smoothly. "It's very good of you to offer your help. However, I've just received word from our link to the surface that the meteor bombardment seems to have stopped for the moment so we can all proceed."

He had his navigation officer provide landing coordinates for Johnny, and communications terminated while the *Custer* darted toward the pockmarked planet, the *Piaf* following.

As they neared the surface, the landscape before them looked even less habitable than it had from the air. Murel had done some computer research on volcanoes while aboard ship, wanting to learn more about the one forming Petaybee's newest landmass. One of the pictures of the field inside the volcanic crater had looked something like Halau's surface. There were large craters pocked with emberous pimples of meteor rock. The comparatively level bits of ground looked back at them with thousands upon thousands of bloodshot eyes, and the air was still spangled with fiery rain.

Ke-ola, his finger trembling, pointed out what had been New Puna.

"You see that big hole there? That is where we had the gardens. And that one over there? That is where the pool was that held the Honu's relatives."

"And your relatives, Ke-ola? Where are they?"

He scanned the viewport in a slow, deliberate way then shrugged. "I don't see the home dome, where the people lived. Not even a splinter. That big hole with the m-melted edges? That's where it used to be."

Johnny quietly placed a hand on Ke-ola's shoulder.

As soon as it was humanly possible they suited up and prepared to leave the ship. The soldiers and Johnny at first wanted Ronan and Murel to stay aboard but the twins were adamant.

"Since we *are* Petaybee's ambassadors," Murel said, "I think we really do have to be in on everything."

"You are only ten years old," Marmion said. "It could be very upsetting out there."

"We won't be any more upset than Ke-ola or his bruthahs and sistahs," Murel said, pronouncing the words the way Ke-ola did, out of respect for what seemed to be a colloquial language mutation, rather than ignorance of the way everyone else said it. "We're here to help and that's that."

"Perhaps we should use the *Piaf* as a base camp, ma'am, and take flitters out to reconnoiter. It would be faster and we'd be less vulnerable in case the rocks started banging about again," Johnny suggested. "Also, if we needed to collect the wounded, we'd have something to carry them in."

"I'm not sure your flitters will work here," Ke-ola said.

"Why shouldn't they?"

"Too heavy," he said.

"Not that much of a problem," Johnny said. "*Our* all-terrain vehicles are just that—vehicles that adapt for all terrains. Terrain includes gravity. Might take a bit of adjusting but I reckon they'll run, all right."

"That's good, man," Ke-ola said.

They took the lift to the docking bay, where they suited up and prepared to disembark. The bay held all kinds of machinery—flitters, cranes, shuttles, and forklifts among them. The main entrance to the bay was cavernous enough to allow smaller ships to enter, but there was also another hatch for personnel only, and Ke-ola veered away from the flitters and headed for the air lock. It irised open, and the others stepped inside while it closed behind them and the gantry—a broad platform with an extendable staircase—extruded itself. Ke-ola took a step out onto the platform. It groaned beneath his weight.

CHAPTER 4

R IGHT, THEN," JOHNNY said through his helmet's mic. "Perhaps we'll try it without the flitters for now." He signaled the bay's control room and gave the order that the flitters should be recalibrated for heavy g.

Meanwhile, Ronan followed Ke-ola. Once he was out of the *Piaf*'s controlled environment, he found it hard work to pick up his feet and put them down again. It was as if he were wading through hip-high snow in heavy boots.

"Use the antigrav setting on your boots," Johnny instructed. "Two ought to do it."

Johnny tapped the control panel on the wrist of his suit. The twins had never had to wear such heavy protection before.

I'm glad the controls aren't actually on the boots, Murel said, following Johnny's example. *I don't think I could see my feet real clearly with the helmet in the way.*

Yeah, Ronan agreed, activating his own boots' antigrav function. *But—hey, that's a lot better!*

Dust and smoke rose from the dozens of meteors smoldering in craters like malign red eggs in nests of molten rock. The steam and smoke from them formed a gray-brown sludge that hung in the heavy air.

Ke-ola swarmed down the ladder ahead of Ronan. He ran like a charging rhino toward the meteor that had landed on the residence enclosure.

"Poor kid," Johnny said. "We probably won't even find bodies if they were under those things when they hit."

"Well, surely not everyone perished," Marmie said optimistically. "If these meteor showers happen often, the inhabitants must have developed some sort of defense."

"Ke-ola would know about that kind of thing, wouldn't he?" Murel asked.

The three of them were on the ground by then. Ronan trudged over to the crater where Ke-ola was. The larger boy was circling it, examining the edges carefully.

"They might be under there," he said slowly, nodding to the meteor.

"You mean crushed under the meteor?" Ronan asked as delicately as possible.

"Maybe not. They might have had time to take cover in one of the root canals before this one hit. There were trapdoors inside the habitats. Believe it or not, we're in the planet's green belt here. The meteors usually hit the equatorial belt, which is a big desert where nobody lives. I remember the elders saying how the showers were changing the orbit of the asteroid belt and shifting the planet on its axis, so maybe they started hitting here because of it. Anyway, usually, when they're not all burned up like now, there are some scrubby trees and other plants that grow here—only part of them grows on the surface, though."

"So how would those keep people from being . . . you know?"

Ke-ola's breath huffed through the mic into Ronan's helmet, and with deliberate patience he explained. "*Because* there are so few nutrients or water in the surface soil, they have these roots that are maybe ten times as deep as they are tall. Where old ones have burrowed into the ground and then died and the roots rotted away—a long time ago—there are the canals or tunnels. They're big enough for people to stand in, or even live in, and some of them interconnect. They're real deep too. My people use the channels sometimes, even though they don't much like being underground. I think the tunnel under this bubble went deeper than the meteor."

"Then all we'd have to do is dig them out," Ronan said, thinking of all of the digger attachments for the flitters he had seen in the docking bay.

"Yeah, if the meteor didn't collapse the tunnel on them," Ke-ola replied grimly. He sank to his knees, pawing at the ground with his heavy gloves.

"Hey, you don't have to do that," Ronan told him, touching the shoulder of Ke-ola's suit with his glove. "The *Piaf* has plenty of equipment to dig way deeper than you can."

But Ke-ola didn't seem to be listening. Ronan decided he must be in shock. Leaving his friend to his own futile efforts, he sensibly galumphed a couple of steps back toward the others to tell them about the underground canals.

"We heard," Johnny said. "These transmitters in the helmets send to everybody unless you narrow the frequency. The flitters are being fitted with diggers and crews are already being mobilized."

Marmie knelt beside Ke-ola so that her helmet-enclosed face was close to his. "Come away now, Ke-ola, before something lands on you and burns through your suit," she told him.

But he ignored her too.

Everyone else returned to the ship's interior and waited until the equipment was ready. When they reentered the airlock, the twins followed Johnny's and Marmie's example and pulled off their helmets but kept their suits on as they stepped through the air lock, back into the docking bay. It was now a hive of activity as equipment was fitted and tested.

Murel stayed close to the bulkhead and looked through the small porthole to the ground below, where Ke-ola continued to dig. *I hate to leave him like that, but it's daft to think he'll be able to dig down to them with just his hands.*

Of course it's daft, Ronan replied, *but if it was Kilcoole that was buried down there instead of Ke-ola's village, would you wait for someone else to try to save them? I think not!*

The interior hatch to the docking bay slid open to admit a small troop of people marching double time toward the flitters.

Watching the flitter crews climb aboard, wearing suits but only carrying helmets, made Ronan worry about another matter. "Johnny, we have to wear our suits when we go outside. If Ke-ola's people were inside when the shower hit, they probably didn't have their suits on," he said worriedly. "They wouldn't be able to breathe without the suits belowground either, would they?"

"I don't know. I suppose the instinct would be to get out of the way of the meteors and worry about suffocation later—or maybe they grabbed the suits as they went down and had time to put them on before they could suffer ill effects. We can hope so, at least. Ke-ola might know."

Ronan pulled his helmet back over his head and spoke into the microphone inside it. "Ke-ola, you told us there's room enough for your people underground, but won't they suffocate for lack of air if they didn't have suits with them?"

After a pause, Ke-ola replied, "No, they won't. Not down there. The air's better belowground than above." A hopeful note had come into his voice, though Ronan could hear his heavy breathing as he continued pawing at the ground. Drawing a deeper breath, Ke-ola continued, "The air up here is okay as far as basic composition goes but it's contaminated by a lot of space junk that gets drawn to the surface by the gravity. Underneath, the heavy root systems of the plants work to purify the air."

"I thought that was because of chlorophyll and photosynthesis."

"With the plants we brought with us, terran plants, that's how it is. But these native plants have other properties that let them do the same thing with their root systems. Also, the planet's water is underground. Something to do with the gravity again."

As Ke-ola spoke, Ronan looked up and saw that the shovel-bearing flitters with belted tracks for surface travel were being flown toward the air lock.

Johnny and Marmie were pulling their helmets back on and heading toward the flitters.

"Okay, Ke-ola," Ronan said into the mic. "The diggers are ready. We're on our way."

Murel squatted down so Sky could jump off her shoulders. She didn't look back, not wanting to encourage him to follow.

Once the diggers and their technicians were offloaded, Johnny, Marmie, and the twins took a flitter to the surface. It dropped quickly and flew low, laboring under the pull of the heavy gravity, but it worked. Another digger that had been ahead of them pulled up to Ke-ola, and after a brief exchange with the driver, Ke-ola crawled into the machine's cab beside him.

"Madame Algemeine, what are you doing with that machinery?" Colonel Cally's miniaturized face demanded from the comscreen on the flitter's instrument panel.

Marmie had had about enough of the colonel, as her expression showed, but she replied sweetly, "I thought I'd use the meteor craters as the entrance for a new mining operation, Colonel. I do hate to let a good disaster go to waste."

"I'm sure even a lady of your position would find that difficult to explain to the council," Cally said pompously, and then realized—slowly—that he was being had.

"I would hope so, if that were the case. But *vraiment*, we undertake now a rescue operation. Ke-ola believes that he knows where some of his people may be trapped underground. If you have digging equipment and muscle to spare, I'm sure we'd all be grateful for your help."

"Actually," he said smoothly, "if you are investigating this area for survivors, perhaps we should look elsewhere and see if we can find other spots where people may have taken cover. Halau held three quite large settlements, you know, and they've become larger as time has gone by. These people bred like rabbits—not that I think anything is wrong with that. Their size and this world's heavy gravity made them very strong, well suited for a variety of jobs involving heavy manual labor."

"Your concern is touching," Marmie said. "Don't let us keep you from your noble rescue efforts."

Murel was seeing red that had nothing to do with meteor fire. "He's awful, Marmie! You should report him. He doesn't care about Ke-ola's people at all."

"Get real, sis," Ronan said aloud. "If the company cared anything for them, do you think they'd have settled them here? I mean, no offense, Marmie, 'cause I know you're on the council and all, but this place is a hole, even without the meteors."

"I do realize that, dear," she said. "Unfortunately, there are so many of these displacement worlds that not even I know about all of them. Since learning about Petaybee, I have made an effort to discover where Intergal has settled as many of the so-called inconvenient people as I can. Most of them were far less fortunate than your people and did not land on so hospitable a world as Petaybee. I'm afraid the colonel's attitude is a mirror of that of his employers. Intergal does not wish for the inhabitants of these places to be happy or comfortable, because they want to draw upon these populations for military personnel, laborers, or other less desirable career opportunities within their ranks. Appealing to the Federation does little good. There are a few who are genuinely concerned and high-minded, such as Farringer Ball, but many are also major shareholders in Intergal and more deeply interested in the bottom line than in the welfare of the people involved in achieving the company's fiscal goals."

"That's terrible!" Murel said.

"It is indeed," Marmie agreed. "Remind me at a more auspicious time to give you my lecture on the uses and abuses of power."

CHAPTER 5

K E-OLA'S FLITTER/DIGGER BEGAN trundling away from the crater. His voice came through their mic helmets. "None of my people are down there after all," he said. "They're still alive, but they've already gone farther into the tunnels."

"How can you be sure of that, Ke-ola?" Marmie asked.

"I can't but Honu can. He says we've got to keep looking."

"How does he know that?" she asked.

Ke-ola, sounding determined, said, "The sacred Honu knows these things. He sees what I see through my eyes when he wishes. He knows the hearts of his people. If the heart has stopped beating, he knows that too."

"Oh dear." Since they had all heard the exchange, Johnny, who had replaced the digger's pilot, followed the lead of Ke-ola's vehicle.

"Marmie, Honu thought-talks to us too," Murel said. "We could cover all the craters faster if we left the flitters to look around different craters. We could ask the Honu if there were people nearby."

"It's too dangerous for you out there unprotected," Marmie said.

"It's more dangerous for the survivors right now," Ronan said. "We'll be as careful as we can but if a big meteor came down and landed on the flitter, in spite of what you told that Cally, I bet we would get hurt. It's not like anyplace in this area is exactly safe."

Marmie gave a Gallic shrug and said, "So, you don't think the shields I invented for his sake would save us, eh? You are of course correct. Remind me never to try to do a business deal with you. You have come to know me far too well. So, proceed, *mes petits,* but with caution please."

The twins pulled on their helmets and gloves, reset their boots, and stepped out onto the wounded planet.

Ke-ola jumped heavily out of the flitter they'd been following and lumbered away from it.

Ronan slogged off in the opposite direction asking, *Honu, you can read Murel and me from the ship too, can't you?*

I can, the Honu replied.

You'll let me know if you sense survivors if they're nearby, as you did with Ke-ola?

Yes, Honu said.

I don't suppose you could tell us where to look for people as well, if we're getting warmer or colder?

I do not understand. It is warm where the sky rocks have fallen. You will be colder when you are farther from them.

That's not what I mean. I mean, warmer by am I nearer to the survivors or farther from them.

Walk on and I will try to sense the answer through you.

Ronan trudged on to the next area where it looked like a structure had collapsed under the onslaught of the meteor shower. *Here?*

Not there.

How about here?

No, no one is there.

Over here?

No.

There's something weird about all this, don't you think?

Murel's thought reached Ronan. She had walked away from the flitter in a position that triangulated his and Ke-ola's. Ronan could tell she was scared of what she might find, and he also caught thought pictures of crushed and burned bodies as his sister imagined what the meteors that had ruined the landscape might have done to living beings.

Meteor showers are sudden, not easy to predict without special equipment, Murel continued. *But there are no people here, not even injured ones or bodies. Why not? How could they have known in time to take cover the way Ke-ola seems to think they did?*

They knew, the Honu said, *because Honus know. My relatives living among the people warned them. The people fled to safety long before the sky rocks fell.*

But how did Honus know the sky rocks were going to fall? Ronan asked. He didn't expect a scientific answer and he didn't get one. He knew what the Honu would say. It was the same thing any sensible creature on Petaybee would say, fleeing before a natural disaster could overtake it.

Honus know, the sea turtle said simply. Then, *Ke-ola knows too.*

Ronan and Murel looked toward their friend and saw him striding purposefully toward something orange. A piece of cloth? A flag? It moved against the stark background of a barren hill.

"What's that?" Ronan asked him through the helmet com. "What do you see? What's the orange thing?"

Ke-ola was panting as he answered, "There's a guy *waving* the orange thing."

Ronan and Murel began to run toward him, but Marmie's voice crackled into their helmets. "Stop. The flitters will be faster."

Even as she spoke, the flitter skimmed the rocky, pitted ground as it swung toward them, pausing long enough for them to climb aboard before chasing down Ke-ola.

There, they could spot the man waving the flag. It might have been his shirt, since he wasn't wearing one.

"Keoki!" Ke-ola yelled. The com unit shrilled painfully loud feedback. "That's my bruthah, Keoki," he explained, his voice, though quieter, quivering with excitement.

"Excellent!" Marmie said.

By then the flitter had set down, the hatch was opened, and Keoki was practically on top of it before Ke-ola and the others could climb out. The brothers wrapped their arms around each other, but while they were still entangled Keoki began steering Ke-ola back into the hill.

After Johnny gave the other flitters their location and told them to stand by, the twins, Marmie, and Johnny followed.

There was a cave entrance in the hill. Keoki lit a torch while Johnny and Marmie flicked the switches in their suits that turned the fingers of their gloves into flashlights and activated another powerful beam on each helmet. Ahead of them a long black tunnel curved sharply downward.

"Lava tube, not the root canal!" Ke-ola crowed to the others. "Of course! Sure! I should have thought of that. These hills are full of them. Old volcanoes from long time ago, way before we came here."

Unencumbered by space gear, Keoki, torch in hand, trotted well ahead of them.

"The meteors never hit our settlements while I lived here," Ke-ola said, "but us kids found the tubes. We wanted to explore them but our folks always said it was too dangerous. Then one of my uncles who'd joined the Corps and come back with one leg missing said instruments on the expeditionary ship that brought him back showed subterranean water, bigger than what was in the canals. But they were really deep down so we never got to go all the way down while I was living at home. They'd make a good shelter, though, deeper than most of the meteors could penetrate and with water for the Honus and the others. Yeah. Makes sense."

He pulled off his helmet and shook loose his dark hair, which had grown to shoulder length since he left school. "Ahh, good air. Better than in the canals."

Johnny referred to the tiny control panel on his wrist again. "It does seem safe enough."

They removed their helmets and continued down the tube.

The tunnel was of black rock that looked as if it had dried after being poured around the cave. In places it was perfectly smooth, in others the floor and walls rippled and undulated. There were no stalactites and stalagmites toothing the passage as they did in the communion caves on Petaybee. Also, deeper and farther along, huge roots pierced through the walls and ceiling of the passage.

It's as if they grow upside down, Murel said. *These roots are more like their branches than the part that grows aboveground.*

The cave smelled pleasantly of life growing and decaying. Moisture soothed their nostrils, dry from breathing the recycled air of the helmets.

Soon they began hearing noises: an occasional shout or even a laugh, some splashing, coughs, the slap of bare feet, the shuffle of shoes, the rustle of clothing or the rattle of rocks displaced by shifting bodies, sniffs, a sob, a low fevered repetition of unintelligible words that could have been a chant or could have been nonsense. There was even a little singing.

It grew louder as they walked deeper into the tube. The twins' knees ached with the steepness of the descent. Their lights bounced off the broadening lava walls as they rounded a bend, ducked under a curtain of low-hanging roots. Keoki waited for them, torch in hand, and made a right-angle turn. The tube flared into a vast cavern and the lava floor gave way to a wide black shining lake. All around it people gathered in groups. Within it several people swam or floated, as did several very large Honu and a few small ones.

Keoki called out something to the other people in his and Ke-ola's language. He pulled Ke-ola forward and thumped him on the back, then beckoned Marmie, Johnny, and the twins.

"Ke-ola, will you tell them—" Marmie began, but Ke-ola raised his hand.

"You don't need an interpreter, Madame, if that's what you think. Keoki doesn't have good manners, like me. But everybody here knows Standard. The company makes us all learn it so we can get along on the job later on."

"Of course," Marmie said. "How silly of me." She raised her voice. "Hello, everyone," she said, but for once her presence didn't work. Maybe it was because her stately form was enclosed in a bulky space suit and she was standing just outside of a shadowy chamber even more dramatic than she was.

The people kept talking among themselves and pointing at the newcomers or splashing across the lake to see what was going on.

"Hey, everybody!" Ke-ola bellowed. His voice echoed through the cavern. Ronan was glad they weren't still wearing helmets. The feedback would have deafened them, maybe permanently. "All of you pipe down a minute and listen to this lady. This is Madame Marmion de Revers Algemeine who runs the school I've been at and a lot of other stuff too."

Keoki gave Marmie a once-over that was pointless considering the sexless space suit, and scoffed, "If she's so important, how come she's with you, bruh?"

"She and these other friends of mine came to save your sorry butt, Keoki."

"From the meteor shower? You're a little late. Good thing for us we got the Honus. They told us to come here. If it wasn't for them we'd have been squashed into poi."

"We got a Honu too," Ke-ola said. "He told us you were still alive. He said your Honus would have warned you about the meteors. He's back on the spaceship."

"You got a Honu on a spaceship?"

"Yeah," Ke-ola said. "A little one."

"We have an otter too," Murel put in, just in case anybody was interested.

A woman wearing the ragged remnants of a ship suit got up and walked over to them, giving Keoki a disgusted look and reaching out to pull Ke-ola into an embrace. "Welcome home, little bruthah. We knew about your Honu. Keoki's just being a pain. We got the message a long time ago from the space-station school 'bout your Honu needing a mate. We wondered when you were gonna bring him home to find one."

"We found another home, Leilani, someplace we can all live if we want to," he told her.

Turning back toward the rescue party, Ke-ola said, "This is my sistah, Leilani, Madame, Captain, Murel, and Ronan. Leilani, Murel and Ronan are my friends from Petaybee. They can explain about the new home better than me."

"First, however," Marmie said, "Leilani, Keoki, is everyone all right? Does anyone need medical attention?"

"Yes, Madame," Leilani said. "We all got inside the tube before the first rocks began to hit. We didn't stay up there to watch the show, though. The Honus told us to take them and take cover so we did."

"It's a good thing," Ke-ola told her. "Your biospheres are nothing but holes in the ground. We thought at first you were in them, then that you'd gone underground in the root canals. That was before our Honu sensed that you were someplace else and okay. The meteors have stopped for now. We got room for anybody who wants to come on board Madame's ship. Who's coming?"

"Not so fast, Ke-ola," Leilani said. "Go where? Why?"

"To Petaybee," he said.

"What's that?"

This is where we come in, I guess, Murel told Ronan, then addressed Leilani and Keoki but turned to include anyone else who wanted to listen too. "Petaybee is our planet. We came to tell you that you're welcome there."

"We're welcome here too," Keoki told her, an angry edge to his voice. "What is this, some new company scam to get us to move again because they've found something they need that makes this place too good for us to live here?"

"No," Murel said. "We're not from the company. I *told* you we're from Petaybee. It's where the company moved our grandparents a long time ago. The company figured it was too cold for anyone to survive there, but the planet helped us and adapted everybody so we've all done fine. Only once you grow up, you can't leave again because of all the adaptations. That's why they sent Ronan and me to invite you."

Leilani crossed her arms over her chest as if she were shivering. "If it's colder than here, count me out."

"Where we'll live isn't going to be so cold," Ke-ola said. "It's in the middle of the ocean, between the poles, and there's hardly any ice there since the volcano started blowing."

"Ice *and* a volcano?" This from a wizened little old man. "Sounds like we'll be homesick for the meteor showers."

"No, really, it's a good place," Ke-ola said.

"The volcano wouldn't bother you folks very much, probably," Ronan said. "All you have to do is keep chanting to it like Ke-ola did and—"

"What chant was that?" Keoki asked. "What you been telling these people? Some of that old voodoo Aunty Kimmie used to talk?"

"Used to?" Ke-ola said, and looked from face to face. He didn't find the one he was searching for.

"She died two turns ago, bruh," Leilani said.

"None of her homemade poison could stop her coughin'," Keoki said. "'Bout drove everybody nuts hackin' her head off till she finally croaked."

"What's the matter with you?" Ke-ola asked his brother. "You didn't used to be like this. You got no respect now for anything. Aunty Kimmie knew about our people. Her medicines worked too."

"Keoki, you should be ashamed talking like that," Leilani said. "Aunty Kimmie may have been kind of old-fashioned but she was important to a lot of people, 'specially the older ones. And most times her medicines *did* work—they just tasted like crud."

She turned back to Ronan, Murel, Marmie, and Johnny. She was a very thin lady, much older than Ke-ola, Murel thought. But he'd said he had a big family, and if she was the oldest sister, she might be almost old enough to be his mum. His real mum was dead, Murel recalled him saying.

Later, Murel realized they could have been there arguing without accomplishing anything until the next meteor shower had it not been, once again, for the Honus. As everyone else chattered, the great sea turtles swam to the bank of the black lake, making their decision on the matter known. As the first turtle reached the bank, three men hauled it toward them and gently lifted it among them.

"The Honus say it's time to go now," one of the men said. "Can you folks move aside so we can pass? Ours is a very old, very well-fed Honu."

"Go where?" Keoki asked.

"They say they want to go to the Honu on the lady's spaceship."

"She can't take our Honus away without us!" Keoki said.

The spokesman for the first turtle's team shrugged, then, in one strong heave, the men lifted the huge Honu up over their heads. His weight was so great, as the twins knew from their acquaintance with their own much smaller Honu friend, that his flippers were too fragile to carry him on hard ground.

Murel got an idea then, and whispered something to Marmie, who nodded.

"Come on, Ro, let's show them the way," she said aloud.

Okay, but that's not really necessary, is it? Won't the Honu guide them onto the ship? her brother replied in thought-talk.

Yeah, but I just thought of a way to make the people feel welcome, only we have to be there in time to greet them the way I plan.

After a few words with Marmie, they scuttled back up the tunnel ahead of the first Honu bearers, who were followed by several more turtle-toting teams. The gravity made the twins less than speedy, even when they used the lightest setting on their boots, but at least they didn't have to carry turtles as big as they were while they climbed.

The first flitter, on Johnny's order, picked up the twins and took them back to the *Piaf*. They looked behind as they left and saw the first Honu and its bearers being loaded into a second flitter.

We'll have time, Murel said. *It's going to take the flitters several trips to ferry all the Honus and people from the cave to the ship.*

THE TWINS QUICKLY pulled off their helmets and suits and raced into the main lounge. In the great tank, the Honu swam excitedly back and forth. He had been stolen as an egg, so this would be his first meeting with others like himself.

The purser, Aidan Carnegie, strode into the lounge. On his wrist, he wore his "brains," a small computer holding the data he required for the smooth operation of the internal organization of the ship.

"Madame and the captain will be joining us soon, I trust?" he asked.

"On their way," Murel said. "But there are also several delegations of Ke-ola's relatives bringing more of the sea turtles aboard. They'll go into the tank, of course, and we should make their human friends comfortable too."

"I've already arranged with the galley staff for refreshments. Madame relayed orders to the bridge about your other requirements. Dr. Eisenbeis is waiting for you in the gardens."

"Great," Murel said. "We'll be back as soon as we can."

MIDORI HAD ALREADY plucked all of the tropical blossoms and started stringing them into necklaces or leis. Ke-ola had presented the twins with leis for their first birthday aboard the space station, explaining that these were greeting, parting, and celebratory gifts his people gave each other. Midori, whose specialty was knowing how natural things were used in various cultures, was pleased to have a practical application for her knowledge, though she grieved to have to denude her tropical garden of its flowers. Murel and

Ronan pitched in and began stringing the bright soft blooms along-side her.

"We won't be able to make enough," Ronan said.

"That's okay," Murel said. "I think it's the thought that counts here. We'll give one to Leilani and let Ke-ola decide where else to put them. Maybe we can give individual blossoms to other people kind of randomly. It's a goodwill gesture. Emissaries do that kind of thing, you know."

"Of course I know. We studied the same stuff. How are we going to get them to sit still long enough to collar them?"

"Collar them? We're not arresting them, we're *honoring* them, Ro. You don't have to make fun just because you didn't think of it first."

"I just figured naturally we'd do that since that's what they do," he said. "I didn't know you were going to make such a big deal of it, though."

She rolled her eyes and continued as if he hadn't spoken. Midori looked up from her stringing and smiled. Murel thought Ronan was showing off for the benefit of the pretty scientist.

Midori helped her out by asking, "When do you plan to present the leis?"

"We have a little time. Once the Honus are settled into the tanks and all of the other people arrive, Mr. Carnegie's crew will offer them something to eat and drink, of course. I don't think they were able to take much with them when they evacuated, and now all of their supplies are destroyed. Even if they don't want to come to Petaybee, they're going to be on short rations until Intergal gets around to replenishing their food, so I hardly think they'll refuse a meal. But first we'll have to lift off again because, of course, we can't just sit around down here and wait for meteors to fall. Johnny will offer to take them for a spin outside the meteor belt. Then we'll present the leis while the food is served and welcome them to the *Piaf* and, we hope, to Petaybee."

"And if they decide not to emigrate to Petaybee?" Midori asked, her fingers flying through deep lavender and cream petals.

"I don't see that they have a lot of choice now. That planet is not fully terraformed. Petaybee in the middle of winter has more to sustain life. I think Marmie is planning on taking any who don't want to come with us to the nearest Federation outpost to lodge a complaint about Intergal's negligence in overseeing their welfare. But why would they want to go through all that? They know how reliable the company's promises, or even the Federation's, can be. And with the Honus on board and wanting to come with us, and a lot of their relatives, I bet everybody else will want to come too. At least they should be in the right frame of mind to consider thinking about coming with us."

"While they're eating, we could show them the holo we did about Petaybee for school," Ronan suggested. "I saw it in the *Piaf*'s memory banks."

One of their first assignments while attending classes on Marmie's space station had been to make a holographic representation of their planet, including the topography, special features, imports, exports, culture, and in fact most things a prospective settler might want to know. Each student in the class had made one to acquaint all of the others with his or her background.

Ronan continued, "Marmie got some good footage of the new volcanic island when she returned to fetch us for this mission. Keola can sing the song he made about the big eruption." He ran out of words, remembering that Keoki had seemed almost hostile and none of others had been ready to leave until the turtles swam ashore. "Do you think they'll go for it?"

Murel looked at him gravely. "They don't have that much choice, do they?"

"I guess not, but they don't seem anxious to make friends."

Midori said, "That's your job. That is why this," she lifted the lei, "is such a good idea. If you show some understanding of their culture, their viewpoint, they may feel that you want them to be comfortable, that you care about them. That should help."

"That and feeding them, maybe," Ronan said.

Marmie's voice came over the intercom. "Murel and Ronan, our guests have arrived."

"We'll be right there, Marmie—only, maybe someone could bring a florrie to help us carry the flowers?" The florries were a cross between a small flitter that could operate in the corridors of the ship and a lorry, or truck.

"Never mind, Madame. We'll take mine," Midori said. She stepped into a bay that was hidden by greenery and drove out in a florrie that still had water glistening off it. "I just washed it after hauling some soil," she explained.

"I'll come back and wash it again for you later," Ronan offered shyly. Midori was very pretty.

"I don't think so," she said with a disappointing lack of gratitude. "I like to care for my own equipment." She added gently, "But thanks for the thought."

CHAPTER 6

THE CARPETING AROUND the huge tank had been stripped away when the tank was installed, and now deckhands busily mopped the slippery surface. Water continued cascading over the top as the enormous Honus glided and swept, dipped and dived around one another in a graceful ballet.

Honus are happy, their Honu told them, his thought tone reflecting his own happiness.

"Glad somebody is," Ronan muttered to Murel. The human evacuees looked as bleak as Halau's surface.

There weren't enough seats for everyone, but those who had no chairs seemed perfectly comfortable sitting on the deck—in fact, a couple of chairs were empty and people were leaning against them instead of sitting. Now that the people were in good light, it was clear they were ragged with exhaustion.

Leilani stood near Marmie, and Ronan overheard her asking, "Have you heard anything about the other settlements?"

"Not yet," Marmie said. "Colonel Cally and his crew were going to check on them. Let's see what they've found."

As the two women walked over to the lounge's com unit, Murel pulled an armload of leis out of the florrie. Looking around, she found the oldest of the island descendants and approached her. She held out the lei and said, "Welcome aboard, ma'am. Aloha."

The old lady blinked up at her, and Murel dropped the lei over her head, less ceremoniously than she'd intended. The lack of interest and bafflement on the elder's face caused Murel to release the flowers as if they'd suddenly turned hot.

She started for Keoki next but he glared at her so fiercely she turned away. "Maybe I'm not doing this right. But this is what Keola did, isn't it?"

"I think they're a little distracted, sis," her brother said.

She looked at the glum and only slightly hopeful faces of the people crowded into the lounge. "Yeah, I guess it could have a dampening effect on a party," she said aloud. "Plus they're worried about—"

"Cally here." The colonel's brusque voice sounded even harsher than it had before. "What do you need now, Madame Algemeine?"

"We have some of the survivors from New Puna here and they are wondering how the other settlements fared, Colonel," Marmie explained.

"The short version is: they didn't. I don't have an exact body count but anybody who wasn't crushed was fried, as far as I can see. There's nothing you can do for any of these people, ma'am. I strongly suggest you get the—heck—out of here before the next shower starts. I certainly intend to."

Cally's face in the large comscreens at each corner was trying to look cool and in command but his left eyelid blinked nervously. It was very clear he wanted the whole incident to be over and done with and to see the last of the *Piaf* and her pesky crew.

"Very well, Colonel. I shall of course take your advice. I also intend to recommend to the Federation that no further settlement be

allowed on this world. It is obviously too unstable for human habi-
tation."

"Right. You do that little thing, Madame. Cally out."

Wow, he was a bit upset, wasn't he? Ronan remarked to his sister.
*He didn't argue with Marmie, didn't say anything about our guests,
nothing.*

*He probably would have made us send them back down to let the
meteors have another go at them if it was anybody but Marmie on this
ship,* Murel replied with a hostile glance at the now vacant comscreen. *I think he was lying about searching for other survivors too.
Did you see how his eye twitched?*

The people around them had been murmuring during their exchange, those closest to the com screen relaying what was being
said back to the others.

The murmur escalated to a mutter, then to shouting. Then a long
wail cut through all of it, accompanied by shrieks and sobs from
others.

An old woman was pulling at her long gray hair, her fingers
bloody from the wounds her nails made on her scalp. The hair
falling into her contorted face was soon soaked with her tears. Ke-
ola knelt beside her and put his arm around her. Later he told the
twins that the woman was his auntie on his father's side. She had a
daughter and five grandchildren in one of the settlements Cally had
pronounced lost.

The elder to whom Murel had given the lei rocked back and forth
moaning, twisting the flowers to shreds in her fingers.

Keoki sat glowering at first, and then, when Leilani touched him
on the shoulder, rose and helped her try to comfort the others.

"Blankets, I think," Marmie said to Purser Carnegie. He had
been standing by the cartloads of food until the conversation with
Cally was over. Now he tried to appear calm as he awaited his
orders. "Then some fairly stiff drinks and sedatives for the worst
cases. When they have quieted a bit, the ones who are still awake
will probably be able to eat the food."

"We have plenty for the one hundred and fifty humans and ten sea turtles I have counted among our guests, Madame, and comfortable sleeping quarters are being provided."

"Excellent," Marmie said, "but I would not be surprised if for the time being the guests preferred more communal arrangements so that they might remain close to each other."

"Very insightful of you, Madame. Should that be the case, appropriate bedding will be provided for them here." He gave a little bow and left.

The twins were standing close to Marmie at the time or they wouldn't have heard what was said. The younger children had picked up on the distress of the adults and started shrieking and crying too. All of a sudden things were far beyond the control of the people in charge. The young ones, whether frantically clutched in a smothering embrace or ignored, were terrified. Taking cover from a meteor storm was exciting when adults were there to assure them that everything was all right. When the adults were crying, everything was clearly out of control.

Murel helped Purser Carnegie's staff pass out blankets and warm drinks. Presently she noticed that the children's sobs began to subside. A moment later she heard a distinct giggle, and even a laugh. Startled, she looked up to see Sky peering out from behind one child, teasing another.

Good work, Sky, she told the otter. *Maybe if the kids calm down, the adults will too. Though they have enough to cry about, it's true.*

Otters do not cry, Sky told her. Then, after a moment in which he seemed to consider his statement, asked, *Is crying the noise the new people are making?*

Yes, she said.

Otters do not cry and otters would not like to cry. Otters like to play.

Yes you do, and very good at it you are too, she said, smiling when she looked at him.

The child behind whom the otter was hiding waved her over and pointed at Sky. "Your aumakua is very friendly. You must take very good care of him."

"We take care of each other," she said. "What's aumakua mean? It's part of Ke-ola's last name, I know."

"And ours. Honu'aumakua," the little one said. "That's us because the Honu is our aumakua. Is this furry little fellow yours? What's he called?"

"Sky. He's an otter. A river otter originally but then he became a sky otter, when he flew in a helicopter."

"So is your name Sky'aumakua or Otter'aumakua?"

"Neither one, it's Shongili. Are your people named after a friendly animal usually?"

"My family is named for the Honu," the child said, as if the question baffled her.

While Murel distracted herself with the little one, a loud argument broke out among some of the guests. Ke-ola was in the thick of it, he, Keoki, and Leilani shouting and gesturing.

They were arguing in their own language so Murel couldn't make it out. *What's the matter with them?* she asked the Honu.

They will not leave this place. Others remain outside, below. They die.

Well, yeah, there were others but . . . Realizing it was useless standing there having a telepathic argument with a sea turtle, she walked over to the group, dodging the gesticulating hands, and asked Ke-ola, "What are you fighting about?"

"I told them there's nothing to be gained from everyone staying behind, that Petaybee may be a cold place but it's better than here. But they say—"

So much for our diplomatic persuasive tactics, Murel thought.

"We say," Leilani put in, "that if the company abandons the planet and we go off with you, what if some of our people *did* survive underground somewhere? They can't live on what the planet alone provides. There may be others, like us, who hid belowground to escape the meteors. They'll starve to death if we just abandon them."

"But we'll starve to death too if we stay," Ke-ola said. "Oh, sure, Madame would leave us food and water and even see that more are delivered later, but without regular supply runs, we can't survive here."

"Wait," Murel said. "I thought you were the only people left alive, and we know that because the Honu knows about that kind of thing."

"Honus know what affects their own people," Ke-ola told her. "With people who are guarded by other aumakuas, Honus don't know so much."

"Fine time to find out they don't know everything," Murel said. "So what do we do now, Ke-ola?"

"The ship and our people stay in orbit. I will take a shuttle back to Halau and explore the waterways and underground. Madame can leave me a way to communicate, and I can let her know if I find someone."

Ronan said, "That's a pretty pathetic plan, Ke-ola. That's about as good as Mum wanting to stay behind with Marmie's yacht while everybody else got in lifeboats to escape the volcano. I know you feel bad about the people who died—or are missing—but . . ."

Murel's imagination had gone to work while they talked. She could see people trapped in little narrow passages, similar to the lava tube but smaller and darker. The passages would be choked with roots, damp underfoot and lightless once the fuel for the torches or the batteries for the flashlights wore out. The people trapped there would stand or sit or maybe only have room to squat in those tight little places. They'd listen, waiting until the meteors stopped crashing and shaking the world around them. Finally, when it seemed safe to go aboveground again, they wouldn't be able to stay. The air mixture aboveground was not safe to breathe without protective clothing or equipment. There was no shelter for them, no food. They would discover they'd been left for dead, and soon enough they *would* die.

"We're going too," she said, interrupting more arguing. "Ronan and me, we'll help you find them."

"Not your job," Ke-ola said.

Leilani, Keoki, and others gave her startled looks. She moved closer to Ke-ola and said in a low voice, "Maybe not, but if those canals are filled with water, as you said, we'll be better able to help than anyone else. You know what I mean, Ke-ola."

"You don't know how things are down there. You don't know where to look. I grew up here."

"So you come too, but we're going to help."

CHAPTER 7

This isn't Petaybee, children," Marmie said when they told her what they intended to do. "There are no rivers or open sea on Halau—it is all underground and in utter darkness, with dangers multiplied by the damage from the meteor shower. No, I'm sorry. It is out of the question."

The twins complained to each other but knew there was no dissuading Madame once she made her decision. Nor would she hear of Ke-ola or the others going back.

"But Marmie, what if that Cally is wrong?" Murel said. "What if there are still people down there? If we just go without finding out for sure, we could be condemning them to a horrible death. And to make matters worse, they'd know they were dying because the other survivors abandoned them."

Marmie gave her a shrewd look. "They are not to know that there are survivors if they have been hiding underground all that time, *n'est-ce pas?*"

"It doesn't matter if they know or not, *we'll* know," Ronan told her. "And Ke-ola's people will know and they'll always wonder. It's no way to start a new life, thinking maybe you've left people to die a—"

"Enough!" Marmie said firmly. "Some things cannot be helped, and I trust that the adults among Ke-ola's people will understand this."

"No, they don't," Murel said just as firmly.

"In time they will."

"One last sweep, Marmie," Ronan wheedled. "It's what we came down here to do, after all. Just because we got some people safe doesn't mean we should go away without making sure there aren't more. You don't really trust that creepy Colonel Cally to find his own arse with both hands, do you?"

"What if the meteor showers begin again?" she asked.

"The Honus will know," Ke-ola told her. He stood a little behind the twins, and it seemed he'd been talking with Leilani and Keoki, but Murel didn't think he had missed a word.

"Perhaps not in time. No, it's too risky. Your parents would never forgive me if something happened to you."

"And these people will never forgive you or us if we don't try," Murel said, hard-headed as a curly coat who wanted to graze when his rider wanted to keep going. Even if it was dark and dangerous underground and underwater, she knew they had to try to look for other survivors and dig them out.

Otters do that, Sky said suddenly, entering the minds of both twins as easily as he did when they were in seal form.

What? Murel asked.

What you are thinking. Burrowing into dark dens and tunnels, coming into water. Otters do that all the time. Sky otters do it too.

Sorry, Ronan said. *We don't have any otter-shaped space suits and helmets.*

Sky stood on his hind paws and looked first one way and then another at a discarded helmet lying beside Johnny Green. *Sky Otters are not large. Sky otters can curl up very tight, fit in helmet. Don't need suits. And Honus say air belowground is good. No helmet.*

What do you think? Murel asked her brother.

I think otters burrow into dens all the time, even sky otters. Might be a bigger burrow than Sky's used to and I don't think he should go alone, but it's worth a try.

"Marmie," Murel said. "Sky says going down into the kind of burrows we're talking about is something otters do all the time. He's willing to let us carry him down there curled up in an activated helmet and let him loose when we get to the fresher air below. Besides, you know, we have night vision in seal form and great hearing too. We haven't needed it much so far, but our dad says we have sonar, so the dark wouldn't bother us either."

"So you think I won't let you go by yourselves, but with a two-foot-long otter to chaperone you I trust you to stay out of trouble?" Marmie asked, then made a moue. A glimmer of humor entered her previously steely glance. "Mmmm, perhaps. But I think maybe we all will go back down and watch aboveground in case you find more than even otters can handle, yes?"

"We can help," Ke-ola told the twins excitedly. "The Honus can hear you and tell us where you are. We can station ourselves above you and keep you from becoming lost."

"With so many hands, flippers, paws, and shells aligned against me, I have no choice but to surrender," Marmie said.

"Count your lucky stars," Johnny said to the twins when Marmie had turned back to tell the survivors of the plan. "She is not usually so democratic. She must have deep respect for otters."

THEY SHUTTLED PEOPLE and diggers to the flattened settlements several miles away from the one formerly occupied by Ke-ola's people. The surface was deeply pocked with giant meteor craters, and blackened and scorched by fire.

The three digger flitters now had added sensor attachments to their array that could detect subterranean water. They resembled the buglike aliens of the old vids the twins had watched on shipboard as they aligned themselves in a more or less east-west line and lowered the shovels.

As many of Ke-ola's people as could fit into the available flitters came too. Through the Honus on shipboard and the smaller Honu accompanying Ke-ola and the twins, the other Halauans hoped to help keep track of the twins' progress and know where they were when they were belowground.

Inside the transparent helmet Ronan held like a fishbowl, Sky twisted his sinuous self so he could peer out the glass, his whiskery face looking strangely distorted and misshapen, his eyes huge and darting around as he tried to make out his surroundings.

"Didn't these people have an entrance to the lower regions, like yourselves? How about lava tubes?" Murel asked Ke-ola.

"I don't think there were tubes near enough to their settlement to give them cover. But they had canals, and an escape route, according to our people who had relatives here. But the meteors changed the landscape so much, it's hard to find the old entrance point. Digging down until we strike a channel seems like our best bet."

When one of the shovels came back to the surface dripping water, Ronan and Murel carried Sky over to the hole and slipped down into it. Literally. The soil was first too warm for comfort, then very muddy, and the twins slipped, lost their footing, and slid down into the water, still clad in their space suits. Ronan hit a rock. Sky's helmet tumbled away from him, landing in the stream of rapidly flowing water, no doubt from an artesian well of some sort.

Before he could find it, he heard a splash.

Hah! Free! Sky's thought reached him. He caught a sense of the otter swimming away, scouting ahead of them.

When they found their footing, Ke-ola carefully handed the small Honu down to Ronan, then slid down himself.

Murel patted the Honu's shell. She couldn't work up a lot of reverence for a sea turtle the way Ke-ola and his people and even Ronan seemed to, but she liked him. And he was very young as Honus went, and she sensed he was worried about them as well as about the other possible survivors they sought. Knowing the things Honus knew seemed to carry a lot of responsibility with it.

Sky, water-slicked and excited, darted back again, shaking himself a bit. *Good water. Deep water. Deep enough for river seals. No salt, but deep.*

The twins undressed in the dark, strapped on their suits, and submerged themselves. Ke-ola and the Honu followed.

The first passage was deceptively easy. Its end was marked by a snarl of live roots that formed an almost impenetrable wall. Even Sky got stuck trying to pass through its openings.

Hah! he said. *No swimming here.*

Honu conveyed the problem to his fellow turtles. *Go back,* he said to the twins and Ke-ola. They backed off a little ways and soon heard the hum, thump, grind, crash of the digger above them. They scrambled out of the new hole. The digger's operator and Johnny conferred, then the driver got back into the machine, drove forward a short distance, and lowered the shovel again.

"It's going to take forever if we have to keep doing this," Ronan complained.

"We could cut through the roots with a laser, I suppose," Marmie replied, "but it seems a shame to destroy the roots of some of the few organisms living on the surface of this desolate place. Besides, the laser might cut through to the far side and injure people who took refuge there."

Caution won out over speed. The twins would swim until they inevitably hit another barrier and once more had to haul out. Again they suited up, and waited inside a flitter with Sky, Ke-ola, and the Honu until the digger opened a new entrance beyond another impediment. Usually the blockage was caused by roots. Once, the water disappeared, hissing, beneath a huge chunk of meteor. Then all of them had to turn around and splash back to the previous hole before they emerged.

It took endless hours. Although their night vision was good, the tunnels were usually cramped and there was little to see.

Murel could feel Ke-ola's spirits sinking a little more during each dark trip, though the Honu thought only, *Noooo, not here. Not yet.*

Often they had to wait quite a while for the digger to make its way over the cratered ground to reach the point above them.

But each time they emerged, some of Ke-ola's family were waiting at the hole's opening, peering expectantly down at them.

Marmie was among them when they climbed out of what seemed like the hundredth hole, muddy and discouraged. "I think that much as we hate to believe he could have been correct, Cally had the right of it," she said. "There don't seem to be any other survivors."

"The Honus feel that there are, Madame," Ke-ola said, although it sounded as if he had begun to believe that the Honus might actually be wrong for once.

"Very well," she said. "But one more dive only before we return to the ship. Everyone is tired and hungry and the operators tell me the diggers need refueling and cleaning to maintain their efficiency."

This time, however, the diggers were not needed. Instead of narrowing to a root-choked wall, the stream broadened and deepened.

Hmmm, I think this must be where the sonar comes in, Murel said.

I wish we'd asked more about it when we were home with Dad, Ronan said. *If we were full-time seals living in the ocean, we'd have been using it already.*

If we were full-time seals living in the ocean, we wouldn't be here, she pointed out.

True. I think maybe this is how it goes. There are supposed to be songs, I think. Individual songs.

He made a noise that was somewhere between a snore and a belch and a little like a growl. *Like that,* he told her, and did it again, modifying and modulating the tones.

Oh, those noises! she said. *Like the ones we used to make under the river ice. I never paid much attention to them before. I thought they were just what our vocal cords do when we're in seal form.* Confined during their earlier childhood on Petaybee to nearby rivers and streams where they went only for short swims, they were so famil-iar with the territory, they had been under the impression that their memories let them know where they were and approximately what things looked and felt like. Even during their brief time in the ocean, they'd relied mostly on vision to find their way.

But now that they wanted to learn to use their sonar properly, they found they'd been using it all along, far more than they'd pre-viously thought. In this alien underground territory where they had no idea what was coming next, the seal sounds they made bounced back to them from shapes of various densities, rather like echoes. Once they were aware of it, they didn't need much practice inter-preting the echoes. Their seal senses recognized the signals so they "heard" how deep and wide the water was, how far they were from the bottom and the walls of the passage. The solid surfaces of the canal were many body lengths away from them.

That's all? Ronan asked. *A big flooded cavern. I'm disappointed. I understood we would be able to tell where the fish were and even plants and things. All I'm getting is these walls.*

I don't think there are any fish down here, or anything else except more roots, Murel answered tiredly. She would have enjoyed a nice juicy fish right then.

And then, suddenly, there *was* something else. Something unfa-miliar. If it was a fish, it was a very large fish.

Murel sent a mental call to Sky. *Come back,* she said. *Stay close. We are not alone.*

CHAPTER 8

S KY DIDN'T NEED to be told twice. In fact, he didn't need to be
told once because before Murel's thought was finished, he was
back beside her, keeping himself safely shielded between her and
Ronan.

Back, back, river seals, the otter told them. *Something is there.
Something large and hungry.*

As if they needed proof, they felt a disturbance in the water, rip-
ples piling against them as something swished back and forth in the
water beyond, back and forth, back and forth, relentless, sinister,
blocking their way forward. In the dark cool silence the water broke
as the something sliced through it with great and churning force,
leaving a broad turbulent wake behind it.

It's really big, Ronan said finally. *Much bigger than us. Bigger than
Ke-ola even.*

Yes, I feel that too.

Hundreds big, Sky agreed. *Eats otters, river seals, Ke-olas, and
Honus.*

Not if we don't give it a chance, Ronan said, and flipped over in the water so he was headed back the way they came. *What are you lot waiting for? Start swimming.*

Murel and Sky flipped in the water too but they met Ke-ola head-on. "Honu!" he called aloud. "Where are you?"

The twins heard no answer from the sea turtle but could feel the creature swimming forward. Each time he paddled, he hesitated ever so slightly, as if listening or waiting.

And then, swift as a diving hawk, the thing that had been swimming before them suddenly turned, shot forward, and was among them.

"Hey!" Ke-ola shouted.

Murel thought he was the one under attack. But then her sonar told her Ke-ola was swimming close beside her, crying, "Honu!"

She heard the *click-crunch* of teeth on shell. The creature had the Honu! Scooping it into its maw, the attacker grabbed the turtle, then abruptly turned and swam away again.

Let go of the Honu, she demanded, hoping that the telepathy she and Ronan shared with other creatures worked as well on Halau as it did on Petaybee. *He's not for eating!* Since the Honu's attacker didn't seem like the sort to take orders from seals, she added, *Also, he has large relatives who could crush you by crawling on top of you.*

She streaked through the water toward it. When a sinewy tail as large as she was slashed close to her face, she leaped on top of it, clamped her teeth into it and hung on.

Let go of my tail! it cried. *I have relatives too and they're circling us now.*

Ronan's sonar confirmed the creature's threat. He leaped onto the tail too and sank his teeth into it.

Got it! he thought. *Let go of the Honu, monster, and tell your relatives to leave us alone.*

Unless of course you've already hurt the Honu. Murel's thought was threatening. *In which case, you can say good-bye to this tail. I'm pretty hungry!*

Wait! the thing's thought cried out. *Mano halau, get back or I will be eaten by these monsters.*

The twins found it difficult to use their sonar while their mouths were full of thrashing tail, but the water churned wildly and they had the distinct feeling that something dangerous was giving them a bit more space.

Good, monster, Murel said. *Now let the Honu go. And he'd better be alive and unhurt.*

He's free! I let him go. I wasn't hurting him. I was only giving him a ride. Aumakuas do not eat aumakuas. So untooth my tail and leave me alone.

Sky piped up, *The turtle is swimming now, river seals. He is swimming in circles. He does not know where to go. But he is swimming.*

Honu?

I live. The thought was feeble. *The Mano's teeth did not penetrate my shell.*

That's good, but your shell broke one of my teeth, little brother, his attacker complained.

You fellows know each other, then? Ronan asked, thoroughly puzzled.

Ke-ola, who'd been swamped by the thrashing and churning water, recovered enough to swim to the Honu and scoop him into protective arms. His voice was shaking as he said aloud, "Ronan and Murel, you have been biting the tail of the great Mano, the shark. The smell of blood excites his kind, and his relatives surround us."

The Honu's thought-voice was a little stronger. *The other Honus say this shell biter is Mano'aumakua, sacred to his clan as we Honus are to ours.*

So you're related? Ronan asked.

The monster swirled in the water so that even in the darkness they saw his teeth. *Do I look as if I am codding related to a turtle, morsel?*

Ke-ola, perhaps prompted by communication with the Honu the twins did not hear, spoke again, "The sacred Honus have intervened to save us. These Manos will eat anything except their own people or another aumakua. Our Honu protects us."

Funny, Ronan told his sister, *I could have sworn it was the other way around.*

Let's not mention that we are only honorary Honu clan, Murel suggested.

The shark was trying to examine its own tail. Fortunately, the part they'd bitten was largely cartilage and was not bleeding heavily.

There was no need to bite me, the shark complained. Had his thought-voice not been so rasping and whispery, he would have been whining. *I wasn't going to hurt him, I was carrying him to some of his two-legged relatives who are staying with our two-legged relatives.*

So what relatives of yours are swimming around us now? Murel asked. *Two-legged or shark-finned?*

Shark-finned, of course, seal. You are so stupid I am tempted to eat you and improve your gene pool.

They are not of our people and do not know our ways, the Honu said. The twins realized with astonishment that the turtle was apologizing for them. *And they are young, but considered quite bright on their world.*

The shark's thought was preceded by a shark's version of a growl. *It must be a very stupid world.*

It is an intelligent world, the Honu replied. *I have spoken with it myself. And meteors do not fall on it in great numbers. That is an advantage. Also, the waters, though cold, are open to the sky.*

You don't say, the shark replied, chewing on the thought, though fortunately not on the Honu.

Murel had not known many sharks—or any sharks—before. Petaybee did not even have sharks, as far as she knew. She was not entirely sure Petaybee *needed* sharks. The planet had invited Ke-ola's people and Honus, not sharks. But it seemed that the shark had the same relationship with some of the people that the Honu had with Ke-ola, so probably it was a package deal.

We came to help your people as well as Honu's people, she said. *If you and your kind can keep yourselves from eating anybody we can save everyone.*

Can't you even let us have the otter? it asked. *We haven't been fed all day and we're very hungry.*

No, Ronan said, and remembered what Ke-ola's people seemed to think. *He is our* aumakua *so you owe him professional courtesy too, right?*

Seals don't have aumakuas, according to any lore I've been told, the shark replied scornfully. *I thought you were Honu people but you're not. Seals look like meals to me.*

They are not seals all the time, Mano, the Honu told him. *They are two-legged children.*

Why don't they have a seal aumakua then, instead of a puny little otter?

Who knows how things work with those from other worlds? the Honu replied. *Perhaps otters on their world are the ancestral spirits of seals.*

Ronan, just to keep the shark confused, said, *No, otters are the ancestral spirits of people just as you are. The seal spirits are our father's—*

What he means to say, Murel said, *is that there aren't many human seals like us. We are aumakuas in training ourselves. So, no eating us or the otter or Ke-ola or Honu. Are we agreed? If so, can we stop discussing cross-cultural theology now and save the people?*

Follow me, but if I feel you looking at my tail, I will tell the Mano halau to eat everyone but the Honu and his human. The shark gave a long shudder. Murel realized he was not refraining from eating them out of any kind of respect, but because he was afraid of them. He was not used to being attacked and he felt instinctively that anything smaller than he was, foolish enough to attack, must be either very dangerous or so deranged, and maybe diseased, as to be unpalatable. The shark was actually quite anxious to get away from them. It shot forward into the water.

They followed the tail, no longer lashing the water but knifing through it so sharply it seemed the shark might leave a dry trench in his wake.

At length the lake narrowed back into the sort of canal they had seen before, then to a streamlet. When they got that far the shark told them, *You go ahead. Too shallow for me.*

I thought you were taking us to your people, Murel said.

They're over there, downstream, beyond the wooden reef.

Murel thought he might mean a ball of roots like those they'd encountered before. *How do you know they're there if you can't go that far?* she asked.

The Honu answered, *Manos know too.*

In spite of the shark's failure thus far to eat them, Murel was very happy to leave him behind in the lake while she and Ronan, Ke-ola, Sky, and the Honu continued.

Can you sense the people beyond the roots, Honu? she asked.

Yes, two Honu people, the Honu said. *I will tell the other Honus and the diggers will come.*

Sky dived and surfaced again a short distance away. *There is a hole in the roots, river seals. Otters can go through there. Maybe Honus. River seals and Ke-olas are too big.*

Be careful, Murel told him. *They might have more water and sharks on that side too.*

Otters are very careful, Sky told her, and dived.

Waiting was not good. They waited with their heads above the waterline while Ke-ola dog-paddled and the Honu swam around in circles. Under the water, everything was very quiet, but once they surfaced the tiniest sound was magnified as it bounced off the water and back and forth in the tunnel, ricocheted through the cavern and lake beyond, and bounced back again. They could hear Mano restlessly sectioning off the lake with great thrusts of his muscular body. They heard the slap of water against the sides of the tunnel and Ke-ola's sigh of weariness.

Odd to be down so deep within this world and not feel anything at all from the planet, Murel said, suddenly very homesick.

It's dead, Ronan replied flatly. *There's nothing to feel.*

It's just strange, is all I'm saying, she replied. *Meteors crash into it, people settle on it, but all it does is wallow around in space like flotsam.*

Of course, he replied. *This place isn't a natural force like Petaybee. If it was ever alive, it was a long time ago. I'm not of a mind to stay here one minute longer than necessary.* He asked the Honu, *Are the diggers coming yet?*

Yes, but far away. The humans also come.

Good, Ronan replied.

The land shuddered. A moment later a wave rolled in from the lake and flung them against the tree roots.

What was that? Ronan asked, trying to see in the dark. His sonar told him something disturbing was happening, that the walls around them were subtly shifting.

The land quakes, the Honu told him. *When its shell was smacked and dented with sky rocks, its insides were damaged too.*

I hope that was it, Murel said. *I don't fancy being down here during a major quake.*

Perhaps it was. Perhaps not, the Honu said, as if it didn't matter.

What happened to "Honus know"? Ronan asked.

Ke-ola spoke up. Through his link with the Honu, he now received a filtered version of the turtle's communications with the twins. "It doesn't take a Honu to know we need to find the survivors down here and get back to the ship before we're *all* smacked, dented, and damaged."

"I wish Sky would hurry," Ke-ola said. "While we're swimming I can stay warm enough but I'm freezing now."

Murel dived and Ronan heard her sonar song from beneath the water. *Aha! Just as I hoped,* she crowed. Surfacing, she told Ronan, *Follow me. The quake opened a river-seal-sized hole in the root wall even big enough for Ke-olas and Honus,* I think.

She dived again, followed by the Honu, then Ke-ola, with Ronan bringing up the rear. The hole on their side was very large but the roots made a maze of the passage they had to weave their way through. Twice Ke-ola became stuck and had to hold on to one of Murel's fins while Ronan body-slammed him through from behind, sacrificing some of Ke-ola's human hide to the rough roots.

Once they were through the root wall, they expected to see Sky, but found only more of the same narrow canal they'd been swimming in on the other side.

At least there don't seem to be more Manos, Murel said gratefully.

They swam on for several moments. Twice more the tunnel shook and the water sloshed, but these quakes were mere tremblings compared to the first one.

Sky popped out of the water ahead of them.

Did you find the people? Murel asked him.

Yes, he said. *Hundreds of Ke-ola relatives.*

That meant there were quite a few, but not necessarily hundreds. Otters were very intelligent but they didn't count. When they first met Sky, the twins had asked him how many were in his family and he had not understood the question, so they asked if it was one otter or maybe a small group of otters or hundreds of otters. Sky usually reported any group larger than two or three to be hundreds.

The canal was more torturous than previous ones, choked not only with tangles of roots, but also littered with chunks of earth and stone that had fallen from above. The twins followed Sky as long as they could in seal form, but then the water ran out for creatures of their size and they had to flip themselves dry and put on their dry suits while they and Ke-ola, hunched over under the low tunnel ceiling, waded through the shallow water, following Sky and the Honu.

At last they rounded a bend and saw torchlight and a shelf of rock extending from the streamlet to the side of a cavernous root canal.

In the flickering of the torchlight, the twins saw a small band of people—not hundreds.

And from above them they heard rumbling. Ronan and Murel could smell the fear and hopelessness emanating from the people as their eyes fearfully searched the sides and roof of the cave while rocks and dirt rained down on them.

CHAPTER 9

THE RUMBLING INCREASED, then stopped.

Ke-ola waded toward the people and spoke quickly to them. The ones nearest him looked startled. Being intent on the quake, they hadn't seen or heard the small rescue party until then.

Many of the adults were older people, though there were a few younger women and a great many children. One old woman, nearly as big as Ke-ola, stepped up to their friend and made loud demands the twins could not understand.

The Honu did, though. *She wishes to know if the Manos still live, and Ke-ola tells her they are well,* the turtle explained.

Ronan's human throat emitted a sealish bark of frustration. *Everybody is just fine, but we aren't going to be much longer if we don't find a way out soon.*

True, the Honu replied as once more the tunnel trembled, the water sloshed, and the dirt and rocks showered them. *So it is a good thing the diggers are above us now.*

"Are these people the only survivors or do we need to look for more?" Murel asked Ke-ola, even though she didn't think she wanted to hear the answer if it was not the one she wished for.

"This is all," Ke-ola answered. "Two compounds were completely obliterated when the first meteors fell. The Manos warned the people, but those far from the water didn't know of the warning until it was too late."

"So we can go now?" she asked. She felt very selfish. These people had lost everything, even relatives, and she was only uncomfortable and tired. But it was enough for her. She wanted to go home.

When the diggers poked through the root-woven ceiling and soil and the first victim was carried to the surface in a sling attached to a rope, she thought it was all over.

But the old woman who had first addressed Ke-ola wasn't letting them off that easily and demanded something of him in their own language.

He tried to urge her to go up in the sling. She shook her head, and Murel thought it was because she was afraid the rope wouldn't hold her. "It's very strong," Murel told the elder soothingly in Standard.

The woman answered her in the same language. "Strong for you, missy, strong for me, but how will it carry the Manos?"

"The Manos?" Ronan asked. "Why would it carry the Manos?"

Ke-ola tapped his forehead with the heel of his hand. "Of course, how could I be so stupid? The Manos will have to come too. These people cannot leave their aumakuas behind any more than we would leave the Honus."

"But they're going to have to," Murel said. "I don't think the tanks will hold all the Honus and the Manos too. There's not enough water."

"Couldn't Madame make more tanks?" Ke-ola asked.

"And put them where?" Murel said. "Besides, it's not that easy. Adrienne said they already had to reinforce the lounge deck to hold the tank that's there now. I don't know how we're going to satisfy everybody, Ke-ola. Can't the people and the Honus come with us now and maybe Marmie can come back for the sharks later?"

"And maybe not, eh?" the old woman interrupted. "We will live with the Manos or die here with them."

Ronan didn't want to ride with the sharks. Swimming with them once was enough. And if it came to that, he didn't want sharks prowling the Petaybean seas.

"Maybe we can send for another ship to take these folks and their sharks to another safer planet somewhere," he suggested.

Ke-ola shook his head. "My people will not come without them. We are all related. The Manos are difficult relatives but all must come or none will. You do not leave your grandmother and grandfather behind."

"That grandfather would have eaten the Honu, Sky, and you too if Murel hadn't grabbed his tail," Ronan said.

While they were arguing, the old woman, who seemed to think they would do exactly as she thought they ought to, saw to it that several children were lifted to the surface. They were immediately put into flitters to return to the ship. They were followed by three young women who appeared to be their mothers.

Once they were gone, the old woman called to the remaining adults. Bearing torches and holding them high, they entered the water and she led them deliberately around the rescue party, away from the escape hole, and toward the tangled roots.

"Where are you going?" Murel asked.

"To fetch the Manos."

"But—" she started to protest.

The Honu told her, *They do what they must. Now we will do what we must. The diggers must uncover the Mano lake. Meanwhile, we will make a place for them.*

The twins looked at Ke-ola, who shrugged, settled the Honu under one arm, and used his other hand to hang on to the rope as it was raised toward the surface.

Sky draped himself over Murel's shoulders as she ascended, followed by Ronan.

Halfway to the surface the rope was enveloped by a tube that blew fresh air from the flitter down at them. Within its protective envelope, they reached the flitter's opening, and Ke-ola helped them in. This was not the simple four-passenger flitter they had seen before, but like a large passenger carrier.

Johnny Green's voice greeted them over the com. "Is that everybody, then?"

"Everybody but the people who stayed behind to wait with the sharks," Murel told him.

"Stay behind with the *what*? Sorry, darlin', but the reception seems to have a glitch. I didn't quite catch that last word." He chuckled. "It sounded as if you said 'sharks.'"

"That I did," she replied. "Sorry, Johnny, but what with all the mind-reading and psychic communicating with the Honu, Sky, the sharks, and Ronan and me, we quite forgot you wouldn't be hearing any of it. It seems that what the Honus are to Ke-ola's clan, sharks are to this group of survivors. They say that if we want them to go, we must make room for the sharks as well."

"Ah," Johnny said. "I decided against marrying a lass one time because she said the same about her mother. Her mother was somewhat less attractive and amiable than most sharks, but she had the advantage of not needing to live in a tank."

"The Honu says the other Honus will let the sharks have the tank," Ronan told him.

"Did they now? That's very interesting. I suppose they'll be expecting their minders to hold them all the way back to Petaybee?"

Ronan shrugged. "They didn't say. I suppose we can sort it out with them when we've returned to the ship."

"Best do it before deciding to take any sharks aboard. I don't recall Petaybee inviting sharks, do you?"

They did not, of course.

The large flitter groaned under the collective weight of the passengers all the way back to the ship, but at length it arrived and they climbed back through the air lock and onto the main deck, feeling as if several tons of rocks had been removed from their heads, shoulders, hands, and feet. The children began bouncing around as if they had invisible wings, laughing and zooming into each other.

Most of Ke-ola's people of the Honu aumakua were still back on the surface, waiting to help the Mano people evacuate their finny friends. So the twins weren't surprised to see the lounge empty except for a few people and some odd-looking occasional tables they hadn't previously noticed.

What did surprise them was that the Honu tank was empty. Where before the giant turtles had glided through the water in an oddly graceful ballet, now there were no creatures in the water at all. There was also somewhat less water in the tank than there had been, and the deck was flooded around the pool at the end of the water slide.

Ronan noticed an old man leaning against a table, his clothing and the ends of his long hair damp, and that others among the remaining people were similarly soggy. "Where are the Honus?" he asked him. "Why aren't they in the tank?"

But it was Ke-ola who answered, after conferring with the old man in their language. He told the twins, "The Honus slid out of the tank on the water slide and the people helped them out of the pool because the Honus requested it."

"Why did they want out?" Ronan asked. "Were they worried about the sharks? Where are they?"

"Right there, of course," Ke-ola replied, nodding at the tables, some of which now had heads, tails, and legs.

"Silly, didn't you recognize them?" Murel asked.

"No, the shells are different, aren't they?" Ronan answered. "The Honu shells are like our Honu's, kind of pointy at the back and streamlined. These are round and have that octagonal cell design on the back."

"Shhh," Ke-ola said.

"Why?" Ronan asked. It seemed apparent to him, not anything to be quiet about.

"Because it's their secret," Ke-ola said. "The Great Secret Transformation of the Honus."

"The one Dr. Mabo was so mad to find out about?" Ronan asked, referring to their former science teacher, a woman who had an obsession with shape shifters and had tormented the Honu because she believed the sea turtle could change shapes.

"Yes," Ke-ola said. "She found out that they made the transformation, she just didn't know what it was."

"Neither do I," Murel said, puzzled. "What is it? That their shells change shape and color a bit?"

"Oh, no," Ke-ola said. "It's far more dramatic than that."

"So?" both twins demanded, still puzzled.

"Well, look at them more closely. It's obvious!"

The twins looked at each other and shrugged, then turned back to Ke-ola.

"Look at their legs. See? No flippers. Big sturdy legs. They've changed, you see. They are no longer sea turtles who live in the water. They have altered their structure so that they are now land *tortoises*."

"Oh," Murel said.

"It's a very big change," Ke-ola declared, as if daring them to say it didn't amount to much, though in fact it was hard to tell there was any change at all.

"Oh, yeah," Ronan said. "Anyone can see that. But it makes me wonder—could the sharks turn into something else too? Like dolphins or salmon, something like that?"

"Not that I've ever heard," Ke-ola said in a wry tone. "Though there is a rumor that perhaps the Mano come to us in the form of recruiters for the Intergal labor force."

AT FIRST JOHNNY said he didn't think they could load the sharks without killing them, since unlike the Honus, the sharks needed the water to breathe. But Ke-ola's Honu pointed out that a shark would just fit into his old, smaller transport tank.

"What do you think, Madame?" Johnny asked Marmie. "It's your call."

"I think if we try and we fail, then at least we will have made every effort to accommodate these people, which I hope they will remember. If we try and succeed, then we'll have to decide what to do next. I'm a bit worried about Petaybee's reaction."

Murel said, "I shouldn't worry too much about that if I were you, Marmie. It's not like there aren't other predatory creatures already on Petaybee. And you know, if it doesn't care for the sharks as they are right now, Petaybee has a way of adjusting things—adapting them, so they are better suited to it."

Johnny, who knew of sharks by reputation and from personal encounters on other worlds, nodded and said, "Yes, I've no doubt that eventually it will all work out. It's just that painful adjustment period that might cause a spot of bother."

The Manos's people insisted on personally handling the sharks during the transfer from lake to tank to larger tank aboard the ship. Nobody contested their exclusive claim to the dubious honor.

Ronan and Murel were perfectly happy to stay on the *Piaf* without the need for space suits or dry suits or having to swim through root-choked tunnels. After enjoying a snack of tea and cakes, with tinned fish for Sky, they returned to their cabin to catch up on their sleep.

When they awoke, the dry area of the lounge was crowded with both turtle and shark people as well as large slumbering Honu/ tortoises. The tank was filled with murderous-looking Manos, who appeared less than happy to be there and seemed to be continually evaluating the nutritional benefits of the various crew members who passed before them.

The sharks' presence made the twins want to avoid the lounge, which was the most pleasant and social of the meeting areas on the ship. Somehow, the sharks glowering hungrily at everyone through the glass put a damper on their own appetites. There were only four—the male they had met, his mate, and two young—but in no way did they blend in with the rest of the company, despite their claim to kinship with some of it.

The new passengers—sharks and Honus/land tortoises aside— were not the cheerful, nature-centered, flower-wreath-making, singing, and dancing folk Ke-ola had told them about. The children, thin and runny-nosed, cried constantly, and the heavy appearance of people like the old shark matriarch, the twins discovered, was more a matter of bone structure than nutrition.

Indeed, after looking askance at the replicated food and nutrient bars that were routine shipboard fare, the newcomers began eating so much that the replicators overheated. As a result, by the third day of the trip home the electronic bits wore out and the replicators stopped working altogether. Fortunately, the ship also carried stores of the dried, powdered, or otherwise preserved staples that had pro- vided occasional treats for the twins. Most of these provisions were bound for some of Marmie's client satellites. The tinned fish went quickly, and the twins later learned this was partially because Sky had raided the stores and hoarded a good stock of his favorite food for his own needs.

Large bags of rice, supplemented by cans of mystery meat, served to keep everyone full. The Honu/land tortoises were shown to the 'ponics garden, and they crawled sedately down the corridors, then loaded one at a time into the lift down to the garden level. There, under Midori's watchful eye, they could graze on the plant life and also on the bugs that inevitably seemed to sprout in the gar- den along with the seeds.

That took care of everyone but the sharks.

"Ritual sacrifice is out of the question," Johnny Green an- nounced before anyone suggested it. "Unfortunately, we have no designated sacrificial crew members aboard at this time."

"The Manos are hungry!" the shark clan chieftainess declared.

"Madame, that is painfully obvious," Johnny told her, darting an uncomfortable glance at the toothy snarling maws staring hungrily through the glass at the lounge full of inaccessible prey. In an attempt to be diplomatic, he smiled his most roguishly handsome smile and asked, "As primary shark liaison officer for your people, have you any suggestions about what we could offer them—other than personnel, that is?"

She looked at Sky and raised her eyebrows in a calculating way.

Sky attempted to look small. Murel and Ronan stepped in front of him.

"I'm afraid Chief Petty Officer Sky, our otter operative for this mission, is essential personnel," Johnny told her. On a more practical note he added, "Besides, he'd be less than an appetizer for the smallest of your cranky kinsmen."

That's when they learned about Sky's secret stores of tinned fish, or at least it was when he admitted it. Since Sky periodically brought the twins a tin to unzip long after the rest of the fish supply was exhausted, they had sort of figured it out already.

When he led them to his hiding place, though, Murel shook her head. *I can see why you'd make the offer, Sky, but there's even less of this than there is of you. And it's not like you can eat just anything. You need this fish just as much as the sharks do.*

"Besides," Ronan said aloud, "the Mano madame says sharks only like live prey."

"What are we going to do then?" Murel asked. "I wish those people hadn't brought those horrid creatures along or that we'd never found them."

"They have some redeeming qualities," Ronan said. "They didn't eat us when they had the chance, though I'm sure they're regretting that now."

"Indeed."

Ke-ola had followed them from the lounge and glanced sheepishly at his new friends. "I'm sorry about this. Sharks make good aumakuas because they're such powerful creatures but they aren't really good space travelers. Actually, they can probably survive the whole journey without eating as long as it doesn't take any longer than it took us to get here, but I wouldn't like to be on the transfer team that takes them from the ship to the ocean on Petaybee."

"They'll probably have to be sedated," Murel said.

"That's it! That's brilliant," Ronan said. "We just need to sedate them—hypersleep would probably be the best thing, but they wouldn't fit in the chambers."

Sedation worked, but in the end they had to sedate the old lady and two other family members as well. There were only a few days left of the journey, too short a time to put the people in hypersleep. However, once the sedated sharks were floating peacefully in their tanks and the old lady and her staunchest followers slept in their bunks, the tone of the entire journey markedly improved.

Ship's maintenance extended the apparatus for the twins' privacy curtain to veil the shark tank, a measure that markedly improved the morale of the crew and most passengers.

The twins and Sky helped entertain the children. While they were at it, Ronan and Murel picked up some conversational vocabulary in the language of their guests.

Sadly, however, the children of Halau knew very little of the colorful customs Ke-ola had described and demonstrated at school and on Petaybee.

"So your people didn't really live like that?" Murel asked.

"We did, or at least tried to, when I was growing up," said Ke-ola, who had reached the ripe old age of thirteen recently. "But Midori and I were talking about it and she says the culture grew from the place we lived, back on our islands on Terra. It makes sense, since we recognized the spirits of the land and sea and other animals. Except for the aumakuas, we don't have any of those things anymore. That land, to hear Aunty Kimmie Sue tell it, was rich and full of food for feasts. The climate was mild and we didn't have to work very hard to live, so we developed our dances and singing and other skills. You've seen Halau. If the people tried to live like they used to, it would kill them. The planet is deteriorating and the company hires away many of the stronger adults and older kids. The people who stayed behind did well just to keep themselves and the aumakuas living and fed. At least the kids know about that part of our culture."

Murel made an *mmm* sound. Ronan gave a snort. He considered the aumakuas a mixed blessing. Honus were fine. Sharks were something he would have just as soon left behind.

More Petaybeans would share that feeling when the *Piaf* docked near Kilcoole and the sharks had to be moved from the only space port on the whole pole to the warm seawater near the volcanic island.

CHAPTER 10

NATURALLY, THE SHARKS could not be unloaded until they had been thoroughly inspected by everyone on the entire northern pole brave enough to enter the ship and face the monsters for whom they coined the Petaybean word that translated as "doom with fins."

The twins' geneticist father, Sean Shongili, was fascinated with the offworld creatures. He immediately buttonholed the shark clan matriarch, whose name was Puna Mano'aumakua. He asked her so many earnest questions and listened to her with such flattering attention that the forbidding-looking woman started smiling a lot. Murel realized, with a mixture of amusement and horror, that the large grim shark lady was actually flirting with their da!

Clodagh, very sensibly, was far more intrigued with the Honu/land tortoises. She expressed surprise that the little Honu she had known previously as a water dweller now crawled along the ground on elephantine feet under a substantial armor of shell. "Practical," she said, nodding approval.

"What does Petaybee think of the sharks?" Murel asked Clodagh.

"Doesn't know them yet," she said. "When they are in the sea, the planet will sort out what to do with them." Meanwhile, fish both finned and shelled were delivered via boat and otter paw as Sky's relatives hastened to provide the newcomers with nonmammalian meals.

Sky dutifully stood near the tank and regaled the sharks with the generosity of the noble otters, both riverine and sea—as well as sky otters, of whom he was the only one—who were to be the shark's greatest guides and allies on Petaybee. And who, Sky pointed out repeatedly, tasted horrible and were known to be poisonous.

On the journey home, Marmie had ordered a second tank the same size as the one aboard the *Piaf,* and a barge to haul it down the river and out to sea.

The new tank was filled with water, and the sharks sedated again. Then one by one they were carried in the Honu's original tank to the new one on the barge already afloat on the river that ran from the Petaybee space port, through Kilcoole, all the way to the ocean.

The tortoises, in the interest of learning about their new home, said that they would walk the whole way.

"I'm not sure that's such a good idea," Yana Maddock-Shongili, the twins' mother, said, as if the tortoises were her kids too, instead of old enough to be her grandparents. "Fall's just begun but there's snow in the air already."

The twins relayed this to Sky, who was anxious to get back into the river again. He had proposed to guide the tortoises to the sea. "Snow is fun!" he told the Honus. "If snow comes, we can all slide on it. Shells slide good!"

By then the twins' mother had hugged, kissed, and had someone else feed her children. The twins' mum was an ex–career military officer, and very good she had been at it, they were sure. Much better at officering than at cooking. She almost had to be.

She had also seen the sharks and was far less enamored of them than her husband. So when the twins asked to swim with Sky and guide the Honus to the sea, she agreed more readily than they'd expected.

"By all means go, swim and enjoy the sea before your ugly guests make it too perilous for me to let you go without an armed escort."

"Oh, Mum," Murel said, laughing. "The Manos are dangerous but they won't hurt *us*. They didn't even attack us when they were half starved, and that was before we saved their lives and all."

She felt it would only muddy the waters, so to speak, if she mentioned that during that first encounter she and Ronan had their teeth firmly embedded in the lead shark's tail.

Sis, she said we can. Let's quit while we're ahead, okay? Ronan said in thought-talk.

"Nevertheless," Mum continued, "I want you to take Nanook and Coaxtl with you."

"Mum, they'll scare the otters," Murel said, winging it a little. The big cats, domestic and snow leopard, had been the twins' reluctant nannies when they were little kids. Though they still loved both of the large felines, they had long ago outgrown nursemaids of any species.

"Don't give me that nonsense," their mother replied in her briskest commanding officer voice, "I know you all communicate telepathically. The cats know the otters are off-limits for chasing or tormenting, much less as prey. Simply explain to the otters and other creatures on your mission—er, journey—that 'Nook and Co' are big pussycats who are there to protect all concerned. I'm sure you can make yourselves understood. Have I made *my*self understood?"

"Ma'am, yes, ma'am," Ronan said with a mock salute, to which Mum responded with a hug and a swat on the butt for them each as they ran toward the river.

CHAPTER 11

THE RIVER WAS almost more of a home to the twins than their parents' cabin. Racing to their favorite entry spot, they stripped down and dived in, changing to seal form as they hit the water. Meanwhile Sky danced on the shore ahead of the Honu procession, which watched the foolishness tolerantly.

Before they could surface, they heard and felt a large splash. Fingers and opposable thumbs caught each of their tails. They flipped around to face a laughing Ke-ola.

"Trying to leave me to all the dull diplomat stuff, were you? Leilani can handle that. The Honu wants to go with his elders, and Keoki can't wait to see the sea."

The twins couldn't answer him directly but over his shoulder they saw Keoki leading two curly coats, their own horses, Chapter and Page. He seemed to be receiving a lot of unsolicited advice from Nanook and Coaxtl. Coaxtl walked in circles around the boy and horses, giving them a thorough inspection while the more domesticated lion-sized track cat, Nanook, rubbed against all ten legs involved in the horse-leading operation.

Ke-ola's Honu friend had been installed atop the shell of the foremost land-tortoise-shaped Honu, where the younger, smaller creature could advise the entire column.

Wouldn't you rather be in the water with us? Murel asked.

I could not swim in this form, the Honu said, *and it would be disrespectful to change before my elders.*

Suit yourself, Ronan said, plunging back into the refreshing depths of the living river.

They frolicked in the currents and eddies, playing leap-seal and having races, snacking on the plentiful tasty fish, loving the freedom of the big wide deep river after the confines of the root-choked tunnels of Halau. It smelled so good, so full of growing plants suffusing it with oxygen, so full of colors and textures in the water's flow. It was as different from the tank and the tunnels as Halau was from Petaybee.

Sky jumped in and out of the water, splashing the ponderous Honus playfully, sprinting back to play peeking games with Keoki. Ke-ola's brother was surly to start with, but eventually seemed pleased to be included in the otter's games.

Chapter and Page pranced restlessly, eager to stretch their legs after too many weeks of receiving the minimum attention due them while their primary riders were away.

The smell of snow was in the air, a shimmer of frost sparkling on the ferns lining the banks.

The river was chilled by ice that formed at night and melted when the sun rose. It felt marvelous, but when the warm sulfurous current from the hot springs flowed into the river, that felt marvelous too.

We should show the Honus and Keoki the hot springs, Murel told her brother. When he agreed, she passed the thought on to the Honu who told Ke-ola what she was thinking.

Then they turned up the little stream that flowed from the pool below the falls that concealed the communion cave.

Ke-ola floated in the current and called to his brother, "Hey, Keoki, you're gonna love this, man! This is the magic place I told you about when we were on the ship. You should come in now. The water is warm, feels great."

"Stinks a little," Keoki said, drawing near and peering into the water from which a light steam rose.

"Get used to it!" Ke-ola told him. "You think that's bad, man, wait till you smell what it's like out near our new place."

Keoki wrinkled his nose but stripped off the three layers of outer clothing he'd been wearing against the chill, held his nose, and jumped in.

When the twins reached the pool at the foot of the waterfall, they saw the Honus tagging far behind them, a line of upturned cauldrons in stately procession. Ke-ola, Sky, and Keoki climbed to the top of the waterfall and slid down it into the pool. Ronan said, *Come on, sis, let's do that too!*

But Murel, suddenly self-conscious, replied, *But we'd have to change . . .*

So what? Ke-ola and Keoki know we change.

Maybe so, but we shouldn't be so careless about it, she said. That wasn't the real reason. She wasn't even sure what the real reason was, but lately, sometimes, she'd felt some differences in her body that had nothing to do with changing into a seal.

Have it your way, Ronan said. The truth was, he enjoyed being back in their own waters so much, he didn't want to come out any sooner than necessary.

So they played the game their own way. Murel hid behind the falls and leaped over Ke-ola when he splashed into the foam at the bottom of the pool. Ronan dived under Keoki when he splashed in. When Sky fell, he didn't reach the pool because Murel leaped up and caught him on her back, shedding him when she plunged deeper into the sulfurous warm water.

While the rest of them climbed, leaped, and dived, the Honus continued to make their way up the side of the stream until the path intersected with the one used by the villagers during latchkays.

After one more circuit in the waterfall by the frolicking youngsters, the Honus came abreast of them, then walked under the fall and into the communion cave.

Ke-ola almost landed on top of Murel's head as she paused to watch the last short triangular Honu tail disappear within the cascade.

Ke-ola surfaced and saw her looking after the tortoises. "Is something wrong?"

She couldn't answer directly. There wasn't anything wrong, but the power of the caves could be very strong. She'd never known others to enter without a native Petaybean, usually someone like Clodagh, beside them.

Catching her concern, Sky scrambled onto the bank and dashed after the Honus. *Otters belong to this world. Otters can show the Honus the world, and the world the Honus.*

Well, so could river seals. She and Ronan were the emissaries, after all. *Keep the Ke boys here, Ro. I'll change in the cave.*

The Honus and Sky were no longer in the outer cave. Murel shook herself off and loosened the harness holding her dry suit, climbing quickly into it. She followed the padding of ponderous Honu feet and the patter of otter paws on the cave's stone floor. Eleven leathery Honu heads craned from eleven shells, and eleven pairs of eyes widened as the heads swayed back and forth, taking in the cave. Sky ran circles around them, chattering away about how this was much better—hundreds and hundreds better—than the caves back on their old world.

You tell the Honus too, Murel, Sky said when he saw her. *Tell them how our world is better.*

She sat on one of the stone benches and shook her head. *You're doing a great job, Sky. River seals don't tell these things any better than otters.*

That was true, of course, though she knew she probably would have mentioned more things the Honus might like and less about how very tasty the fish and river grasses were and how many wonderful muddy places there were to slide in the winter and icy ones in the summer.

But as Sky regaled the tortoises, the cave grew welcoming and warm, as it did at the beginning of the night visits for a latchkay.

Although none of the more spectacular expressions of the planet's personality manifested themselves, the tortoises seemed well aware of Petaybee's presence. They craned their wrinkled necks and widened their eyes and appeared to be listening with their invisible ears to something beyond Sky's sales pitch. At last they seemed satisfied, lowered their heads, and with deliberate steps turned their shells toward the entrance to the cave. Then they paraded single file out from behind the waterfall and down the path. Murel followed and watched until their shells appeared no larger than a nut's. Ke-ola and Keoki, seeing the Honus were leaving, stopped playing. Keoki awkwardly mounted Chapter and led Page, while Ke-ola struck out swimming back to the main channel, following the Honus.

Sis? Ronan called.

Coming, she called back. Stripping off her dry suit, she harnessed it to her back again, then dived into the pool, transforming as she shot deeper into the steaming warm water.

By the time she reached Ronan and Ke-ola, Ke-ola was ready to climb out and join his brother. "That hot springs water wears you out," he told the two seals watching him from the stream.

It did indeed, so much so that when the stream rejoined the river, the twins had to catch a few fish to keep up their strength.

As the day ended, the twins flopped themselves onto the bank. Murel chose a particularly ferny spot that provided her with privacy to finish changing and dressing. Then the twins helped the brothers to find the best wood for a fire. When it was just right, Ronan dived back in and caught enough fish for all of them, though Sky brought his own, the largest fish of all. They got little warmth from the fire, though, for the Honus were feeling the chill of the evening and ringed the blaze with their giant shells, blocking the warmth from the unshelled members of the party.

The twins and the brothers slept in bedrolls carried on the horses. Sky joined the two-leggeds in a companionable way, snuggling between Murel and Ronan, though normally he would have slept in a den in the riverbank.

Long before the sunrise, an event occurring minutes later each day, the Honus announced that they would be off again. Moving was warmer than not moving, and by now they thought they smelled the salt of the sea.

At midday Sky streaked ahead of the others, returning in an hour with some of his hundreds of relatives. They greeted the twins with diving and nosings, and thoroughly explored the tortoises, running around, between, and over them. One even tried to peer inside a huge shell but the Honu discouraged the bold otter with a hiss.

You were quick, Murel said to Sky.

Yes, otters are quick, that is so, Sky responded. *But the sea is close. Very close.*

Is it? she asked. *I thought we still had miles to go.*

It moved, Sky told her. *My relatives' old dens are far beneath the sea now. They moved too. Even the sea otter cousins moved from their island. The sea is near.*

He was right. In another half hour or so, even with all of the otter foolishness, they soon reached a place where the river broadened, covering hills and land, even trees, until there was only water and no banks to be seen on the surface. The water grew suddenly salty.

Murel dived and swam out a short distance. Beneath her, fish swam among the bare and rotting tree branches, while seaweed and crabs decorated the trunks, making of the drowned trees a forest of individual wooden reefs.

The water smelled ever so slightly of sulfur, like the spot in the river where the stream drained from the hot spring.

Murel returned to the shore. Ronan and otters of both riverine and sea variety swam in the shallower waters. Keoki and Ke-ola dismounted and turned to face the approaching Honus.

Now we change, the smallest Honu announced on behalf of the others. *The seals must change as well. We will need them.*

Murel and Ronan hoisted themselves onto the shore, Murel finding the upper branches of a submerged tree to conceal her while she pulled on her dry suit. Then she joined the boys.

The small Honu needed only Ke-ola to help him transform, but when it came time for the larger ones to do so, the brothers slid into the water and supported the front ends of the heavy tortoises while the twins supported the back end from the shore. In this way, the tortoises were able to change their stumpy legs to long flippers on the front and shorter wedge-shaped ones in the back without injuring themselves, while first the lower shell and then the edge of the upper changed. At that point in the transformation, each half sea turtle/half tortoise could complete the transformation by dipping his head under the surface without drowning. This accomplished, the Honu swam gracefully out to sea.

All four youngsters were exhausted by the time they had helped all eleven tortoises convert.

"I can see why they don't do it more often and Dr. Mabo thought it was so secret," Ronan told Ke-ola.

"They need our help usually," Ke-ola said. "At least to go back to sea. They're very vulnerable to attack while they change. And their flippers won't support them for long on land, unless it's sand. If they take the tortoise form into the water, they can't survive either. So as far as I know, they never change without some of us around to help them."

"As an adaptive mechanism, then, it's not very convenient, is it?" Murel asked.

"I think they're still learning," Ke-ola told her. "I don't think Honus have always been able to do it."

Ronan, who was very interested in learning about other shape shifters and shape-shifting in general, said, "That's funny. Dad, Murel, and I have always been able to change."

Ke-ola shrugged. "Maybe the shells make it harder. Or maybe it's because they're older. I don't know if they even know."

"Did you ever ask them?"

"No. See, we've always had Honus, but I don't know anybody who's ever been able to talk to one as personally, I guess you could say, as I have been and you guys are able to do. What we usually do—used to do—was wait till we had something important to ask them, or maybe they waited till they had something important to tell us before we talked to each other."

"Not much for idle chitchat, then?" Murel asked.

"Not as such, no," Ke-ola said.

"I'll ask," Ronan said, and waded back into the water where the turtles were now swimming toward the horizon.

"Wait for me," Murel said, a bit late.

"I'm coming too," Ke-ola said.

"Me too," Keoki said. "They're our Honus after all."

They swam after the turtles until the smallest swam back toward them, up under Keoki, inviting him to hang on to the shell.

Murel decided Honus were probably good at psychology. It was easy to see that Keoki was disgruntled by the changes, by being up-rooted and separated from Halau, horrible as the place had been. She'd felt a bit that way several years before when she and Ronan had been sent off Petaybee to school on Marmie's space station, even though it was a beautiful and luxurious facility. Ke-ola, who had already visited Petaybee, had met the planet and been accepted by it. He was much more at home here than his brother. The newly transformed sea turtles gave off an intense feeling of relief and ease at being able to stop crawling and start swimming.

Keoki, having literally taken the turtle by the shell, was embold-ened enough to ask the question. "Sacred Honu, how did you and the others happen to learn to change from sea creatures to land?"

CHAPTER 12

THE ELEVEN TURTLES, two humans, and two selkies—plus a number of otters who were busy chattering and splashing each other and were not paying any attention at all to the others— had been swimming out to sea. But as the small Honu answered Keoki's question, the other turtles paused to swim in a circle around the small Honu and Keoki, Ke-ola, Murel, and Ronan.

The Honu's Story

Here is how it was. Long time ago we always had the sea to swim in, the warm bright sea full of delicious things to eat and soft clean beaches to lay our eggs. No Honu ever went hungry and the food in the sea was so good, few among the other sea folk preyed upon us, for our shells were hard and our bite was harder. We lived long and became wise and numerous as grains of sand on the beaches.

Then men came and found us easy to catch and less danger-

ous than Manos or stingrays or other animals. They ate us and
thought us tasty and thus we were doomed. They used our very
shells as bowls from which to scoop our poor flesh, then made
our shells into implements. Other creatures stole our eggs too,
but the people harvested so many that our young did not hatch
into the world.

One day a whole family came to take the eggs, a mama, a
papa, and their young, a baby. The mama laid the baby on the
sand while she helped her husband collect the eggs. They were
laughing and talking and didn't notice the big bird circling
overhead. He heard the baby laughing to herself and saw her
waving her arms and legs around, playing with her toes. He
thought she looked tasty and swooped down to get her.

Most times if we saw a bird like that when we were on the
beach with our eggs, we'd make a circle around them so the bird
couldn't get at them. We saw the bird. We made a circle. That
day five of us had been watching the people take our eggs. We
could do nothing about that. But we could keep that bird from
taking another young thing. We circled close around that
human child. The bird screamed with anger when he saw he
couldn't get her, and her parents looked up and drove him away.
Then they thought we were trying to hurt their child. When we
moved away and they saw that she was fine, they were glad.
They thanked us and were surprised when we talked back and
told them they were doing to us what we would not let the bird
do to their daughter. They put back the eggs and promised that
they would tell their families what had happened and what we
said. After that, those people were our family.

That was good. They sheltered and protected us from others
among them who did not revere us. If not for them, we might
have all perished.

The Honus collectively gave the sigh hiss the twins had come to
know as a Honu's expression of frustration or relief.

Soon they themselves were preyed upon by other men who took their lands and waters and harvested the living things they contained as if by right. Again our people saved some of us, though many more were lost. Then the newcomers built great nests that shat poison into our waters. Sores and growths worse than barnacles covered our skins, our shells grew soft, and we died in great numbers. Many wise elders who had escaped hunting died from this poison. But we could do nothing to save ourselves because our homes were in the sea and all the sea had become poisoned.

Then one day a clutch of eggs hatched young who looked strange and behaved differently from all of their ancestors. Perhaps the poison changed them or perhaps the forces that created them took pity, knowing that if they did as forebears had done, they would not survive long in the world. They had strong stumpy feet that carried them easily across the land. They grew hard heavy shells that could shield them from the sun and hide their tender parts from enemies. But they could not join their parents or the other remaining Honus in the sea. They were too heavy and their stumpy feet did not let them swim as easily as flippers or webbed feet.

In time some mated and laid their own eggs, but others, remembering what they had been, yearned toward the sea and its dangers and found their fellow tortoises unappealing. Only the turtles of the sea pleased them when they thought to mate. But it was difficult for the sea Honu to go ashore to mate, and so the land tortoises jumped back into the sea. They would have drowned, and perhaps some did, but some part of their beings recalled what they had been and changed them to it once more. In this way, more turtles were born, some starting life on the land, some in the sea. We who change are the descendants of the tortoises who returned to the sea. The children of the tortoises who mated with other tortoises on the land produced only land creatures who could not breathe the sea. Eggs that hatched into sea turtles who returned to the sea never changed into land creatures.

This was their bad luck. Those who could not change died off and only we who can survived.

Murel thought about the story for a moment, then said, *While I don't want to be rude or anything, it seems to me that a change that is as difficult to make as yours is not a very useful one. You need quite a lot of help to make it, after all.*

The Honu gave a frustrated hiss. *That is true. But it is also true that change is usually more difficult than not changing. It is true as well that changing often takes help. Our change has served its purpose. We have survived a long time.*

Ah, so the story had a moral, Murel thought. Overall, the Honu's tale was a bit like a Petaybean song.

After the story, all of the other Honus had things to say. *Basically you have it straight, young one, but the way I heard it, we started on the land and then went to the sea,* one said.

Yes, and I distinctly remember, said one whose mental voice was old and creaky, *that some of the ones who stayed in the sea turned into something else—warthogs, was it? Octopuses? Let me think now. Maybe it was jellyfish.*

It's been a long trip, Grandfather, said another turtle, just as big but sounding much younger. *Let's give it a rest now, shall we? The youngster got it mostly right.*

No, no, not octopuses or jellyfish, the older turtle continued, correcting himself. *Could have been clams, though. Or lobsters or crabs. Shells, you know. Our sort will always have an affinity for shells.*

Sky swam up with a dozen or more sea otters. *Are you going to the volcano, river seals? Otters like to go there for the giant white clams.*

Ronan said, *I guess with no deep sea otters there to object, the sea otter cousins can have all the clams they want.*

Deep sea otters do not care how many clams sea otters take, one of the sea otters replied. *Deep sea otters give clams to sea otters.*

How can that be? Murel asked. *The deep sea otters' den was buried by the volcano. We threw clamshell leis down to them, remember?*

The sea otter somersaulted in the water and came right side up facing her. *That may be, but there are still deep sea otters living out there. Maybe all of them did not live in the strange den. Maybe some swam away.*

Maybe so, Murel replied, feeling a bit excited but also a little worried. The deep sea otters' "den" had resembled an odd human city, or the ruins of one. A very unotter-like presence sent thoughts from within, and the city had seemed impenetrable to Ronan and her. Still, the deep sea otters, or whatever they were, had saved her da when he was injured. That made them good, didn't it?

Ronan caught her line of thinking. *Unless they were the ones who hurt him to begin with,* he said.

Yeah, she said. *There is that.*

How big is the volcano now? Ronan asked the otters.

Big. Bigger than before, was the answer. *But quiet now.*

Perhaps it's done, Murel mused. *Perhaps it made the island and settled down so Ke-ola's people can move there soon.*

It should be safe to swim out there now.

Yes, but we promised Mother we wouldn't.

I know, but if the deep sea otters are still alive, someone should warn them about the Manos. We won't be able to swim out there safely once they're let loose, so we'd better do it now.

You don't think we'll be safe around the Manos? They did promise not to harm us.

You trust them?

Not really.

Me neither. So on the whole, what do you think Mum or Da would do in our position, if they knew all the facts? Would they just leave these deep sea otters or whatever they were who saved Da to face the sharks without warning?

Otters could warn them, Sky said.

Only if otters remembered to warn them while they were harvesting clams, Murel replied. In some ways she didn't trust otters either, Sky being an exception. She and Ronan liked to play, but compared to otters, they were party poopers. Sky might have been the only one among them who was a sky otter, but they were all a bit flighty.

It's not like there's time to go back and ask permission, even if we could, Ronan rationalized. *We promised to keep them secret, after all.*

Just a quick trip, then, she agreed. The volcanic flow had covered so much of the ocean floor that the closest approach to where the "den" of the deep sea otters had been was nearer than before. They had discovered this when they went to pay their respects to the presumably dead denizens with clamshell leis, as Ke-ola had showed them.

The Honus, usually patient creatures, were chilled by the wintry waters close to the polar shore.

We wish to go to the new home, one of them told the seals, otters, and the brothers.

Ke-ola and Keoki, back on shore, looked unhappy. *We want to go too but we can't,* they said.

If you are too weak to swim all that way, grandsons, you may hold onto our shells and we will tow you, the Honus offered.

We can't, the boys said. *It's too cold. We'd freeze if we swam in that very long.*

Ronan and Murel agreed that the only way they could all go together was to find the brothers a boat. Murel and Sky turned north and swam along the coastline, while Ronan and some of the sea otters turned south. But they discovered that the entire length of the shoreline was abandoned. Where normally there might be boats and nets and small villages or camps, now the sea was bounded only by rocks, drowned trees, and sheer cliffs. The water was higher than at any time in Petaybee's history.

I know the volcano made high water and waves, but I can't believe people moved so far from the sea, Murel called to her brother. *They make their livelihoods from it! Surely they can't be far. Maybe we should change and walk inland a bit and see if we can spot anybody.*

Of course, if we do find a boat, we'd have to carry it back to the shore. I guess Ke-ola and Keoki should help us search. If we're not around to guide them they could get lost.

And we couldn't? Ronan asked. *We should have asked Mum and Da about this sort of thing. They'd know.*

So will Sky's hundreds of relatives. So, race you back to the river. Last one there's an otter's uncle.

The twins raced through the icy waves, enjoying the freedom of the sea as they had the rivers. The Honus waited for them near the river mouth. They were not pleased with the new plan.

It is too cold to wait here. We must swim to the new warm water. You have fur and no shells to shatter in the frozen tide. We must go now.

We'll not be long, she told the turtles. *We'll just change and get into the dry suits and—* She stopped talking to the Honus and said to Ronan, *That's it! The dry suits! We can let Ke-ola and Keoki wear them. They keep out the wet, but they keep out the cold and the wind too.*

The suits had hoods, mittens, and booties that could be attached as firmly as a space suit's boots, gauntlets, and helmet. They were also expandable to fit the twins as they grew.

Honu, if you would tell Ke-ola to take the packs from the harnesses strapped to our backs, Ronan said, *he and Keoki can wear our dry suits to keep warm and dry on the trip out to the volcano. Since Murel and I are in seal form, we'll not be needing them till we return from the volcano.*

Ke-ola and Keoki did as the Honus instructed and removed the twins' packets from their harnesses. The two boys, though older and larger than either twin, easily skinned into the suits.

Then, booties, gloves, and hoods secured, they waded into the water. The largest of the Honus waited for them where the river became the sea. Each boy grabbed the top of a Honu shell and was carried away as easily as driftwood.

With the Honus in the lead, Ke-ola and Keoki trailing in their wake, and Ronan and Murel following, they set off for the volcano. The sea otters did not go. Sky did not want to go either, at night and in salt water, which was not what a former river otter preferred, but he could not bear to be left behind, so in the end he too hitched a ride on the shell of a Honu.

"Their" Honu, the small one, was a little slow since he didn't have as much paddle power as the larger ones. Before long Ronan surged ahead of him. Shortly thereafter, he amused himself by letting off a continual stream of the snore-fart noises he used for sonar.

Ro! she called, her head aching with the force it took to get through to him. *Cut it out. You're not even stopping long enough to let the sound bounce back to you.*

Am too, he said. *For your information there is a sizable iceberg off our bow at two o'clock.*

That's very interesting but we're not ships. Even if we ran into it we wouldn't hurt ourselves. We can't go that fast.

Ouch! For your information, you can so hurt yourself if you run into this iceberg while you're listening to your stupid sister instead of the echoes from your sonar. Ran right into it.

And over the top of the next wave she saw it, her brother outlined against it before he dived. The Honus, not relying on sonar, swam neatly around it.

Undeterred, her brother called back, *If you don't want to navigate properly, please don't distract me.* Then he recommenced his series of snore-fart blatting, managing to sound pompous this time.

She stayed purposely behind the Honus, feeling somehow that their rear needed guarding. If she lost sight of them, she used her own sonar, emitting a sound that was not nearly so rude as the one Ronan produced. Hers was a throaty roar with a high-pitched tweak at the end. It sounded to her almost musical in its range.

She noticed that there weren't as many icebergs as there had been even in the summer, when they'd rescued Da and first saw the volcano spew.

But the water seemed warmer too, even so far away from the

crater. Of course, the big volcano wasn't the only one warming the waters. Though they were still some distance away, there were smaller chimneys of gas and liquid venting from the planet's belly in the same volcanic caldera. These were called black smokers because, well, they were black from the solidified mineral deposits left behind when the hot gases cooled off rapidly in the frigid waters. And they continued to smoke as the gas continued to rise. All around them were the rich beds of specialized sea plants and animals, including white crabs and clams. The otters loved those so much they risked dodging the hot water and acid pumping from the active vents in order to snatch up some of the delicacies.

And even though the bed of smokers began farther out to sea, the warmth from them raised the temperature of the sea enough that it explained the relative scarcity of icebergs.

She had thought that the higher watermark on the coastline was due to displacement from the volcanic island, but now she reconsidered. Farther up the coast, where there was a year-round ice pack, that ice would have been touched by the warmer flow too and melted, perhaps for the first time in many years. For the first time *ever*. Petaybee was definitely rearranging its furnishings to accommodate its latest creation.

At some point during the night, Murel fell asleep, which she had never done before while still in the water. She didn't mean to. It just happened. She opened her eyes and found herself floating below the surface. How had she breathed? Her nostrils were closed. But then, without intending to, while still half asleep, she surfaced, breathed, and submerged again. Interesting. You never knew what you could do until the occasion arose, just like Mum always said.

However, she had no idea how far ahead of her Ronan and the others were. No doubt he had been having way too much fun making loud noises to think to check on her or the Honus or anyone. She sent out her signal and listened as it enveloped the sea within its reach. Four more icebergs floating on either side of her and three black smokers beneath the waves—she had drifted a long way in her sleep! She also detected eleven Honus—two weighted down with humans, one with a river otter—and a seal making rude noises perhaps five kilometers ahead of her.

She had been swimming at a leisurely pace, to stay behind the Honus. With a powerful undulation of her sleek body, Murel pulled out the stops and torpedoed ahead, using her sonar not as wantonly as Ro did, but judiciously emitting her helpful—and yes, quite musical—signal at even intervals to keep her on course.

Then, suddenly, where there had been nothing, there was something very large. Very, very large, and it was coming straight toward her. When she changed course, so did it. Apparently she wasn't the only one with sonar in her immediate situation.

The thing drew close enough for her acute hearing to confirm her theory, at which point Murel realized that the large creature was not one entity, but many, all large. *Very* large. She swam for all she was worth, calling to Ronan as she did, hoping he would tire of the sound of his own signal long enough to hear her thought.

Something's chasing me, she said. *A school of something, I think.*

We'll come back for you, he told her.

But she realized that probably wasn't a good idea. She recognized the shape of her pursuers now, first by the shape of their sound, then as her eyes caught the white markings on their black hides. Orcas. Seals were part of their diet, she remembered from some natural science lesson. She and Ro had never had to worry about the creatures when they were allowed to swim only in the rivers. She couldn't remember whether they ate otters or not, or sea turtles.

Probably. There were so many of them and they hunted in schools, like wolves in packs. In fact, weren't they called the wolves of the sea? And they looked so friendly and cute when she was walking on two legs and safely dry on shore.

CHAPTER 13

S HE WANTED TO tell Ronan not to come and at the same time she also wanted to yell for help, but she had no chance to do either. The grinning whales circled past then surrounded her like a lot of footballers intent on the ball, only they were much noisier. They used their voices not only for sonar now, but to bewilder her. Swimming in an ever tightening spiral, they frothed and churned the water so that all she could see was their dark shapes whizzing around her and under her; that and flashes of humongous mouths filled with teeth the size of her foot, when she had feet.

It was great sport to them, which was all it could be since even one of them could gobble her down in a couple of bites.

Over here! To me to me! three of them cried at once.

An underpass! another sang out as he swam beneath her so close she could have hitched a ride had she had opposable thumbs at the time.

Something solid and black shot toward her, then into her, knocking her over and over in the water.

A side pass and a coup! Score one! called her attacker.

She had almost stopped spinning when another one did the same thing and cried a triumphant, *Coup and score!*

She spun dizzily away again, but this time pushed herself down as she spun, and actually landed on the back of the orca underpassing her. She was thoroughly confused, and she hated being confused so she was mad too. What worked on shark fins should work on whales as well, she thought, then clamped a black dorsal fin between her sharp teeth and bit.

Hey! the victim bellowed.

Score one for the seal, she called back to the lot of them. *You lot leave me alone or I'll make a meal of your fin before you make one of me.*

Us leave you alone? You've got my fin. You're confused about who's the prey here, seal. Orcas eat seals, not the other way around.

You're the one who's wrong, she said. *I'm not just any seal. I'm Murel Shongili, a girl and a selkie, and my family is going to be pissed if you kill me and will come after you with harpoons and guns.*

Back off, pod. There's something strange about this one. We may have made a mistake here.

You bet you did, Murel said. *I did not swim this far to be a whale snack. I'm on an important mission for Petaybee.*

We are too. We cull the seal population of specimens too slow to avoid us, said a voice above her. She looked up into a door-sized, spike-lined mouth.

Okay, eat me. I hope the sharks return the favor.

What's a shark? they asked in unison.

It's a fish as big as you guys with teeth as big as yours and a nasty attitude.

There's no fish as big as us in the whole world, the toothy whale scoffed.

Didn't used to be, she said.

Pod members, wait, said a calmer whale voice. *This is all familiar. Remember the stories our elders told of fish like that long ago on an-*

cient Terra, when we ruled the coastlines? The fish were called—yes—
they were called sharks. And they were fierce good sport. But they did
not prey on us. We preyed on them!

The orca she was riding flipped over suddenly, then righted himself, and she felt the fin tear as she slid off his back. He let out a
high sound that made her head feel like it was going to explode, and
flipped again, leaving her by herself with a mouth full of torn fin.
She spit it out and tried to swim under the pod but they were too
many, too large, and too fast.

Once more she was entombed in a wall of darkness with teeth.
She felt/heard another attacker an instant before he slammed into
her shoulder and neck, but he was too large and she was too small
and too surrounded to escape.

High on the inside! Strike! Her attacker gloated.

Swim aside, she's mine. She took a bite of me. Now it's my turn.

She screamed the scream of a terrified seal, and silently she cried
for help as she had not done before, though she knew there was
nothing Ronan, a bunch of sea turtles, a little otter, and two un-
armed boys could do except become whale food too.

RONAN HEARD HIS twin's first cry of alarm and didn't wait for further explanation. He felt her fear charge through his spine. Flipping
over, he swam back toward her.

"What's the matter, little bruthah? Where're you—where're we—
goin'?" Ke-ola asked, revising his question as the Honu whose shell
he held spun around to follow Ronan.

Ronan couldn't answer him but the Honus could. *Murel is under
attack.* The Honu was silent for a moment then continued, *Whales,
she thinks, orcas.*

"Whales wouldn't do that," Ke-ola protested, remembering his
stories. "Whales are good people. They wouldn't hurt a girl like that
without—"

She is no human child to them, but a seal who is their rightful prey, another Honu told him.

"If we explain it to them?" Ke-ola asked.

"Bruthah, you are such a dreamer!" Keoki, who also understood the Honu's thoughts, told him. "You don't know any of these things, any of this land. You got a head full of Aunty Kimmie's tall tales about the old days, which she never really lived through either. Things are different now."

Keoki had to sneer at his brother's notions very quickly because the Honu he was on was swimming much faster than he would have thought possible.

Ronan sent out one sonar signal after another.

Slow down, boy. Pace yourself so you can receive, a Honu cautioned.

What do you know about it? Ronan demanded rudely, because he was in a hurry and upset and he didn't want to slow down to listen. He had never felt such fear and panic from his sister before.

I may not have sonar, the Honu replied, *but it just makes sense that if you ask your world a question, you should wait a second for the answer.*

Ronan forced himself to wait a nano between signals and immediately sensed an enormous presence dead ahead about three klicks to the north. A mass of enormous presences.

The sonar didn't pick up Murel at all, but for another few furious lengths Ronan felt her desperately trying one thing after another to elude or dissuade her attackers.

He didn't send anything toward her. He didn't want to distract her. Maybe he should send to Da? But no, what good would that do? Da was far away, too far away to help. But what if the next thing he had to send to his father was that Murel was gone?

No!

The waves rose and he dived, cutting through the currents with strong undulations of his torso. Eight of the Honus dived with him, but those carrying Keoki and Ke-ola hesitated. The one carrying Sky dived too, in a moment, and the otter loosed himself and darted forward.

Otters are very brave and ferocious in battle! he cried. *Your sky otter friend is coming to save you, sister river seal! Do not give up!*

The seas ahead of them grew confused and murky. Ronan's sonar detected something shooting upward from the sea floor and swimming toward Murel and the orcas.

He couldn't tell what it was but it did not feel like a single creature.

Da! he cried. *Da! Help!*

Then, realizing, as Murel had earlier, that the whales could kill him and the others as well, he added, *Killer whales are trying to kill Murel. We're on our way but—* He didn't finish the thought: that their efforts might be fatal as well as futile. Instead he said, *We love you,* including both parents.

ODDLY ENOUGH, YANA was the one who first knew her daughter was in danger. She was working late, finishing up some paperwork, while Sean escorted the shark tank as it was being transported to the coast.

In the middle of a stack of immigration applications, she suddenly felt a bolt of panic shoot through her. A seasoned veteran of the Company Corps, Yana was not personally given to bolts of panic. But although this one didn't originate with her, it caused her a bolt of her own. "Murel!" she cried, and stood straight up, knocking her chair over.

Then she sat back down again and called her husband.

The com unit to his mobile beeped five times while Yana paced and snapped her fingers repeatedly. Finally, Sinead, Sean's sister, who also was working on the shark relocation project, answered.

"Sinead, where's Sean?"

"He just now sealed out of here without an explanation and

started swimming coastward," Sinead said. She didn't sound sleepy, but then, moving the sharks was a tricky operation. The barge and the powerful but makeshift tugboat towing it had brilliant lights so they could see the waters around them far enough to avoid trouble. Sinead didn't even sound particularly tired, but like Sean, she was apt to focus on the projects she undertook to the exclusion of creature comforts. Yana recalled when she had been like that herself, before motherhood and bureaucracy became her projects. Now she got plenty tired plenty often. "I had to fish the mobile out of the river. Why? What's wrong?"

"It's the kids—Murel, I think. I just got this terrible feeling that she's in trouble."

"I think Sean must have had the same feeling, Yana. How can I help?"

"I don't know. If I think of something, I'll pick you up on the way out to the coast."

"Okay, I'll continue shark wrangling until then."

Yana's next call was to Johnny Green at the helipad, and Marmie, who promised to make a call that would have what Yana thought she needed loaded and ready to go.

Meanwhile she went out to the moonlit corral and whistled for her favorite curly coat, Pi. When Pi came to her, she patted the horse and vaulted onto her bare back, hanging on to her mane as they jumped the corral fence and galloped along the river to the old Space Base, where the helipad was.

She saw the landing lights and the copter's beacon from a mile away. The rotors were whirling. She jumped off Pi before her mount became startled, swatted the horse on the rump, and sent her home. Johnny and Rick O'Shay, Yana's flight instructor—a former Company Corps pilot now retired to Petaybee—waved at her from the cockpit.

Pet Chan, Marmie's security chief, leaned out and gave her a hand up onto the inner deck. Beside her sat a burly barrel-chested man with grizzled hair and mustache. Pet introduced him as Raj.

Raj handed her a headset, like the ones everyone else wore, and Pet stopped shouting. "Raj is Marmie's personal jeweler and armorer," Pet explained. "When Johnny told us Murel was in danger, Raj grabbed a few of his favorite toys."

Raj shook her hand. "Raj Norman, Colonel. You're the mama, right?"

She nodded, and he said fiercely, "Don't worry. If anything's got your little girl, we'll make it beg us to take her back. Now this is a Colt dual mode laser mini mortar . . ."

He continued describing the arsenal of weapons that were strapped to his and Pet's bodies and were in a compact array at his feet. "You're welcome to anything," he said. "Help yourself."   .

Yana thanked him and wondered briefly if she was going to feel foolish for overreacting if Murel's trouble turned out to be little more than a bout of preteen histrionics. But no, the sick sinking feeling left over from that first shock was still fluttering at the bottom of her rib cage. She took the mini mortar and two air-to-sea missile launchers as well as a stun gun with settings that ranged from a mosquito to a small moon, should a small moon ever need stunning.

Johnny was flying copilot since Rick was more intimately familiar with the landscape.

The glow from the lights of the barge and tug on the horizon let them know they were near even before they saw the covered shark tank and the boat. As the chopper drew closer, Yana briefly considered stopping for Sinead, but decided that making time was more important. If this was happening to someone else's kid and she was advising them, she knew she'd be thinking that it might already be too late.

CHAPTER 14

S EAN SHONGILI HAD been helping pole the shark tank barge away from the sandbar when Murel's cry reached him. Behind him was another river channel and the darkened forest. In front of him the lights of the barge sparkled off the rippling water with an almost blinding effect. Since he was concentrating heavily on directions from his fellow polers and his own physical exertion, it took a little longer for his daughter's terror to register than it had with her mother.

Shortly afterward, the barge cleared the bar. Sean was stripping down when the mobile call came, but the mobile itself was in the way of ridding himself of his trousers. When it fell in the water, he didn't bother retrieving it. Making an arrow of his slim sinewy body, he dived into the river and changed, his sleek seal form maintaining the arrowlike speed and purposefulness of his dive.

The barge, towed by one of Marmie's boats, had made excellent time, taking only the whole of one day and half the night before they reached a point about three-quarters of the way to the coast. There, the channel widened and sandbars became a problem.

Sean swam past the brilliant lights cast by the barge, swimming as hard as he could to close the distance between himself and the sea.

The river mouth looked deserted without otters, but unless they had some information about his children, Sean had no time to chat anyway. He had been using his own sonar all along to keep his course straight through the swiftest current of the river channel, but once he hit salt water he slowed and sent out a throaty roar of a signal to try to get a heading.

That was when Ronan's call reached him.

I'm coming, he answered. He sought Murel, but received no clear response. How long he searched, he didn't know, though he had begun swimming hard again. He sent another call to Ronan, *I'm not getting anything from her, son, but that doesn't necessarily mean anything.*

Ronan's alarmed thought reached him a few minutes later: *Da, it's a pod of orcas.*

Stay calm, okay? Sean told him.

He waited for a response from his son but it was not forthcoming.

Instead, he picked up a confused babble of thought, the orca pod, and homed in on it.

Where'd they go?

I dunno. I don't have 'em. Who has 'em?

Bitfin, you didn't eat both of them, did you?

No! This thought was disgruntled, pained, and angry. *I was all set and—*

Father of seals! Another, clearer thought cut through the pod's chatter, which had begun to recede. They were swimming away from where the children had been. *The Honus greet you.*

Where did my kids go? he asked them.

We do not know. Murel fell behind without our knowledge while we swam toward the new home. The next thing we knew, she cried out. The swifter among us swam with Ronan and the otter to try to save

*her, but although we were swift, your son was swifter. He dived into the
pod of orcas and that is the last we saw of him. He made no outcry. The
orcas have gone but no seals remain. On the bright side, neither is
there much blood taste in the water.*

Sean felt as if he would sink to the bottom and stay there at the
mention of blood where his children had been.

Picking up on Sean's distress, one of the Honus suggested, *One
of the orcas had a wounded dorsal fin. Perhaps the blood was his.*

Thank you for that. We'll hope so.

*We will continue to dive. As soon as it is light enough for them to
use their weak human senses, Ke-ola and Keoki will also dive.*

*Thank you. But tell Ke-ola and Keoki I am coming and can search
before sunrise. I don't know how those boys got out there but we don't
need to lose them too.*

Well before sunrise, though, Sean heard the chopper flying overhead and figured that Sinead had called Yana for backup. By the
time he surfaced, the chopper's searchlights and its noise were fad-
ing in the distance. It was on course for the emerging volcano.

He reached the Honus as the indigo skirt of the sky bloomed
with the scarlet of the rising sun. This had the unfortunate effect of
bathing the sea in blood.

THE HELICOPTER HAD picked up Ke-ola and Keoki by the time Sean
arrived. He wondered how the boys had survived the long swim
from shore, which would have been far too cold for them to stand
for long, if nothing else.

*The seal children gave them the shells they carried on their own
backs,* the Honus answered, although Sean had not posed the question with an intention of receiving a reply.

So the kids gave the boys their dry suits. That would make one
less piece of evidence he might find in the water to indicate what
had happened to them.

Yana was aboard the chopper, as were Johnny, Rick, Pet Chan, and another man Sean didn't know but whose face seemed familiar. Pet Chan squatted with Yana in the open side door of the aircraft. Both were dressed in diving gear. When Yana spotted Sean, she waved and said something into the mouthpiece attached to her headset. Shortly afterward, the copter hovered close to the water.

Sean looked up at her, trying to meet her eyes. Escaping strands of her black hair whipped in ribbons across her face. More than ever, he wished Yana and he could speak telepathically as easily as he could with the children. She wanted him to board the copter, he thought, and explain what had happened. She also wanted to dive in with him. In as large a gesture as he could make, he shook his sleek gray-brown head from side to side three or four times and dived. No need for her and Pet to risk themselves. Besides, they could obscure evidence of what had happened to the children. He had a better chance of sorting out the situation alone. Water was his natural element—well, one of his natural elements.

His dive was not solo, however. The Honus dived with him. All of them.

We have searched clear to the bottom but there is nothing except rock, they told him. Silt, plants, and animals were already covering most of the rock. Although the water was very murky, he saw no sign of anything from that quarter that might have taken his kids, nor was there anyplace for them to hide. Not that they would be hiding. If they were here, he would know it.

Sean searched in an upwardly spiraling pattern from the black rock to the surface, combing a square mile without a trace of either of the children. He did, however, spot a piece of black bloody flesh. Before he could reach it, it had become breakfast for a large fish.

That would belong to the whale with the maimed dorsal fin the Honus described. Those whales had been closest to his kids when they disappeared. From their conversation, Sean had the impression that the whales had not killed Murel, though not from lack of trying. Still, if he questioned them, perhaps they had seen what became of the kids, or remember something that would help him find them.

He surfaced again and leaped up and down to show that he was ready to board the helicopter. It extruded pontoons from its landing platform and Rick set it down upon the waves.

Ke-ola and the burly man hauled Sean aboard. Yana wrapped him in a tarp till he dried off and completed his change. Rick tossed him a duffel bag. "Extra duds in there, Sean. You're welcome to them."

Thankfully, he pulled them on. The wind was cool, and though the tarp kept it off, it didn't do much to warm him.

"Nothing?" Yana asked. "The boys told us what the Honus got from Ronan and Sky before they vanished too." She sounded annoyed that they hadn't had more information. Yana did not so much resemble other grieving mothers as she did an eagle with an eye out for prey. He knew she was holding back her emotional reaction while making a mission out of finding the kids. It was her training. Act and think first, feel later, when you had the luxury of time to fall apart. He took her hand and squeezed. A flicker in her eye betrayed her fear, then vanished when she squeezed his firmly in return. She was in control. Good. He agreed with her. There was much to be done.

"I overheard something I want to question our black-and-white boyos about but I want the copter. I want to be in my human form when I confront them. Unfortunately, seals are fair game for orcas. I'll need more of their attention on my questions than on licking their snouts over how I might taste." The mother of his children winced. "Sorry, love. I don't believe they hurt either of our kids." He summarized the conversation among the orcas. "It's not their way to lie among themselves, and they wouldn't have known I was eavesdropping. But one of them may have noticed something he didn't feel was relevant to the argument or interesting enough to share with the others."

She acknowledged this with a sharp nod, the kind she might have given a report from another officer. "You know where to find them?" she asked.

"I do," he said, and gave her a heading that she relayed to Rick.

They were out of headsets and he couldn't make himself heard over the chopper's noise to explain to the others what he had to Yana, so she relayed that too, and made introductions. When she got to Raj Norman, he shook Sean's hand and patted his own belt, which bristled with armaments Sean could not begin to identify. "Don't worry, buddy," he bellowed above the copter's roar. "If those whales give you a hard time, tell 'em the trigger-happy dude," he jerked a thumb at his own chest, "will be happy to make black-and-white puddin' of the lot of 'em."

"A comfort to me and none to them I'm sure," Sean said politely, though the idea of anyone attacking Petaybean creatures with high-tech armaments made him a bit nauseous. "But I don't think it will be necessary. I intend to pull rank."

Yana interrupted, pointing to the water, "Tall fins at 2200," she said.

Sean looked down and there they were, a flotilla of them in Y formation, proud as you please. The copter overtook them but did not set down. Instead, at Sean's urging, it circled high enough to keep from frightening the whales while keeping them in sight as long as their fins remained above water.

Sean could not copy their verbal speech aloud but he could think at them in their own language, and so he did. *Hello there, boys, and isn't it a lovely morning and the water fine?*

So it is, if it's any of your business, replied the lead whale, turning first one way, then the other, then flipping upside down trying to spot him. Even over the noise of the copter he heard them sending out their sonar signals, seeking him.

Up here, me fine finny friends. Don't worry about it. I am one of the people who put you into this lovely ocean with all of these tasty fish and other things your sort find agreeable.

Very good of you, we're sure, the alpha whale replied cautiously. *What is it you want?*

A while ago you made a little mistake. Oh, not that I blame you. You had no way of knowing, of course. But me and my—er, calves—some-

times take the form of seals, and it seems you mistook my daughter for a light snack.

I didn't eat her! came a protest from the ranks. Sean wasn't close enough to tell which one, but he suspected the speaker's dorsal fin had a piece bit out. *She deserved it, mind you. She is vicious. She bit me but—*

Frankly, I was about to call the game off when she disappeared, the alpha whale interrupted, with an aside he apparently thought Sean would not hear to the speaker—now known as Bitfin—to let him do the talking. Whales might not lie, but like anybody else, Sean suspected they probably wanted to put the best spin they could on an error in judgment when called to account for their actions. *I knew there was something peculiar about that one. And then, you know, she said she was actually not a seal but a mur—*

Moray eel, boss, one of them supplied, based on what she thought she'd heard. *She said she wasn't a seal, she was a moray eel.*

There you have it. Of course, I've been known to gnaw on one or two of those too if I'm a bit peckish, but she didn't seem like a seal or an eel to me but another more dangerous creature altogether. I've no doubt that if she hadn't disappeared when she did, she'd have made us all sick at the very least so, as I said, I was about to call it off when she vanished in a cloud of murk and bubbles.

And my son? Sean asked.

Looked like another seal, did he?

He did.

Never laid an eye on him, much less a tooth.

He'd have been swimming with an otter. Not the usual kind. A wee brown fellow.

Had whales possessed shoulders, the pod would have shrugged them. *I saw no strange-looking otters swimming along with the strange seal. I didn't see either, did you?*

Not me!

Nor did I!

There you have it, the alpha whale said again. *Now the normal sort of otter, we'd have probably gobbled up without a thought, but after meeting your she-calf, I should have felt it my responsibility to warn my pod off any funny-looking animals in the vicinity. But that reminds me. The little—your she-calf—said something about some sharks, thinking to frighten us, I think, though pretending she was giving a warning. What was that about?*

She was warning you indeed, Sean replied, the thought giving him a pang. That would have been part of what took his kids to sea. They'd have thought it necessary to warn the other creatures about the new predator in the waters. They were like that. *And yes, sharks are coming.*

As I told your calf, sharks are our natural prey, not the other way around. I hope you've no objection to us eating them? No relation, are they? Aunties? Uncles? Mothers of mates perhaps?

Sarcasm really didn't suit orcas but Sean let it pass. *No, no relation, but it would be in your own best interest to let them breed and multiply for a few years so there's enough for you to eat and enough to breed more sharks as well. Also, you should know there'll be some new humans coming this way soon.*

Well, that's all right, the alpha whale said. *By and large your sort have treated us well enough here, and you're not all that tasty—so it's said. Wouldn't know personally, of course.*

Sean was pleased. They seemed to be on very good terms in spite of a potentially hostile situation. He felt that the alpha whale and the others were being truthful insofar as they understood the truth.

Yana cocked an inquisitive eyebrow at him and he nodded and made a hand sign for her to be patient just a bit longer.

Of course, he said. *But now that we understand each other better, I want to ask you all to think if you can remember what happened just before nobody ate my kids and the otter.*

That's a bit more difficult, the alpha whale said. Sean could feel the whole pod, spurred by their keen instinct for survival in the face of a massively mucked-up situation, giving thought to his inquiry.

Did you for instance notice the sea turtles swimming after my son? Sean asked, probing.

Well, no, we wouldn't have noticed those, would we? Bitfin replied. *We were circling at the time, you see. Using the sonar to confuse the prey—I mean, your calf, not that we knew she was your calf, as we said. By the way, she has teeth. Very sharp indeed.*

What Bitfin means to say, a whale thought-form that was distinctly feminine interjected, *is that our attention was directed inward, toward your calf and each other. I did not see turtles or another seal or an otter, just that bubbly whirlpool thing before Bitfin's tail blocked my view.*

What was that? the alpha whale, eager to get to the bottom of this and leading the pod away, asked. *I was up near the surface. Seemed a bit turbulent there for a bubble or two, and next thing I knew, we were all bumping into each other and the seal was nowhere to be seen or heard.*

I couldn't tell, Bitfin said with true regret. *You see, I opened my mouth to bite, and you know how it is when you open wide, you can't see the morsel anymore. You sense them, feel them there, but you don't see them. She was there, she was trying to get away, I open me gob, but when I bit down I nearly break a tooth gnashing them against each other. There was a tickling at my chin, a feeling something was whirling.*

The whirlpool thing, another female said. *I was down below Bitfin and could barely see the prey—sorry, the calf—as it was, but I saw a bit of flipper. Then all of a sudden there was nothing but whirly water in my face and we were scattering. I did—*

She hesitated, then continued more tentatively, *I did get the feeling that there was something inside the water. And of course, that might have been the calf, mightn't it? Almost had to have been, come to think of it. Still, it seemed to me there was something larger there, something not afraid to come into a pod of us in feeding frenzy. I think we were right to scatter when we did.*

Sean could not decide if this was good news or bad.

CHAPTER 15

RONAN CHANGED COURSE, deciding it wasn't a good idea to attack a pod of killer whales even to save his sister. Instead, he dived deep, thinking to intercept whatever it was rising from the ocean floor. If it was an additional threat, well, at least he'd have done *something* before making a sealburger of himself. Sky followed, peering inquisitively into the incredibly turbulent murk directly in front of them. Then the whirling cone swallowed the otter. Ronan followed half a length behind. Once inside it, there was nothing to see but a strange glow illuminating its midst.

They looked up, where the whales had been.

No Murel! Sky said. Then, *No whales.*

He was right. Light from the surface suddenly replaced the hunting shadows looming above them. Something else was there for a moment, blocking part of the view, but they couldn't tell what it was except for more whirling debris and bubbles. No blood, though. No . . . scraps.

Ronan was startled from that gruesome thought by something gyrating past them, almost taking the fur from his skin as it whirled wildly toward the ocean floor.

Below, the faint glow brightening the murk had turned into a spinning column of clean water beaming with light as if from fire at its core.

A speck of darkness was silhouetted against it.

Murel? he called.

Sky's reactions were quicker. *That looks like fun, Murel! Otters like fun! Watch out! Here comes Sky!*

The otter streaked past in a brown blur and plunged into the center of the column.

Hey, wait! Ronan protested, and not to be outdone by the daredevil otter, plunged after him, diving ever downward. The light blinded him as the spinning water sucked him into its vortex.

MUREL? SIS? YOU okay? At some point while whirling around in the waterspout, Ronan had lost consciousness. He awoke lying next to his sister on a hard surface. He had the feeling they were enclosed, and when he sent a sonar probe, it told him he and Murel were surrounded by walls. Not sea grotto, but real walls, like the ones in their cabin.

Ro? Her thought-voice was shaky and scared. *Am I—did the whales bite off a very big piece of me? It doesn't hurt yet.*

The sonar probe had revealed an entire seal lying next to him, not a maimed one, so he felt safe saying, *I don't think the whales even touched you. This weird underwater waterspout typhoon thingy pulled you out from under them. I dived in after you.*

Thanks.

No problem, really, any time. I'm glad we were in seal form, though, because if we'd been human I'd have wet my pants.

You're not the only one! She stirred, sat up. *Where are we?*

I dunno, but not to worry, Da is on his way.

How?

I called him. Guess he wasn't too far off when he heard me. Or maybe he heard you first. Anyway, all we have to do is sit tight and wait. He'll find us.

I just wish I knew where we were.

He rose too and began to explore their confinement. Small, maybe ten by ten, bare. And it felt made. Like man-made, only what man would make something down here? He'd read about shipwrecks and sunken vessels on other planets, but Petaybee had yet to develop an active shipping industry.

Petaybee . . . well sure.

Duh, he said. *The planet saved us. It didn't want the whales to eat you so it made this waterspout that sucked us into it.*

And into a room? Murel was exploring too. *Is there a door?*

Do we want to know what's behind it if there is?

As they spoke, one of the walls grew lighter and brighter. It also became transparent, and soon it popped out of existence altogether. A tall sleek presence stood in its place, one fish in its mouth and one in each front paw.

Are you hungry? it asked.

Who are you? both of them asked. But just then Sky scampered in front of the larger creature, which actually looked like an exceptionally big otter.

She's one of the deep sea otters, Sky told them. His paws each held a sea urchin and he still seemed to be chewing. *They made the waterspout for Murel so the whales couldn't eat her.*

Thanks, Murel told the big otter. *I bet you, uh, folks are getting tired of saving selkies. First our da and now us.*

Yeah, Ronan added, *we're glad to see you're okay. We were afraid the volcano got you.*

Deep sea otters like volcanoes, said the deep sea otter, sounding a lot like Sky, except somehow more feminine. *We like living under them.*

Must get hot, Ronan said.

In spite of being grateful to the deep sea otters, Murel couldn't help feeling this tall creature was in disguise and mimicking Sky. She was an otter impersonator, Murel was sure. The so-called deep sea otters who had rescued Da hadn't talked like Sky at all. And though they never showed themselves, they didn't "feel" like otters. Besides, otters were mammals, and it wasn't scientifically possible for real otters to survive totally immersed in water all the time, not to mention under volcanoes.

Your father is well? the otter asked. Most unotterly again. The otters she knew, Sky included, always assumed everyone and everything was well until clearly proven not to be.

He's looking for us, Ronan told her. *He'll be here soon and can thank you for saving him and us as well.*

Have a fish, she said, again proffering the ones in her paws.

Thanks again, Murel said, and snapped it down. She'd been through quite a bit and, otter impersonator or not, she needed to keep up her strength.

You may go out to him when he comes for you, but for now you seals must stay with deep sea otters, she said, most of her speech again sounding unotterly. Then she added, *Whales, you know.*

Murel's skin shivered all down the length of her spine. *I know,* she said, accepting a second fish that had somehow appeared in the paw when the first one vanished. *Are we inside your city now? Didn't it get destroyed during the eruption?*

No. Our city is designed to withstand the living force of the planet. To us and our habitat, volcanoes give life. And yes, you are safe in our city now.

She means their den, Sky said. The concept of a city was still not one he understood. Kilcoole was the biggest settlement on the northern pole of Petaybee and it was still little more than a Nakatira-cube-enhanced village. *It is a big den. Hundreds of holes. These deep sea otters are very big, so they cannot all fit in one hole.*

Though the twins hadn't felt as if they were floating inside the room, it occurred to them that they were still in the depths of the sea and that water—or something similar—was all around them. It was very clear. All they had to do was to think about swimming and they could swim instead of staying on the floor. What was that all about?

The tall otter, who stood on her hind paws during their conversation, stepped aside, inviting them to leave their temporary harbor.

They were in the strange city they had seen only from the outside before. The multicolored lights streaming from the top of the tallest buildings to the bottom of those at sea floor level were less apparent inside, where you could only see a few at a time, glowing first in one place then another. They looked more random than they had from outside the protective bubble that cloaked the city in what seemed to be a protective force field. The first time the twins had seen it, Ronan tried to swim into the city from several angles but hadn't been able to get inside. *Our security system,* the tall otter explained, picking up his thought.

I didn't realize otters had them, Ronan said.

Most do not. You are bright youngsters. It will not have escaped your notice that we are rather more evolved than other varieties of otters.

What is evolved? Sky asked.

More developed, Murel told him, unsure how to further explain it with images he would understand. *Like living in cities instead of regular dens.*

Regular dens are nice, Sky said, puzzled. *Otters can build new ones when they get messy or filled with water or if we want to go somewhere else.*

But although making dens is natural for river and sky otters, Murel said, *these otters use things that are not exactly natural.*

Hah! Sky said. *Sky otters fly in sky machines that are not exactly natural, and they still swim, walk, run, and slide. Sky otters are evolved too.*

And evolving more all the time, Murel agreed. *Besides, sky otters are real and I think this is all a dream. Ronan and I used to share dreams when we were little. This can't be happening. Some of those other big otters are walking around the city and some of them are swimming. It doesn't make any sense. I fell asleep in the water and then I dreamed the orcas were after me and that this big waterspout pulled me away from them at the last minute and I thought I woke up, but I'm still dreaming, really.*

If I'm in the dream too, Ronan replied, *you're not going to believe me if I tell you this seems to be pretty real to me.*

It is good that you feel that way, their hostess said. *You will remember none of this when you return to the surface, so it will be much like a dream that way.*

I didn't realize otters dreamed, Murel said.

Not to be left out, Sky said, *Sky otters dream!* then asked, *What is dream?*

Stories you see after you're asleep, Murel said.

Oh, yes, sky otters do that. So do river otters. I do not know about the sea otter cousins but if river otters dream, sky otters dream, and deep sea otters dream, then sea otters must dream too.

Ronan asked the tall otter, *Do you have a name? And why do your people—otters, I mean—like living near volcanoes so much?*

You may call me Kushtaka, she said. *We live near volcanoes for the power of their life force, for the food they provide, and because we have always done so.*

Kushtaka? Murel asked. *But that's the name for—* She decided against finishing the thought. Kushtaka was an archaic word brought to Petaybee by Eskimo and Indian ancestors who believed there were whole communities of otters, called Kushtaka, that could steal souls. If she had been in human form at that time, looking into this Kushtaka's cool appraising gaze would have sent goose bumps up her arms.

Yes? Kushtaka asked.

Er—it's another name we have for otters. Not specific otters, I mean, just otters in general. I thought deep sea otters, since you seem quite different from your smaller cousins, might be called something different. But then, you're the first one we've ever met so we have no way of knowing really.

She was aware that she was chattering on and on, her thoughts tumbling over each other to keep her real thoughts and fears from surfacing. She wanted to ask a lot of things, but she was afraid if she did and learned the answers to her questions, the deep sea otters wouldn't let her and Ronan leave. But then, well, Kushtaka had said they were going to wipe out the visitors' memories of this place. That was probably what had happened to Da's memories when they took care of him. Murel continued to feel very strongly that whatever these creatures were, they were not otters, Petaybean or any other kind. She wanted to ask why they were pretending to be, but that was rude since it amounted to calling them liars.

You use geothermals to power all of this? Ronan asked, looking around at the towering spires, the spiraling towers, the domes, the thousands rather than hundreds of what certainly seemed to be entrances or doorways. Glancing back, he saw that the room they had been in, the one in which the wall had dissolved rather than a door opening, also appeared to have a hole-shaped doorway, which seemed odd. Many of the doorways seemed open to lots of traffic, with other large otters swimming or walking around the city, some carrying food items, some carrying other less easily identifiable objects.

Where do you live, Kushtaka? Murel asked. Although she didn't trust this creature, she felt they needed to make friends with her. After all, her folk had saved Da and now them. They certainly couldn't be evil. *Do you have—* She started to think "a mate," but then remembered that sea otters had casual mating habits so she continued, *Any young still at home?*

I have two young still living with me, she said. *I did have a mate but he met with an accident and was killed. I do not intend to take another. Deep sea otters have their own mating customs, different from our smaller cousins.*

Do deep sea otters ever mate with sky otters? Sky wanted to know. *I have not mated yet, but soon I will need to do that and there are no other sky otters. I am the only one. Deep sea otters look interesting.*

Kushtaka had no answer for a moment, then replied thoughtfully and with what Murel thought was a hint of humor, *You are small, we are large. It would not work.*

Maybe a small deep sea otter? Sky suggested, undaunted, but then he swam forward and dived into another hole and said, *Come and see this, river seals! Deep sea otters have strange hunting habits!*

With assent from Kushtaka, they followed their friend into a chamber that had no ceiling and no floor but a flexible device floating in the middle. It was aimed downward, toward a broad rift in the sea's floor. Deep within it a volcanic vent emitted a cherry-red glow, but Murel thought that might be several leagues beneath them. Between them and the cherry glow, the rift blossomed with all sorts of plant and animal life.

Like a frog whipping out its tongue to catch a fly, the device shot forth a beam of light. Water wrapped around the beam, creating a waterspout, a concentrated whirlpool. The practical reason for this, when it wasn't being used for rescuing selkies, became clear when it swirled back into the room with its waters full of shellfish, seaweed, and the sort of plant life they had seen before near the undersea volcanoes.

You use that to hunt? Murel said.

As you see, Kushtaka replied.

Don't you ever leave your city for anything, then?

Occasionally, when it seems safe.

Oh! The sharks. I almost forgot. The reason we came here was to try to find you, once the sea otters told us you were still around. You see, some new people are coming and they brought the sea turtles with them, but their relatives also brought along sharks. I'm afraid they might eat you if they catch you, so we wanted to warn you about them.

What are sharks? Kushtaka asked, exactly mimicking the way Sky had asked the meaning of "dream."

Mean! Sky answered immediately. *And dangerous. Sharks are very mean with huge teeth and they always want to eat you.*

And yet you escaped to warn us? Kushtaka said, sounding as if the idea that they would do so was an entirely alien concept to her.

They won't eat us, Ronan said, more confidently than he felt. *We saved them from dying of starvation on another world.*

And they acknowledge this, these mean sharks? Do you think them trustworthy?

No way! Murel said. When Kushtaka looked puzzled, she tried to explain. *Trustworthy is not the term I'd use for them if I happened to meet them in the open sea, but that's not the case. We helped them and they know if they hurt us, they and their people might suffer.*

Their people? Kushtaka asked.

Murel tried to explain. *These sharks are special to some of the people who are coming, like we said. They're sort of clan totem animals— the people think they have the spirits of their ancestors living in them and are here to protect and help them. That's what the Honus, the sea turtles, are too. They're the aumakuas of some of the other people.*

Sky piped up again. *The aumakua of river seals is the sky otter— me! Except this otter is not the ancestor—that means father's father, to you deep sea otters who do not understand two-legged terms as well as this otter—of these river seals or even a blood relative. I hope to be the ancestor of many river otters soon, but Ke-ola's people think I am the aumakua because I am good friends with the river seals and we help and protect each other.*

It was a lengthy speech for Sky. It seemed to Murel he was learning quickly about their world and thought concepts. Well, why not? Otters were not stupid animals by any means. And Sky was particularly smart.

You speak of two-leggeds as if standing on two legs means human, Kushtaka said. *Deep sea otters stand on two legs.*

But you have otter legs—the right amount, Sky said. *And your hind paws are flippered like those of the sea otter cousins. You cannot be real two-leggeds like Murel and Ronan.*

What do you mean? They do not have legs at all. They have flippers.

Not always, Murel said. *We are not the regular kind of seals. We're selkies, like our father.*

That means as soon as we dry off we turn into people with two legs and two arms, Ronan explained helpfully. *Most of our lives we've been stuck on dry land or in space—you know what space is?*

We know, Kushtaka told him without hesitation.

This otter is a space otter as well as a sky otter, Sky told her proudly. *I am the first otter in space!*

Not precisely, Kushtaka replied, half to herself. Sky didn't catch her thought. He was preoccupied with a fish from the catch inside the hunting chamber and looked over at Ronan with an amiable expression consisting of wide eyes and chewing.

Murel, intrigued by the big otter's remark, pretended she hadn't understood it either. She was beginning to have suspicions, however—how could she not? *So, how did you come to be deep sea otters?* she asked, seemingly conversationally. *Are your species one of Petaybee's adaptive mutations—originally the regular kind of otters but for some reason specially adapted to live underwater and near volcanoes?*

Mutations? No, we are not mutants, Kushtaka said with a hint of indignation.

No, no, Murel said hastily, *I didn't mean anything bad by that. We're mutations ourselves—almost everybody on Petaybee is. The planet does it, see, so we can live here. Our grandfather and great-grandfather and our father too helped decide which original plants and animals belonged on Petaybee, but then a lot of those changed, so they could survive. Usually it takes a long time but on Petaybee it happens really fast. Take our mother, for instance. She came here when she was grown up and had traveled in space her whole life, but now that she's been here a while, Petaybee has changed her so that she can't go off-planet anymore.*

We can only go because we're still kids, Ronan added. *The change doesn't happen until you're past puberty.*

Kushtaka displayed no interest in that explanation at all. Instead she repeated, *We are not mutants.*

Murel decided finally to be direct and say what was on her mind. *You're not really otters either, are you?* she asked.

Not always, Kushtaka admitted.

And let me guess, Ronan said, having shared his sister's doubts about the deep sea otters almost since they first met Kushtaka. *You haven't always lived on Petaybee either, have you?*

Always is an inexact term, Kushtaka replied.

I think this is the part where we ask to be taken to your leader, Ronan said.

I am the leader, Kushtaka said, then added curiously, *Our otter shape has worked well for us until now. Other otters accept us as otters. What makes you think otherwise?*

Well, you live in a city with a force field, for one thing, Murel said. *Normal otters don't tend to do that.* Of course, the other otters, Sky included, were funny and active, playful and curious, and Kushtaka displayed no more of those qualities than an iceberg.

But had we not saved you and allowed you to see our habitat, you would not have known? she asked. Her whiskers drooped. She was downcast at having been found out, and seemed to consider it a personal failure of some sort.

No, and your point is taken, Murel responded quickly. *We're really, really grateful to you for saving us, and our father too, so we know you're good, of course. But why do you want to keep your presence and what you really are such a big secret? I'm guessing you must be some other sentient species from some other world, but there are lots of people here now who've lived on other worlds. If Petaybee doesn't care that you're here, we sure don't.*

And neither will anybody else, Ronan added, as reassuringly as if Kushtaka had been abducted from the sea by a giant waterspout and deposited in *their* shielded fortress instead of the other way around. *You're safe, really.*

We never doubted it, Kushtaka said coldly. *However, we prefer our privacy and discretion to wider exposure to the land population— particularly humanoids.*

I guess we can understand that, Murel said.

During this part of the discussion, Sky, oblivious to so much con-

versation when there were things to explore, darted off to poke into
one hole after another.

Now he returned, followed by a smaller version of Kushtaka.

*Mother, this strange little fellow came into my den. What is he
doing here and why are you talking to these seals?* the small deep sea
otter asked in a girlish mind-voice, suggesting to Murel that this
was a daughter otter.

Tikka, this is colony business, Kushtaka said sternly. *These are not
simple seals. They are the children of that other seal we pulled in during the eruption. They were the ones who came for him and insisted
that we release him. They say that they and their father can transform
into human form.*

Really? They have another form? Like us? Can I see? Tikka asked,
addressing the last question to the twins with more of the otter en-
thusiasm they had come to expect of Sky and his relatives.

Sorry. We can't do it in the water, Murel told her. *We're seals as long
as we're wet. How about you? What is your other form?*

Kushtaka bristled at Murel's friendly interest. Tikka, however,
answered immediately. She suddenly slipped out of her otter skin as
if it were only a wrap. Inside of it her skin was a smooth translucent
gold, with an inner light that cast soft pastel colors over her. Like
them, she had a head and a trunk, but four arms ending in long
web-fingered hands and four legs ending in flippers. Her eyes were
huge, blue green and somewhat prominent. From the middle of her
forehead and extending down her back, a delicate fin waved and
floated like a solid sheaf of gleaming hair.

Wow! Murel said. *You're beautiful!*

Tikka, change back this instant! Kushtaka demanded.

*But why, Mother? You heard them. They like how we look in this
form. And I like being able to use more than two legs and two arms at
a time. Otter form is so inconvenient that way.*

*You know we must be discreet for the good of all. Your brother was
supposed to be watching you. Where is he?*

He wanted to see the humanoids and that new species that just arrived. They were on the sursurvu.

The what? Murel asked.

One of our surface surveillance viewscreens, Kushtaka told her. *We are constantly studying this world around us, so of course we have sensors of all sorts to help us monitor our surroundings. That is how we realized your father and then you were in danger. It is also how we observed the sea otters enough to see that they are sociable, curious, and clannish, and would respond well to our presence if they were told we were distantly related.*

Tikka jiggled all eight limbs impatiently during her mother's explanation, then said, *Mother, Jeel was highly impressed by the new species. He liked their teeth. I did not. I don't think I've ever seen such ferocious-looking fish before. But he wants to inspect them more closely.*

I hope you mean he's just zooming in with your device from here inside the dome, Ronan said anxiously. *He wouldn't be likely to go outside, would he? Your people don't ever leave here, do you?*

Of course we do, Tikka replied. *That's how we met the otters and learned to be deep sea otters. It would be way too boring to be cooped up here all the time. Besides, we're supposed to be exploring and learning about new species, right, Mother?*

Your brother went outside the colony without telling me? Kushtaka demanded, whiskers bristling.

Jeel could tell you were busy with your guests, Mother, and didn't want to interrupt, Tikka told her.

They would be the sharks that we were telling you about, Kushtaka, Ronan said. *They eat anything and anybody in their path, and these ones have been cooped up and hungry for a long time.*

What's the quickest way out of here? Murel asked. *We'll go fetch him back for you.*

I will call him, Kushtaka said.

It's better if we go, Ronan tried to insist. *Like we told you, the sharks know us and they won't hurt us.* Truthfully, he was not all that sure how long shark gratitude lasted. But surely the shark-people refugees would have come with their aumakuas so they'd help control them if necessary.

Also, Murel said, picking up his train of thought even though it was a bit buried for anyone else to catch, *there'll be humanoids with the sharks probably and they know us already. We could help hide Jeel so they wouldn't find out about your colony.*

Very well, Kushtaka agreed reluctantly. *But first we must clear your minds of this place.*

How can we help get Jeel back here if you do that? Ronan protested.

He knows the way. If you must stay with him to protect him, you can follow him.

Okay, but hurry up. He's really in danger, honest, Murel said.

It is not a process that can be hurried, Kushtaka replied stubbornly.

Then for his sake let us go now. We won't tell. We promise. We didn't tell before. You can wipe our memories when we get back if you want to, but if I were you, I wouldn't. You need somebody to warn you about dangerous stuff like this.

Kushtaka finally agreed. *This is not according to our protocol, and I will have to answer to our security team for the breach. However, since the situation is an urgent one, I hope they will understand my unilateral decision to compromise. One of you may go to bring Jeel back, but the other one must stay here until Jeel is safely returned. To save more time, we will locate Jeel in the sursurvu so you can find him more quickly and bring him back. Your small companion otter may remain here too, for his own safety.*

While Murel and Ronan argued about who would go and who would stay behind, Kushtaka beckoned them to follow. Thrusting her paws to her sides, she kicked her legs in a smooth undulation, and shot upward. She led them into a domed room at the top of the invisible dome enclosing the city.

Tikka, who had not bothered returning to otter form, took Sky's paw by the end of one of her beautiful web-fingered tentacles, and asked, *Do you like to slide? See that building over there? It has a spiral slide all the way from the top of the dome down to the sea floor.* He ran around her in excited circles as she led him away.

The room was surrounded by what seemed to be open sea, and for a moment the twins thought Kushtaka had changed her mind and led them to freedom. However, when she said *Scan,* the seascape outside changed so rapidly it felt as if the room were moving, racing in circles toward the surface.

As more light filtered through the water from the sunlit day above, the sharks prowled into view, swimming back and forth beside and behind the hull of a medium-sized boat. Periodically one or more of the sharks dived to scoop up a mouthful of fish, though it looked as if they'd prefer to bite something larger instead. Murel thought the off-limits prey—seal, human, and otter—would remain off-limits only as long as the sharks knew they were being watched.

Then the scene outside the room—though it seemed to be the room itself—swung around to the outside of the sharks and the boat, scanning it first near the surface, then back down again.

A sleek brown shape that looked amazingly small in the vastness of the sea was pumping its way toward the boat and the sharks.

There! Murel said. *That's him, right? Call him back now!*

He's out of range, Kushtaka said, frantically scanning from the sharks and the boat to her son and back again.

Can't you send your beam thing to get him? Murel asked. Jeel was already so close to the sharks that she doubted she could save him.

By the time we reset the beam, you could be there, Kushtaka said.

I'll go, Ronan said. *Lead the way.*

No, Kushtaka said. *The female will go. It is well known that females among your species—both of them—are more ruthless fighters in defense of young—or in this case, my young. My son is the one in jeopardy because your species, of whom I gather your father is a leader, brought this peril to us. Therefore your father's son will stand surety for Jeel's return.*

Murel shot a triumphant "So there!" look at her brother. It nearly masked her fear of returning to waters where other large predators had almost killed her a short time before.

Ronan would have argued, but there was no time. Jeel was on his way to be shark bait. If one of them—and Kushtaka had decided on Murel—didn't get the silly git back before he became a shark snack, Ronan didn't want to think what Kushtaka and her people might do.

Suddenly four of the big otter aliens appeared beside him, each taking hold of one of his flippers in one of their clawed paws as they carried him back down into the city.

Don't worry, Ro, Murel called after him, putting into her thought much more confidence than she felt. *I'll be back with Jeel in no time.*

Kushtaka guided her beyond the domed room, which looked solid from the outside, to a point somewhat higher where the sea enveloped the city. Then she dropped her otter form, revealing herself to be a larger version of her daughter. She waved a tentacle in front of her and then beckoned Murel forward. Murel felt a little resistance, as if she were penetrating some kind of membrane, then with a slight pop she was free in the cold salt water. Although the interior of the city dome had felt similar to the seawater, now that she was outside the enclosure the difference was marked. Although the water near the volcano was warmer than that closer to shore, it was still much chillier than inside the dome. Nor had the dome smelled as strongly of sulfur as the water out here did, despite the fact that the dome was near enough to a volcanic vent to draw energy from it.

She swam away quickly, her torso undulating and her back flippers propelling her toward the surface. She feared the sharks might not remain on the surface, but reckoned that as long as their people were with them, the predators would probably stay somewhat close to the boat.

Her sonar picked up the Manos and the hull of the boat as she had seen in the sursurvu. On board, the shark people and the crew that brought the sharks to the sea would be watching. Da too no doubt. She thought to send him a message, but then she'd be breaking her promise and probably putting Ro in danger. Besides, there wasn't any time. She had to reach Jeel before the sharks did.

Her sonar didn't pick up any deep sea otters anywhere, or other otters, for that matter. Just sharks, the boat, and millions of terrified sea creatures who had no idea what was gobbling them up like popcorn.

MUREL SWAM UP toward the volcano, where the boat with the shark people was heading, with Jeel closing in. Her sonar search soon picked him up. However, she found the sharks as well. They seemed to have detected him and were diving to investigate. They were faster swimmers than she was.

She called to him, *Jeel! Jeel, you need to go back to the city. These animals are dangerous. Don't go near them, they'll eat you.*

She felt the alien—otter? boy? he felt like a boy in her mind—turn from the sharks to her. *Who are you?* he asked with curiosity as acute as a real otter's.

Murel. I'm one of the seal people your mother rescued. She sent me to get you, to warn you about the sharks. Come with me now. Hurry!

Why didn't she come herself? he asked. *She would have if I was really in danger.*

The sharks won't hurt me, but your people are fair game for them.

Why would they eat me and not you? he asked skeptically.

Please just come and stop asking so many questions. There's no time to argue. Look over your shoulder. See those shadows? They're closing in on you. Come here to me where I can protect you.

Instead he backed away, though he did look over his shoulder.

By now Murel didn't need sonar to tell that the sharks were almost upon them. She could see the white of their teeth. *Dive!* she cried. *To me, to me!*

He looked around for her instead. She swam up toward him as hard as she could, but he couldn't see her yet, and otters had no sonar. He saw the sharks, though, bearing down on him.

She drove herself toward them with powerful thrusts of her tail and pulls of her flippers. *No! Manos, no!* she tried to command them, but she might as well have been addressing empty water. *That is not prey. He's a—*

But they were between her and Jeel. She heard his thoughts, sensibly terrified at last. Then she heard his last water-strangled cry, the like of which she had never heard before and hoped never to hear again.

White teeth gnashed and the sea darkened with a deep blue stain that was Jeel's alien blood. She felt him, heard him, saw him no more.

She swam forward and was surrounded by sharks. They still looked horrible and hungry but she was too angry and appalled to be afraid. *You ate him!* she cried. *I told you not to but you ate him anyway!*

Not me, said a Mano who she identified as the one they had first met. *I didn't get so much as a nibble. There wasn't enough to go around.* He wasn't apologizing. He was complaining. *It's not like it was a seal or an otter.*

It was an otter. A deep sea otter, she told him.

I didn't notice any of those bringing fish to our tank. Just the brown slinky ones like your friend. Besides, it was feeding frenzy. Everybody knows you don't stop a Mano in feeding frenzy. We haven't had enough to eat for a long time so don't gripe when we eat something that isn't taboo or we might forget what is and eat you so we don't have to listen to you.

Two Honus swam past the sharks to flank her. Nothing hostile, just there.

It is futile to argue with Manos, the Honus told her. *And foolish.*

She knew that they were right, but she would almost as soon stay with the sharks as return to face Kushtaka. The colony leader would have been watching on the sursurvu. Kushtaka would have seen her fail and Jeel swimming into the jaws of the sharks. How would Murel ever explain why she couldn't save Jeel when she'd promised that she would? How would she convince Kushtaka to release Ronan anyway?

She swam slowly back to the domed city, weary from her hard swim and sadder than she had ever been. The Honus swam escort for a time and then she asked them to go away, so Kushtaka would know she hadn't betrayed the colony to anyone.

The sea trembled as it had during the quake when Petaybee was birthing the volcanic island. It shook, the water even more violently agitated than it had been during the shark attack or when the orcas hunted her.

As if she were a bit of flotsam instead of a strong swimming sea creature, Murel felt herself caught and flung round and round so fast she could not see and could not use her sonar. But she felt it when something solid shot past her toward the surface, and felt a void yawning beneath her.

CHAPTER 16

SEAN AND YANA kept searching for their children. He returned to the sea. She used Marmie's best sensors to probe for some sign of two young seals and an otter. The Honus remained near the volcano, agreeing that it was making a very fine home for them, a comfortable one in keeping with the home in the memories that lay buried inside their ancient heads.

On board the barge and tug were several of the Mano'aumakua clan, chief among them their matriarch, Puna. Sean had found her fascinating, but Sinead didn't have much time for her. The old woman's smile, in spite of sporting few teeth, showed a strong family resemblance to her aumakuas.

Even though Puna was new to the planet and hadn't even been to a welcoming latchkay yet, she was trying to run things her way. It didn't seem to hurt anything since most of the Petaybeans simply pretended they didn't understand if she told them to do something they hadn't already intended to do, but it was irritating.

Once the sharks were released, the tug followed them out to sea, so the people aboard could see where they were to live.

The tall black cone bezeled in black lava rose from the sea as the boat chopped across the waves. An escort of diving, surfacing, circling, and feeding sharks played around it. Sinead couldn't help feeling as if she were to be the main course at a shark picnic. Bears, moose, wolves, and all manner of other wild things held no terrors for her and few mysteries, but the sharks gave her the willies. The sea was Sean's element and he could have it, as far as she was concerned. She used to feel left out that when their grandfather messed about with their DNA, Sean was apparently the successful experiment while she comprised a control group of one. But she was glad now to be more or less normal. It made her life less complicated. She didn't know if her partner, Aisling, could handle a woman friend who grew fur and needed to go for a swim below the ice pack periodically. Now, if Grandfather had made it so she could turn into a wolf occasionally, that might have been different.

Ah well, she had enough on her plate as it was.

Puna grinned maternally at her seagoing relatives. "They like it here. It is a good place."

Sinead nodded but privately thought it had been a good place before, but the other creatures were probably thinking the neighborhood had gone to hell now.

She watched three of the sharks dive and saw that they were converging on some hapless prey, but she couldn't see what it was, despite the clarity of the waters. She felt sorry for it, whatever it was. She was a bit surprised when a few moments later the water on the surface was dyed a deep indigo.

An octopus or squid perhaps? She thought their ink was black.

She had little time to think after that because suddenly the boat lurched and she fell hard against the railing. It listed severely onto its starboard side, spinning in a huge circle. She had a fleeting impression of Puna and the others thrown into the water amid the sharks, who were also whipped around helplessly. An enormous whirlpool drilled into the sea floor.

Suddenly, Sinead was torn from the boat and gulping frigid saltwater. She spun in an ever narrowing and deepening spiral as she was sucked downward to the bottom of the sea. At the same time she was being pulled apart, she felt crushing pressure from her burning lungs and freezing body. A primordial roar filled her ears, and her eyes were blinded with churning water.

By the time the whirling ceased, releasing her, she hung in its depths like a broken doll.

KUSHTAKA'S CITY WAS gone! Murel swam straight to where it had been. Only an open trough remained. The volcanic vents within the trough glowed dully, their heat momentarily dimmed by the push of cold water from above.

Murel blinked. *Ronan? Ro?* she called, but heard nothing, sensed nothing. Her twin was gone.

But when she looked up into what had been the vortex of the whirlpool, she saw her aunt floating in the water above her. For a second she didn't react except to think, *What's Sinead doing here? She doesn't swim.* Then she thought, more clearly, *She doesn't swim!* and rushed up to the drowned woman, grabbing her by the back of her windbreaker and hauling her to the surface. The water was full of sharks with people attached to them. The sharks had rescued their own human relatives, but the boat and the other Petaybean crew members were nowhere to be seen.

Murel had been so shocked by what happened to Jeel, the whirlpool, and the disappearance of the undersea city, that she hadn't realized what the maelstrom had done to the boat.

This was horrible, horrible. Without someplace solid to lay Aunt Sinead, without someplace dry to transform herself, she knew she had no hope of reviving her aunt.

Da! Mum! she cried into the sea and air, not knowing where her parents were or even how long she and Ronan had lain unconscious in the room in the underwater city before Sky awakened them. *Sky, oh, Sky,* another loss—her otter friend gone with her brother, her aunt, with the boat's crew. Everything was suddenly too awful to bear. It couldn't possibly be worse.

Then she saw the black fins bearing down on her. The killer whales had returned.

CHAPTER 17

THE WHALES CHARGED straight at Murel, and though she tried to outswim them, she was hampered by the need to keep Sinead's face above the water. She wasn't sure it mattered, since it seemed her aunt was already drowned, and it wouldn't matter if they were both eaten by orcas, but she was afraid that dragging her aunt facedown would mean certain death and she couldn't bear that. If she hadn't been so focused on warning the deep sea otters about the bloody sharks, if she hadn't stupidly fallen asleep and become separated from Ro and the Honus, the stupid whales wouldn't have almost got her, and the wretched aliens wouldn't have sucked her and Ro into their stupid city. And if Jeel hadn't been so stupid about sharks, and if Kushtaka hadn't been so suspicious and poky about letting her go rescue him, she could have saved him from the sharks and Kushtaka would have let Ronan and Sky go and they would have had their memories wiped and none of this wretched stuff would have ever happened.

Meanwhile, she had to swim backward, towing her poor drowned aunty, while those awful orcas came on faster, ready to ram into her.

As the lead whale drew close enough for her to see the water running down his head, he dived. Suddenly, the surface was full of black-and-white whale tails.

Oh, great, they were going to attack from underneath and scoop Sinead and her into their open mouths! On the positive side, there was no longer a shark to be seen anywhere.

Murel felt something brush her tail and called a mental good-bye to her parents and Ronan.

Then she was hoisted aloft, precariously balanced on her back on the back of one whale while two others flanked him to catch her or Sinead if she fell off. Not a single thought did they send her, but she saw the rest of the pod split from the group and swim away. Keeping her balance was impossible. When she started to fall, she released her hold on Sinead, who was now well above water, and twisted her body out from under her aunt's. She slid down the whale's side into the space between him and one of the adjacent whales. The whale on the side moved to allow her to fall into the sea but made no move to retrieve or attack her. Sinead still lay on the back of the middle whale.

For the first time one of them thought-spoke. *This way. Land is near.*

You're saving us?

Isn't it obvious?

Why didn't you say so?

We didn't want to alert the sharks. They are a nasty-looking lot indeed and wouldn't have been above attacking us while we were answering your distress call.

But I called for Da and Mum. I didn't cry "Whale!" at any time, she argued—peevishly, she knew, but too much had happened and she wasn't feeling very rational at that moment.

We heard. We, uh, knew there was a father missing some younglings, although frankly we expected you both to be seals.

We are! That's my aunt Sinead riding on your back. She's my da's sister but she's always human.

Where is your sib?

He's—it's kind of complicated. Look, why are we headed for the volcano island? It's dangerous. It could erupt again and kill us at any time.

Do you see any other land where we could release your father's sister without beaching ourselves? The island is the only place. And you will not be alone.

That turned out to be true. Puna and her human family members were already sitting on the folded black rock far beneath the rim of the volcano's summit. To Murel's relief, Seamus and Liam were there too. The Honus who had apparently saved them were swimming away, having just deposited them. There was one more form, smaller, furrier, and looking slumped and unhappy until Murel flopped onto the beach beside him.

Sky! You escaped.

Otters are very cunning, he answered. *But not cunning enough to save Ronan.*

She felt no need to cover herself this time as she turned into her human shape. None of the other people had retained many clothes after their dunking either. If Aunt Sinead hadn't laced her warm clothes to her so securely, she might have lost hers too—which could have lightened her burden enough so she might have been able to reach the surface, Murel thought. Her boots alone must have weighed a ton.

The other able-bodied occupants of the island lifted Sinead from the obliging orca's back and began trying to revive her.

She was glacier blue with cold and lack of oxygen. Now fully human, Murel tried mouth-to-mouth to help her breathe, but Sinead's chest didn't move. Seamus pushed her aside and bent over her aunt, sticking his hand into her mouth and pulling out a glob of seaweed. Then he pushed her onto her side to let water run out. Some spilled from her mouth and nose but she didn't stir of her own accord. He tried mouth-to-mouth and thumping on her chest with the same results.

He flipped her over and pumped on her back three or four times. Now more water gushed out and she gave a weak cough. Turning her back over, he resumed the mouth-to-mouth until she fought him off, weakly but determinedly, and tried to sit up.

She spoke but Murel didn't hear what she said. Her words were lost in the thrum of the helicopter engine as the aircraft flew close, to hover above the marooned people.

The copter couldn't land on the island and there wasn't room aboard for the stranded shipwreck—or boat wreck—victims. It set down on its pontoons just offshore, and Da dived into the water, changing, then took a packet in his mouth as Mum, clad in a wet suit, carrying another small bundle, joined him, and both swam to shore.

"Where's your brother?" Da asked as soon as he changed shapes.

Murel, without meaning to, burst into tears. "They t-took him!" she sobbed.

"Who? Where?" Mum asked, as if she planned to dismember whoever had her son, wherever they might be hiding. She tossed a bundle to Murel.

The packet contained clothing.

Sinead sat up on her elbows then, with help from Seamus and Da, propped her back against a rock, and reached into a zippered pocket in her snow pants. She pulled out Da's dry suit. "I thought you might be needing this when we met up again."

Da tugged on the suit. Murel dug into the packet Mum had given her, donned a shirt that covered her to the knees, and handed the rest to Seamus, who was nearest.

Da opened the bundle he'd carried in his mouth. It contained medical supplies, compressed packets of thermal blankets, nutrient bars, and purification/desalination capsules one of Marmie's scientists had invented.

Puna reached for the supplies. "I am the clan healer," she told him. "I can tend our own injured and yours too."

In the open door of the copter, Ke-ola, wearing a pair of pants far too small for him, shouted to them. Although the copter had shut down its engine, his voice was lost in the roar of the surf. Da shook his head and started for the water, but Ke-ola shook his head in return, pointed his finger toward shore, and dived into the water.

Once there, he handed Murel her dry suit, back in its packet. "You need this more than me." She slipped into it under the shirt, then handed the shirt to one of the shivering shark people.

"Captain O'Shay wanted me to tell you that the coastal fishermen are on their way to fetch the survivors," Ke-ola told them.

"Excellent," Da said. "We need to organize another search party too. Murel says someone has taken Ronan."

"Da," she told him, "the someone isn't human. They look like big otters, they pretend to be otters, but they're not. Well, at least not all the time. They're aliens."

"As if it weren't bad enough that we're plagued with friendly offworlders wanting to immigrate, now we've hostile kidnapping ones to contend with," Seamus grumbled.

"They weren't hostile," Murel said. "They're the ones who saved Da, and they saved me today and probably Ro as well when the orcas attacked us. They were just curious, I think—the aliens, I mean, not the orcas. They were studying Petaybee's sea life, from what we could tell. They pretended to be deep sea otters so the real sea otters would trust them.

"They could change shapes, like we can," she said to her father. "Ro and I found out about them when we got you, Da, back from their city—or I guess maybe it's a vessel. But they made us promise not to tell. After they rescued me—and Ronan and Sky, who were caught up in the waterspout when they followed me into it—they let us rest up. They were going to wipe our memories before we left but one of Kushtaka's—she's the leader—kids, J-J-Jeel—left the enclosure to get a closer look at the sharks. I said I could talk the sharks out of eating him but I c-couldn't, I d-didn't get there in time. And Kushtaka kept Ro and Sky there till I came back. But she must have seen what happened to Jeel on the sursurvu—that's the big receiving dome for their surveillance sensors."

Murel's voice rose to an embarrassing wail, her nose ran, and her eyes filled with more salt water than they ever seemed to when she was swimming. "It was awful, Da, and she is his mum and she saw it all! I know she did. That has to be it. She decided the sharks made this spot too dangerous for them to stay so she moved the city. Sky got away somehow but Ro's still inside the city, vessel, whatever. It's all my fault!"

Ke-ola beat her parents to putting a comforting arm around her. "No, no, little sistah, it's my fault mostly. If you hadn't wanted to help me bring the Honus and my people here for a better life, then the Manos would not have come to eat the alien kid."

"We never made any deals about alien kids," Puna said, stoutly defending her clan's sacred animals. "The Manos were hungry. You kept them asleep on that ship but you didn't feed them what they needed. It's a wonder they kept their promise as long as they did—back on the old world, they'd eat their own wounded sometimes."

"Petaybee's started changing them already," Da mumbled to himself.

"Well, I wish it had done a better job, and done it sooner!" Murel's grief was turning to anger. "It was horrid. Just poor Jeel screaming and the sound of all those teeth and that blue stain all that was left of him."

Now Mum moved to put her arm around Murel's other shoulder. "Not Petaybee's fault or yours or Ke-ola's, pet, or even the sharks'. They weren't to know what Jeel was."

"But I told them and they just didn't care!" Murel howled, hating how she sounded even as she did it. "And now his mum doesn't have her kid and she took Ro to get back at us for bringing the sharks, even though that's why Ro and I came out here—to warn them."

"Is it your opinion that this Kushtaka is angry enough to harm your brother?" Da asked.

"N-no, but if she took him into outer space we'll never see him again!"

"Here now," Mum said. "None of that. Ke-ola, ask Rick and Johnny to buzz the *Piaf* and get the navtrack records from the ship's computer. That should let us know if any vessels have left Petay-bee's atmosphere within the time since *Piaf* entered it. If the alien vessel has left Petaybean space, have the *Piaf* notify the Corps and the Federation patrol to intercept it. Tell them to use level-three diplomacy in dealing with the alien vessel—speak kindly while casually aiming a big laser cannon at it. They wouldn't use the laser under level three, but the aliens don't know that. Probably the threat won't be necessary anyway. This Kushtaka sounds like she might have cooled off enough to see reason and return Ronan if she's given a chance."

Ke-ola returned to the water, walking out a short way until the lava shelf dropped from under his feet. The water was a deep transparent blue, and the ocean floor was visible here when the water wasn't agitated. Ke-ola flattened out into a long dive and swam to the copter.

"Hmph," Da said. "The way I see it, those bloody orcas have a lot to answer for."

"But Da," Murel told him, "they were sorry—they saved me and Aunty Sinead from the whirlpool that wrecked Seamus's boat. I was trying to rescue her myself but if the whales hadn't picked us up, I'd never have been able to pull her this far in time to—to . . ." That was just it. Everything had been just too-too. She couldn't remember the word she wanted and finally said, ". . . to undrowned her."

Sinead coughed. "Thanks, pet. It's me that's undrowned, and alive to be proud of you, I am."

Murel managed a small smile. She realized that Aunty must be pretty upset herself. She didn't usually sound so much like the Irish side of the family.

Puna rose from tending a shark man's broken arm, planted her feet as firmly as she could on the drastic sloping lava rock, and put her fists on her hips as she faced the Shongilis. "So now there is trouble, what you gonna do with us, huh? You gonna do the same as the company? The Manos make a little mistake and eat something you don' want them to eat and you gonna send us away again some-place worse than the one we come from?"

"Don't be daft, woman," Da said, far more irritably than he usu-ally would. He was too worried about Ronan to want to worry about the shark people's fears. "It's enough of the taking and giving of the blame we've been doing here. Let's leave that until we get my son back from the undersea otters or aliens or whatever they are. Had they been a bit more open about their presence, we'd have known to ask your Manos not to eat them, wouldn't we? Everything has to eat something. While I'm sorry about the loss of the alien lad, that was no call for the undersea folk to go runnin' off with our Ronan. I trust we will get him back, and in time your Manos will learn—with your help—what prey they may take and what prey they may not. Right now there are more urgent issues to deal with, so don't you be givin' out to me about eviction notices I've never sent and have no intention of sending."

Puna gave a huff as the wind left her sails. She pretended to see another wound on someone and returned to her bandaging.

CHAPTER 18

B<small>Y THE TIME</small> the giant otter guards dumped Ronan into another of their poky little rooms, his flippers ached from being used as handles. There was no need for them to be so pushy. It was fine with him to stay here while Murel swam out to negotiate with the sharks. He had hoped to spend the time taking a closer look at the city, though, and was disappointed to be penned up again.

Then Tikka vanished a wall, which seemed to be the alien equivalent of opening a door. If they closed a door, no opening was visible in the wall at all, and when they opened a door, the wall vanished. Otherwise, people just came and went through the open holes in the walls. He didn't know if that meant those rooms were without doors. From what he'd seen, they were probably more public places.

He was alarmed to find that the formerly playful Tikka was angry with him. *It's all your fault, you and your mean fish!* she told him, sending her thoughts so hard that his poor furry head seemed about to burst with the force of them. This was the downside of being telepathic. If someone yelled in regular talk, it was possible to ig-nore or escape them. When someone started yelling their thoughts, however, it hurt. It was impossible to think of anything else until they stopped.

Whoa, whoa, lassie, he told her in the tone he'd heard his father use with the female family members when they were upset with him. *Slow down, will you? I hear you but you're sending so hard I don't understand what it is I'm hearing. What exactly is my fault? Has some-thing happened to Sky? He's not with you, but as you can see, he's not with me either.*

They ate him! she wailed.

Someone ate Sky? Who would do such a terrible thing to such a great little guy? I thought your people were friendly to otters. You are otters part of the time. That's cannibalism, eating Sky. He was as upset as she was by then, and close to tears.

She didn't seem to understand his questions and didn't answer them. Instead, she continued her rant. *Mother saw it all. Your sister swam too slow and the mean fish got Jeel and ate him.*

Oh, no! he said. *So let me get this straight. Sky is okay but your brother was eaten?*

I don't care about the otter. I don't know what happened to him. Jeel is gone! Your new fish ate him.

Tikka, Tikka, please, I'm sorry for your loss. I truly am. He was re-lieved Sky was okay but tried hard to conceal his gladness. Of course, he wasn't glad Tikka's brother had been killed by the sharks, but it wasn't as if he *knew* Jeel, and Sky was his friend.

You just think you're sorry, Tikka said spitefully. *We didn't hurt any-one or anything. We saved your father and your sister but you couldn't leave us alone. You had to bring those new people and those horrible big fish here to eat Jeel. I hate you!*

Somehow, he hadn't thought life-forms as alien-looking as these deep sea otter/jellyfish people would love or hate anything or any-one. All the offworlders he had ever met were human like himself—well, mostly like himself, transplants from old Terra. Kushtaka

sounded as cold and scientific as Dr. Mabo, as if everything was
some big experiment and she was above temper tantrums. She certainly hadn't been affectionate with Tikka like a real mum would be.
But Tikka wasn't a bit detached about this. She was furious, and
now that she'd shut up for a moment, he could feel her grief, and
her fear as well. He understood then what her thought-yelling had
been too loud to say. These people, as adults, weren't all that comforting to be around, but Jeel and Tikka had been as close to each
other as he was to Murel.

That's right, Tikka said, reading him and giving him an appraising
look that was worthy of her mother. *I'll never see Jeel again, and now
you'll never see your sister again or your parents or your nasty fish either.*

At that, the room seemed to elongate, all of the other walls disappeared, and outside the city's invisible force field the sea spun
like the rotors of a copter.

THE SEA HAD quickly subsided to comparative calm shortly after
the whirlpool's localized typhoon. Its once more crystal blue waters
lapped the volcano's skirts with small wavelets.

The first thing Murel and the survivors of the boat accident felt
was a slight tremor in the black rock beneath them. Then the clear
blue-green pools in the rocks shimmied and sloshed in their stone
bowls.

Murel wrinkled her nose as she caught a strong wave of sulfurous
stench. Above them a pillar of smoke pumped into the clear blue
sky.

"How fast is it a fishing boat can go, Seamus?" Da asked the captain of the wrecked vessel.

"Not fast enough, I fear. If our friends immediately put into the
water when they were called upon four hours ago, they won't be
more than a third of the distance."

"Puna, will your Manos give you a lift again out of these waters?"
Da asked.

"Those who are not wounded, yes. But the wounded will not be able to hang on, and besides, you can't expect a Mano to ignore the scent of blood indefinitely."

"No indeedy," Mum said with a quirk to the side of her mouth. "That would clearly be an imposition. So what we'll do is get the able-bodied personnel off the copter except for Rick and Johnny, making way for the wounded to ride. If they've time for two trips, well and good. If not, well, we clearly can't trust the Manos with nonrelatives, so perhaps, Sean, you had best go see if you can find some of those apologetic orcas to provide the taxi service to the rescue vessels for the rest of us."

Da saluted, as he sometimes did when Mum was being bossy— if efficient and right, of course—"Ma'am, yes, ma'am," stepped into waist-high water, stripped off his dry suit, and let Mum harness it to his back.

"Wait, Da, I'm coming too," Murel said, and made her transformation in the same manner. She lingered a moment, though, to see what happened. If the volcano erupted all of a sudden, she would save Mum if she had to slap her silly with a flipper to get her to come.

Mum swam to the copter to tell the others her plan, and Murel saw Pet, Ke-ola, Keoki, and a man who reminded her a bit of a small bear jump into the water and head for shore. They began carrying the injured people aboard. The copter waited until they were ashore once more then lifted off, whipping up waves that made it hard for Murel to see more as she bobbed up and down in their hills and valleys.

MARMION STAYED WITH the *Piaf* while Johnny, Pet, and Raj flew out to help look for the missing twins. Someone had to stay there and host the new refugees still lodged aboard the ship while accommodations were being arranged for them. This was something of an inconvenience, since Marmie felt she had neglected her own business enterprises while assisting her friends. The lack of reliable interplanetary communications from the volatile Petaybee made it difficult to keep in touch with her managers, vice chairpeople and presidents, her boards and department chiefs.

In some ways, being so isolated was restful, but she had begun to feel that she had rested too long. She had every confidence that the twins would be located soon, unharmed. Probably, their elders would learn in time that during their absence the children had gained some benefit for their planet and all concerned. Once the Maddock-Shongilis were thus reunited, she and her crew must bid their erstwhile guests adieu and return to Versailles Station. Some intermittent stops at this world or that moon along the way no doubt would be necessary to quench corporate brush fires. She had that to look forward to as soon as they were clear of the magnetic interference from Petaybee.

If she spent any more time here, she might become like Yana, so used to the planet she too would develop the odd adaptation with the ugly name "brown fat." Then she could travel through the coldest weather like some spacefaring voyageur. Perhaps she should have a parka designed for her from the ancient striped blanket of the Hudson Bay Company? But once she developed that characteristic—not that she seriously imagined that she would—she would be no more able to leave this world for any prolonged period than Yana, Sean, or Clodagh.

No, no, it would not do. She must be on her way as soon as the *bébés* were found and the newcomers lodged locally, pending completion of their own housing. Most inconvenient that she was not even able to send for more Nakatira cubes. Perhaps she would convince dear Yoshi Nakatira himself to deliver them and see to what good use his product had been employed.

"Madame, the helicopter has returned. There are wounded aboard."

"Wounded?"

"A freak typhoon, Madame, upset the shark tug."

"No one was eaten, I hope?"

"No, Madame. But four injured. One rather badly. Shall we bring them aboard?"

"I think not. If you can discover their family names, I will let their families know that they are safe now and you may take them to Clodagh in Kilcoole if they are able to travel by rougher means than copter, or send for her to come here. The twins?"

"Ronan is still reported missing, Madame, though apparently Murel reappeared in time to assist with getting the shipwrecked passengers safely to the volcanic island."

"Hmph," Marmie said, "however safe that may be."

"With your permission, Madame, we will attend to the wounded as you instruct and give the copter clearance to return for the other shipwrecked personnel, including Chief Chan, Captain Green, Governor Maddock-Shongili, and Mr. Norman."

"By all means," she said. "That particular area of Petaybee remains most tempestuous in nature. Is there room for all aboard the copter?"

"No, Madame, but the fishing fleet is en route to transport the stranded people as well. The copter can ferry them quickly between the island and the boats."

"Then they must go immediately," Marmie said.

"One more thing, Madame."

"Yes?"

"The governors ask if you will employ the *Piaf*'s sensors to see if any vessels have launched from Petaybee within the last few hours. The typhoon is said to have been the result of some sort of launch, but it is uncertain whether or not a vessel left the planet."

She toggled the com switch to her navigations officer and explained the situation.

She spent the next half hour to forty-five minutes notifying the families still aboard the *Piaf* of the situation, consoling them and urging the adult family members of the injured to go to them. The children would be perfectly safe aboard the *Piaf* while Clodagh healed her patients.

When the com unit played her personal code again, she felt sure it was First Officer Robineau notifying her of the information gleaned from the sensors. It was a bit early for the copter to return but perhaps Ronan had been found after all or, heaven forbid, the volcanic island was too active to approach.

But it was another sort of disaster altogether.

"An Intergal Company Corps vessel just docked in the next bay, Madame."

"Without authorization?" she asked. Had Yana or Sean authorized such a landing, they would have mentioned it to her before they left.

"They have authorization under Federation Code IM87492XP. They request—and I use the term loosely, Madame," Com Officer Guthe's voice betrayed some of the wry humor he showed off-duty but generally managed to avoid while handling ship's business, "permission to board. They claim to have a warrant for your arrest and the confiscation of the *Piaf*."

"*Merde alors!* What now?" Marmie exclaimed.

CHAPTER 19

THE VOLCANO PUFFED again, and this time the smoke billowed from it. The people on shore bounced around a bit with the trembling of their steeply pitched perch.

As Murel turned from them, she heard Ke-ola's voice raised above the others as he began the volcano-birthing chant he had taught them only a few weeks ago, though it seemed a lifetime.

Murel flipped over and started swimming away. A wall of tooth-studded snouts faced her.

Hel-lo, little seal-girl. Got any more tidbits for us? the leader taunted.

Get on with you, you great bloodthirsty lot, she told them. *You're wanted elsewhere.*

She wondered if even Puna knew how nastily sharks could laugh when they wished. But she dived under them and sped on out to sea.

Da? Where are you? she asked mentally while sending out her sonar signal.

Dead ahead, darlin', but much as I hate to lose track of you again, I think it best for the sake of time if we split up to search for the orcas. If I find them, I'll call out to you and then I want you to return to the volcano to help with the rescue. If you find them, do the same.

Right, she said.

She struck off to the east, where the whales had headed after delivering Aunty and her to shore. They could be most of the way to the south by now.

Murel River Seal, wait! Sky called.

Sky, what took you so long?

Wise otters wait until Manos have other things to do than eat otters before getting into the water, he told her. *The Mano people are riding Manos, the hurt people are riding the copter. Only the people of the river seals are on the volcano still. I would have the sea otter cousins help them but they do not trust the Manos.*

Neither do I. The Honus would help but I don't trust the Manos not to bite our people off their backs.

Manos are not good rememberers, not like otters, Sky said.

It was grand having him swim with her again, but she missed Ronan. *How did you get out of the city before it left, Sky?*

Very easy. The walls went away and I saw the beaming place so I slid out and swam fast before the whirling caught me. Otters can swim very fast when they have to.

I wish brothers could do the same, Murel said.

After we save everyone else, we will save Ronan, Murel. It is what river seals and sky otters do, saving others.

Except Jeel, Murel thought mournfully. *This river seal wasn't fast enough to save the alien kid. I wish I hadn't been so cocky. If Kushtaka had gone out with enough of her people they might have scared the Manos away.*

Or the Manos would have had a bigger feed, Sky said. *Manos do not fear.*

Out of the minds of otters, she thought softly, *or one in particular,* the first comfort she'd had since Jeel's death. *I wonder if Ronan is afraid.*

Deep sea otters will not harm Ronan, Sky said. *They are not people to harm others.*

I was under the same impression, but since they took Ronan, I have to wonder. I have a feeling they did it to harm our family.

Not real harm, Sky contended with surprising conviction. *Not the kind that opens skin or makes dead.*

Harm enough, she insisted. *But I'll find him if I have to search the galaxy.*

Searching the sea is closer, Sky said.

Right now we're searching for orcas, she told Sky. While they thought-talked, she emitted her sonar signals at regular intervals.

Orcas! she sent out, a mental call. *Bitfin! Boss! We have a situation here. Your help is needed again. My father and Petaybee will be very grateful if you'd show up right away.*

Orcas, Sky called in a different direction. *This is me, the sky otter, calling you too, reminding you that otters taste terrible but can show you where there are great shoals of herring!*

Murel felt like adding, *And sharks. Really yummy sharks. The kind you said you like to eat.* Puna's people wouldn't like it if their aumakuas got gobbled by whales the first time they went to sea, so she supposed it was very bad of her. If Petaybee was going to mellow the sharks, as Ro had suggested, she wished that particular adaptation would happen in double-quick time.

Someone is coming who is not whales, Sky said at the same moment her sonar picked up several creatures heading toward them. Sky was right. These were not whales. Not unless they were midgets. They were about her size, maybe, or a little larger.

Hey you, solo seal! a mental call reached her. *What are you doing, calling for killer whales? You get caught in somebody's net too long and damage your head? It's not healthy calling orcas. They eat seals. We ought to know.*

They would, of course. These were the regular kind of seals.

They swam up to her and Sky, who backpaddled until he was hiding under her flipper. Then she remembered that when she first met him, he thought seals ate otters.

What you got there, pup? one of the new seals said. *Lunch? That's too much for a young one like you. You should share. Otters are delicious.*

Not sky otters, she said. *They taste awful. Besides, this one is a family member.*

I don't know how to break this to you, pup, but otters of any kind are not related to seals of any kind.

Ah, she said, remembering the superior tone of some distant dialogue from an ancient vid. *But this is not just any seal you're dealing with when you deal with me. I am Murel Monster Slayer Maddock-Shongili, a selkie and Petaybean shepherd seal.* When this didn't get an immediate reaction, she added hopefully, *I don't suppose you lot have seen my brother Ronan Born for Water anywhere around here in the last few hours, have you?*

A female ventured close enough to sniff at her. *She does smell funny, Rork.*

Then there's the business with the uneaten otter, another one said. *Unsealy, that is.*

No, wait, a third said. *I remember. It was a long time ago—she ought to be an adult by now, but I remember when Murel Monster Slayer and her brother were born. Their father is a selkie too and their grandfather before him.*

Murel wanted to protest that her grandfather had been the scientist who made his son into a selkie, which was what Da and Aunty always said, but she didn't want to contradict this seal who believed her and seemed to be on her side and was also maybe older and wiser than the rest of the lot.

We were living closer to the coast back then and all of us felt it, the older seal continued. *Somebody new and exciting had entered the world. Someone to be a leader among us, maybe, or at least a protector.*

So what is she doing calling those orcas back to eat us again? Rork demanded.

I need them to help my mum and some other people stranded at the foot of the volcano, Murel explained. Even where they swam now the stench of the sulfur was sickeningly strong. Looking back, she saw the black smoke billowing into the air, a hint of red at its base.

We could help, the elder said.

I wish I could say that would work, she said, *but there are sharks in these waters now and they'd eat you and maybe some of my people too. No, we need the killer whales. They say they eat sharks, so they're not afraid of them.*

They'll eat you too, the elder said.

No. They tried it and almost managed. Only the aliens—deep sea otters—saved me, and then Da talked to them—the whales I mean, not the deep sea otters—and so when the aliens kidnapped my brother after I couldn't save the leader's son and my aunt Sinead almost drowned, the whales saved us both to sort of say they were sorry.

The seals seemed to be trying to untangle the threads of her story.

Then the elder spoke again. *Well, if you really need orcas, you're going about it the wrong way. Follow us.*

Where?

Back to the reef, of course. The whales know they're not supposed to eat you, but nobody told them they can't eat us. Only we need to be where we can escape from them while you explain your problem.

Their new reef was on the southern side of the volcano, formed by an earlier series of undersea chimneys that had gone dormant but sported new colonies of life-forms on their surface. The southern lip of the volcano met up with the bottom of the reef, partially cupping a beautiful blue-green pool.

Our private tub, the female, named Sorka, told them.

Right, the elder said. *Now, you keep quiet, Murel, and let us do the calling.*

Pork, you get into the pool and call for help because you've, uh—

Caught my flipper in a crack when the reef moved? Pork asked. She might have been large, but she wasn't slow.

That will work. The rest of us will make a big fuss over how you are too large, fat, and juicy for us to free. If the orcas are anywhere at all close they won't be able to resist trying their luck. Once they get within range, Murel can tell them what she wants while you beach yourself on the reef.

Pork assumed her position and began barking something to the effect of, *Oh, dear! Oh silly me! I've caught my flipper in this rift in the rock and I can't free myself. Someone get me out of here!*

Poor Pork, the other seals cried over and over, and, *She's stuck.*

Get her out, others barked.

Oh, she is too big and fat to move far enough to get at the fin! two others barked back.

No, no, be careful! You'll hurt me. My flesh is very tender, Pork complained.

They carried on that way for quite a long time, getting more and more into their act.

Bring me something to eat! Pork called. *I feel weak. A seal of my size needs lots of fish to keep up her strength.*

We are growing weak too, Pork, too weak to feed you. So weak that if an entire pod of orcas came to eat us, we could barely escape.

Orcas! Oh no, not orcas! Save me! Save me!

They were enjoying themselves so much, hamming it up, or maybe Porking it up was a better way to put it, that they weren't paying attention to their surroundings any longer.

Murel had never met full-time seals before and was surprised at how smart they were and how much fun they had. She and Sky sat up on the rocks, the waves washing over them often enough to keep her in seal form. The two of them watched the seals' antics, while also watching for the orcas. Sky suddenly stood on his hind feet and said, *Hah! Black fins, seals. Black fins are coming.*

The seals practically flew out of the water and up onto the rocks, even Pork.

Murel wiggled her way through them to the edge of the reef. She didn't want to get into the water yet, not until she was sure they recognized her and remembered that she was off-limits as a food item. *Orcas, hello!* she called. *It's me, Murel. I need your help again.*

We heard. That poor little seal is stuck in the rocks and she's too large, fat, and luscious for you and her little friends to help her?

No, she's fine now and they're all back up on the rocks.

Everyone? So fast? The game hasn't even started!

Well, there's another game my father and I need your help with.

What is it now?

Some people are stranded on the edge of the volcano and it's been rumbling. There are fishing boats coming but they're very slow. Could you carry a few people out to them?

We could do that. We'd be happy to carry some of those seals too.

Yeah, Bitfin said, *carry them in our bellies!*

The seals started barking insults and taunts.

The volcano belched a cloud of smoke bigger than it was. *Please hurry,* Murel said.

Okay, but tell the seal side of your family not to worry. We'll be back.

Murderers! the seals shouted.

Don't go into the water with them now, Murel, the elder told her. *They're ready to eat seals. I wouldn't trust them.*

They eat otters too, Sky told her. *Those are otter-eating whales.* He did not seem happy. Some of the seals were regarding him in the same way the whales had been regarding them.

Murel waited until the orcas were heading toward the north side of the volcano before sliding into the water, Sky close behind her.

Thanks, seals, she told them. *You were great. There's one more thing . . .*

It doesn't involve more whales or sharks, does it? the elder asked. *Because we can use a rest.*

No, it's about my brother. Did any of you happen to see that odd-looking city near the volcano?

We've seen it. It's always been there, Pork said. *It's where the deep sea otters live.*

Well, it's not there now and my brother is inside of it. If you see it anywhere else or hear reports about someone else seeing it, please tell me. I think they have to live near volcanoes. So if there are other active ones in the sea right now, they may have moved there.

Near the fjord the humans call Perfect Fjord there are more sea chimneys, the elder told her. *Maybe they moved there.*

Thanks, she said. *As soon as we get everyone else to safety, we'll check it out.*

The sea otter cousins will look too, Murel, Sky told her. *They will like to find a new place with giant white clams and no sharks.*

CHAPTER 20

YANA, PET CHAN, Raj Norman, Ke-ola, Keoki, and Sinead huddled on the volcano's shuddering hem, hoping rescue would reach them before Petaybee's labor pains resulted in a further eruption of lava. Sea turtles bobbed just offshore.

Yana watched Ke-ola and Keoki squatting at the edge of the water, apparently consorting telepathically with Honus, until Ke-ola turned back to the others.

"The Honus say they would keep us afloat if Dr. Shongili and Murel don't find the whales," he said. "They are very strong and fast in the water. Two of them supported Keoki and me out here."

"Yes, but you'd have frozen to death in the water without Murel's and Ronan's dry suits," Yana said. "The water near the volcano may be warm enough to swim in, but closer to the land it's starting to freeze already. I'll survive by wearing my wet suit. Sinead is a native Petaybean and would probably survive as well, but those of you from offworld certainly wouldn't. And the turtles would have to carry us out of the warmer waters to escape the eruption."

"She's got a point, Ke-ola," Keoki said. "And also, the Manos might be a little careless about keeping their pledge to take us off their prey list if they thought they could pick us off with no survivors, no witnesses, no one of their relatives to tell the tale. And they will be back as soon as they've delivered Puna's people to the rescuers. That water back landward is too cold for Manos too."

Keoki still wore Ronan's dry suit. "I have this on. I could go with the Honu to try to get help too."

"Missus is the one who should go." Ke-ola nodded toward Yana.

"I could do that," Yana agreed, "but I think our best chance is staying together and waiting for Sean or Murel to find the whales. I have complete confidence in them." Her chin jutted as she looked each of the others full in the face, as if trying to inject them with her own faith and resolve.

"I'm sure you're right, Yana," Sinead said, "but I'm still thinking we should be ordering more wet suits from Corps surplus once we get home. With all these new sea creatures to keep track of, we'll be after needin' an update to our planetary fashion statement of mukluks, snow pants, and parkas."

Pet Chan, her youthful almond-eyed face scrunched up between balled fists, said, "Stupid, stupid, stupid. Why didn't we prepare for this? We should have had them on board before we left Space Base. I'm getting rusty is what. Versailles Station is usually so secure I've relaxed, forgotten how to be alert and prepare properly for things. I'm resigning as soon as we get back."

"Marmie won't accept that, Pet," Yana said. "I was prepared to dive because I know my family. Whenever they get into trouble, water is almost always involved. You were prepared for a copter rescue—"

"No, no, she's right," Raj Norman said. "It was inexcusably careless. I didn't think about getting in the water myself. It's been a while. I brought all those armaments and forgot basic survival measures."

Beneath their feet, Petaybee rumbled and bellowed, and this time the smoke carried a spray of fire.

"Boy," Raj said to Keoki, "I suggest you give your suit up to Miss Sinead or Miss Chan. We men can take our chances with the cold."

"He's a kid, Raj," Pet said.

"I think Yana's right," Sinead said, ignoring the implication that she was helpless merely because of her gender. "I'm thinkin' I could make it with the Honu as far as the fishing boats. They'll surely be entering the warmer waters by now. But the young newcomers aren't used to Petaybee's extremes at all."

"So what you're saying is you think it's time I hop the nearest turtle?" Yana asked.

But the Honus were no longer there. Instead, like an attack fleet of black-sailed boats, the dorsal fins of the orca pod knifed through the waves, heading toward the beach.

Murel and Sky swam around the volcano to the spot where they'd left her mum and the others. By the time they reached their destination, the air was filled with smoke and fiery sparks. The sea was very rough. Swimming underwater was easiest.

The whales swam offshore, back and forth, while the people looked on.

What are you waiting for? Murel demanded. *Can't you see that the volcano is about to erupt?*

We can see that fine, Bitfin said. *Can't you see that if we swim any closer we'll beach ourselves and be even more stranded than your people are? You didn't mention suicide mission when you asked for your little favor.*

Which you tricked us into, don't forget, one of the females added.

Don't be such big babies! Murel said. *This is important. Of course, I don't want you to commit suicide.* She felt extremely cross, but not so much with them as with herself. It hadn't occurred to her that the people on land might not realize the whales could not swim close enough for them to simply hop on and ride without endangering themselves.

She swam closer to the shore. The smallest Honu poked its head out from under a lava ledge. *We can help, Murel,* he said. *Ke-ola and*

the others may hang on to our shells and we will swim them out to the
whales if you will make sure the whales know Honus are not for eat-
ing.

Murel swam back to the whales and explained the plan.

Can't eat sharks, can't eat seals, can't eat otters, can't eat turtles,
can't eat humans. You got a lot of rules for a minnow morsel, the
leader said. *We orcas are big people. We need our nourishment.*

Get on with ye, Murel said in a prodding tone she'd heard her
aunt Sinead use. *Two of the species you mentioned are new to the*
planet and you never had them to eat before, nor have you seen that
many humans. You have tons and tons of fish to eat like everyone else.
Then she added, pleading, *Come on, please. My whole family will*
spend the winter catching fish for you if you'll just help.

Oh, very well, but don't worry about fishing for us. You're so slow
we'd starve before you'd caught enough to keep one of us alive for a day.

Once the Honus were reassured, they conveyed the plan to Ke-
ola and Keoki.

Keoki set the example, under the Honus' direction. One of the
turtles swam close enough for him to grab on to the sides of the
shell. The Honu then ferried him out beyond the lava shelf. Murel
felt its trepidation as it faced the pod of whales, but the leader dived
and came up under Keoki's lower torso and legs. Keoki released the
Honu's shell and instead held on to the whale's dorsal fin.

Ke-ola beckoned Murel's mother toward the next waiting Honu.

The entire volcano cone quaked, and Mum dived into the water.

Change of plans, Ke-ola told the Honus and enough turtles to
carry each of the stranded people surfaced close enough to the
shore to be boarded.

Ke-ola came last, after a brief argument with Raj Norman. Pet
Chan backed Ke-ola, however. "The youngster communicates with
the turtles, Raj. Both boys do. They're the logical ones to ride point
and to cover our rear."

"One Honu is gonna come with us so we can keep in touch with
Murel and the whales," Ke-ola told him.

"Geez, haven't you people ever heard of com units?" Raj grumbled, but belly-flopped into the surf and grabbed on to a Honu. Pet did the same right beside him.

Murel and Sky were joined by the smallest Honu, their original turtle friend who had come with Ke-ola when he first came to Petaybee, the one she and Ronan had helped rescue from the "experiments" of the unscrupulous Dr. Marie Mabo.

Mum and the others had only been whaleback for a klick or so when the rumbling behind them overwhelmed the roar of the sea. Looking back, Murel saw the volcano cone crowned with fire. It spewed from the top and then coursed down the sides of the mountain, a broad red swath bleeding into the sea at the spot they'd just left.

SEAN LOCATED THE fishing boats well before he spotted the orcas. When his sonar picked up large swimming objects, he thought he had found his reluctant allies, but the approaching creatures turned out to be the sharks bearing Puna and her family. They passed him, encountering the boats before he did.

So where were the orcas? Perhaps they were more disturbed by his threats than he'd supposed. Maybe they didn't want to risk his wrath again, so after the peace gesture of rescuing Murel and Sinead, they'd deliberately made themselves scarce for a while? Considering the circumstances, he didn't think he'd been overly harsh in the thoughts he'd communicated with them. However, mental communication could be tricky, and orcas were a very intelligent lot, more so than humans, according to some studies.

Perhaps they picked up on his buried desire to harpoon the lot of them for endangering his children? That would be unfortunate, since he would never stoop to such destructive behavior. Still, that was the sort of thought that his reptilian brain—the most primitive section of any human brain, albeit one with some necessary seal modifications—conjured up, whether one liked it or not. The so-called reptilian brain was the section most responsible for violence, predation, war, and the cruder and more hostile forms of mating behavior. Whales had their own equivalent. Reptilian was a misnomer, actually, assuming a relationship between all creatures and early saurians on Terra. He wondered if alien races would also have it. What if they were highly evolved races of reptilian origin? Would they have developed more sophisticated mental or emotional organs, processes, or responses to overcome it? Most animals had. Even the most seemingly benign creatures, as many viewed the orcas, could behave in a fairly savage fashion, as they had with Murel. Rabbits could behave savagely, using their claws and teeth to shred each other.

The scientist in him could only hope the orcas would understand that his display of justifiable anger did not mean he would act upon it. He hoped they hadn't left the area over an unintentional and unexpressed impulse. Of course, it could be that among whales, acting on the impulse happened immediately after having it, but he couldn't recall reading any studies on the subject.

The sharks, having delivered their cargo to the fishing boats, escorted the other boats for the remainder of their journey. Their motivation and attitude was less ambivalent than the whales'. They doubtlessly were hoping someone unrelated to them would fall overboard. Sharks, at least this particular variety, were probably the best example he could conceive of of a species that seemed to contain nothing *but* reptilian brain. And yet, they maintained a mutually protective relationship with Puna's people. The wonderful thing about science for Sean was how much you could discover and how much still remained a great mystery to be explored. He hoped he could collect his strayed or lost family members, return to land and human form, and get back to his lab soon. The relationships between the Kanakas—as Ke-ola's people preferred to be called—and their totem animals fascinated him.

Perhaps he could infuse the sharks, orcas, and other predators with some sort of inhibitor to prevent them from attacking humans or selkies or even other species that needed time to develop populations, as the sharks themselves did. It would need to be easy to manipulate in future generations, however. The creatures, like all creatures, did need to prey on something, after all.

He dived deep to avoid the sharks and continue his search for the orcas. He hoped that the sharks might attract the larger predators. New underwater chimneys had formed on the outskirts of the volcanic field, closer to the mainland. Were other volcanic chains developing as well? He and Clodagh would need to consult with Petaybee when they returned. Perhaps the planet could also give them a clue if the alien city or vessel was now hidden elsewhere in the sea.

If so, surely the inhabitants would realize that keeping Ronan would only attract attention they did not want. They would realize that the least troublesome course for them was to simply wipe his memory, as they had Sean's, and release him.

Sean surfaced for air and first heard the rotors, then saw the shape of the helicopter. Rick had spontaneously dubbed it the Flying Otter in Sky's honor. It was heading back to the volcano. To his dismay he also saw that the sky into which the copter flew was crimson and orange underlying billows of black, gray, and white smoke.

He dived again to escape the surface turbulence and swam faster. Yana! Would the copter make it in time to lift her off the volcano?

Then his sonar picked up a number of bobbing shapes and others moving rapidly toward them, while still others, the sharks, swam equally rapidly away.

The bobbing shapes were the fishing vessels. By the time Sean reached them, they were engaged in the tricky business of transferring passengers from whaleback to boat decks, apparently under the supervision of sea turtles.

Sean spotted Yana as she slid into one of the boats, and he swam alongside her.

She sat down, caught her breath, checked the others, and finally glanced at him. "Oh, Sean, it's you, thank the cosmos. Now then, if Murel—where is she anyway?"

Sean dived again. Whales, turtles, humans, boats, lots of fish, and other life-forms, but no other seals and no otters of any sort at all. Where was Murel?

CHAPTER 21

MUREL AND SKY swam with the whales until they inter-
cepted the boats. She and Sky hung back as the whales
slowed their swimming so as not to swamp the boats, and the people
on the boats were able to help Mum and the others board their tiny
crafts. Though Murel no longer felt afraid of the whales, Sky was
smaller and his survival instincts were stronger since he used them
every day, not just when his relatives weren't around.

Murel's mother is safe, Father River Seal is safe, Sky said, spotting
Da before she did. *Other human people are safe. Only Ronan is not
safe. Murel will find him now so he will be safe also?*

She considered this for a moment. Mum and Da would want to
go look for Ronan too but they had all of these other people to tend.
It was their job as governors to look after more than their own family. She could just hear Mum saying, "In a bit, Murel. First we
must . . ." and see Da having to change again to take care of some
other aspect of the crisis that was bound to take too long.

While she was thinking all of this over, Sorka, her new seal friend, called to her, *We were right! At the underwater fire mountain in Perfect Fjord there is a different thing with living creatures in it.*

How did you get there so fast? Murel asked.

We did not go there. Our relatives called to us, frightened by a great whirlpool. They wanted to know if we knew what it was, if our fire mountain made a whirlpool too. We said yes and told them it was made by a giant bubble that was home to a herd of otter creatures and that you had lost it with your brother inside. They looked, and though they did not see your brother, they saw the bubble.

Thanks, cousins! she replied. *I'll go right now.*

Even knowing they would be too busy to go with her, she was about to tell her parents where she was going so they wouldn't worry, and then the copter returned. Hovering overhead, it lowered a rope ladder. Responding to Mum's gestures, Aunty Sinead carefully stood and prepared to climb up. The noise and waves generated by the wind of the copter's rotors made it hard for Murel to hear herself think, much less contact Da. She couldn't see him for all of the boats and whales. The echolocation used by the whales also interfered with her own sonar.

She thought the copter would load and take off again but Johnny climbed down the ladder and shouted something at Mum, though Murel could make out none of the conversation.

She didn't know which way Perfect Fjord was, and if she waited to ask Mum and Da, she was nervous that they might insist she return to Kilcoole with the copter while they waited for it to finish evacuating people before they got around to fetching Ronan. Meanwhile, the aliens might decide to take off and take Ronan with them for good. Adults could be so poky, and time was of the essence! She decided on a compromise. First she asked the closest whale how to get to the fjord.

You've got a lot of tail asking anything else after you tricked us into fetching and carrying for you all day, the whale replied, blowing a fountain of water through his blowhole in a decidedly derisive manner. But he added, *Swim north along the coast. You can't miss it.*

Then she found the smallest Honu, the little one she and Ro thought of as their personal friend, and told him where she was going and why. She asked him to tell Ke-ola so he could tell Mum and Da when they asked. *Tell them to come too, maybe with the copter, though it should land on the fjord's shore and wait a reasonable amount of time for us to surface before trying to find us,* she said. *I don't think the aliens will let Ro go because I say so, but they might if they think the adults will find them if they don't. They want to avoid contact as much as possible.*

Then, with the copter still hovering and her Mum and Johnny still shouting at each other, she and Sky struck out, veering north and paralleling the shoreline as the orca had directed. They rapidly left behind the rescue boats. She hoped that with both her and Ro gone again, Mum and Da would decide their children needed rounding up before anything else happened.

FINALLY THE WORLD stopped spinning and whooshing as the city settled over a new vent. Outside the city's shield the deep sea waters teemed with fish. Beneath the pathways winding among the buildings, the deep geothermal rift glowed a bright cherry red. Ronan guessed it was closer to the surface than the last vent had been. So they'd moved, but they seemed to still be on Petaybee, maybe not too far from where they'd been before.

Ronan supposed he should probably be afraid, but he was sure his family would find and fetch him before long, even if he didn't exactly know how they'd go about it.

With Tikka mad at him, he had no one to talk to. He was wary of Kushtaka. Even though she might not be mean, she was grieving over losing her son and therefore not in a very good mood. But there were a lot of the other alien otters swimming around, and he decided to try to find someone else to talk to. There was still so much he was curious about. Even if they wiped his mind later, he'd be satisfied now, and it would pass the time until his family came to take him home.

But the first thing to do was find Sky. Tikka said the little otter was okay so he must be around somewhere. If she had showed him where to slide, being an otter, he might be sliding still. Lucky for him that these aliens enjoyed sliding too. Probably because they'd taken otter form, some of the otters' other characteristics had rubbed off on them. Ronan hoped Sky hadn't been sliding when the city started whirling or he could have had a wilder ride than even otters liked.

Since the walls of the room where Ronan was incarcerated did not reappear even after Tikka departed and the city settled, he simply swam out of it. Looking up and down the streets, he tried to get his bearings. He remembered Tikka gesturing toward a tall spiraling tower, but now that he had time to look around, there were more of them than he'd thought.

Who could he ask? There was that beam thing they used to gather food. His relationship with Kushtaka had been fairly friendly when they last visited, so maybe those aliens didn't realize he'd been demoted in status from guest to prisoner.

He found the right hole again after poking his head in a few others first.

None of the places he investigated initially were residences. One of them seemed to be some sort of power plant, and its floor opened directly onto the cherry-colored vent below. Oddly, the room wasn't hot, but Ronan guessed this was where the city's lights came from. More tubes of spinning water drew fire from the vent, and at intervals big otters added some sort of rocks to it that caused it to turn colors.

There were valves over openings in the walls where the water tubes disappeared. Ronan tried to ask the big otters coloring the water about the slide, but the collective sound of the water tubes might have made it hard for them to hear. Or maybe they just didn't want to talk to him.

In the next room shells were stacked and racked by kind and color, but there were no giant otters stacking or racking them.

He saw some odd-looking equipment in the next two rooms and alien otters very intent on images hovering in front of them, but none of them responded to him either. He thought they might be monitoring the surveillance cameras, possibly focusing them on different areas surrounding the city's new location.

He didn't recognize the room with the "hunting" beam until he happened upon it, and even then he wouldn't have recognized it without the baskets of neatly sorted fish and shellfish that filled the room. Two of the aliens were tossing more fish and shells back and forth, catching them in baskets with a playfulness that reminded him of Sky.

I'm hungry, he told them. *Where could I get a couple of fish?*

Catch! the nearest one said, and flung a fish back to him. Ronan ducked under it, caught it on his nose, and after it hung there for a moment, opened his mouth and ate it.

Good trick! one of the aliens said. *Mraka, he balanced that fish on his olfactory organ! Do it again so she can see!*

I'll be needing another fish, then, Ronan replied. *A nice fat one like the last.*

Mraka was so impressed she threw him another so she could see the trick again. Then she asked, *Can you show us how to do that?*

I think it's a seal sort of thing, he replied, but he coached them nevertheless on how to duck under the fish so it landed just so, and how to hold your head so that even if your whole body moved, your nose kept the fish aloft until it just smelled so overwhelmingly good you had to eat it. *I can hold a regular ball for a lot longer,* he told them. *But you have to eat the fish. It's mean not to when they can't breathe. Huh.* He paused as it occurred to him that there was something a bit—well, fishy—about the state of these fish.

Before he could ask about them, however, Mraka caught one on the end of her nose and balanced it for a couple of nanos before opening her mouth to swallow it. Ronan clapped his front flippers together appreciatively, startling both of the otterlike aliens. *Good, Mraka! I guess otters can do it too.*

I can too, I can, Mraka's friend said, fumbling his tenth fish.

Calmly, Puk, she said. *You get too excited and twitch too much.*

I can't be calm and concentrate with you staring at me, Puk complained, but when Mraka threw the next fish, Puk balanced it, more or less, for a brief and tottering time before it dropped from his nose and began to fall into the whirlpool beam. Reflexively, he dived under it and this time caught it at exactly the right place on his nose and balanced it even after he stood on his hind paws again.

Very good, Puk, Ronan told him, applauding with his front flippers again. *I bet even Sky couldn't do that.*

Your little friend the odd-looking otter? Mraka asked.

Yes, I wanted to ask you if you'd seen him or knew where the big slide is Tikka took him to play on. I'm worried that when the city moved—

I'm sorry about your friend, Mraka said. *I tried to catch him but he was after a fish, and when the beam went out, he fell into it and—well, he didn't come back with it.*

He esc—he left the city? Ronan asked.

Yes, I'm sorry. He probably drowned. The turbulence created by our drives is very strong and he was very small.

Sky? Drowned? Ronan couldn't see how that was possible, having watched the otter swim and knowing how quick-thinking Sky was. *No,* he thought sternly to himself. *I don't believe he drowned. I think he escaped.*

But meanwhile he decided to act as sad as if he thought Mraka was right. *Oh, no. He was a very good friend.*

Yes, it has been very bad recently, Puk said. *First Jeel is killed, and then your otter friend. Jeel was often difficult, not quite right, but Kushtaka and Tikka were fond of him. And I liked the otter. Sky?*

Yes, Ronan replied in a regretful way, *Sky, because he was the first sky otter—he flew with us in the helicopter and went into space too. He was proud of being the first Petaybean otter ever to do so.*

Then it is good he did not find out that his assumption and yours are incorrect. All of the beings in this vessel have also flown and been into space.

Mraka added, *But we are not otters all of the time. Just as you, Ronan, are not a seal all of the time.*

I know. You're from outer space, right?

No, we were born on this world, in this sea.

I'm a little puzzled, Ronan told them. *Our grandfather was the one who chose the animals to come to Petaybee after the terraforming. I'm pretty sure your people weren't among them.*

Nobody put us here, Mraka told him. She set one of the fish baskets in a certain place and it disappeared through the wall. On the other side of the room, Puk was doing the same. *Our people have been here since this world's first life, before it died and your science revived it. This vessel is a remnant of our original civilization.*

But how can that be? The terraforming made new life on Petaybee, but before the process started, the company had to make sure there were no sentient life-forms on the planet. They lie sometimes but they wouldn't lie about that.

Even if they didn't recognize us for what we are? Mraka asked. *Even if there did not seem to them to be enough of us to matter?*

No, Ronan said. *They've done some pretty questionable stuff but I don't think they'd do that.*

Perhaps it is not policy, Puk said. *But there are always individuals and circumstances. Kushtaka would not normally keep a being from the outside world here longer than they wished. But with Jeel's death, she is not behaving in her customary fashion. Perhaps the person who was supposed to make sure there were no life-forms on this world also had reasons for departing from the usual protocol.*

Mraka paused as she lifted a basket. *Or perhaps they simply overlooked us. We are not many and the rest of our world was dead. Only those of us living in this enclave that is now our vessel clung to life.*

But how? According to everything, including the planet itself,

Petaybee was a dead world when the Intergal terraformed it. No water, no plants, no animals, nothing to sustain life.

Oh, well, if you count that time, it very well may have seemed unoccupied. We weren't physically here during that period. When the great ice age came, the volcanoes died and the waters froze and most of our people froze as well. Our city was on the last vent of the last remaining volcano and we had enough power to send a final distress signal before resigning ourselves to extinction. Fortunately, offplanet observers more similar to ourselves than we would have thought possible detected our plight and sent engineers to convert our city to the life-sustaining vessel it is now. It seemed a prudent time to take a holiday and discover what lay beyond this world.

So you were on vacation when the terraforming happened? Ronan asked. *I get why you left but why did you come back if you thought Petaybee was dead?*

Our rescuers took us back to their home world. It seems our race began on that world but as its population grew it decided to colonize another planet. Our ancient ancestors were those colonists, the original settlers of this world in its first life. There was commerce between the worlds originally but they are not near to each other. Though our people are technologically and scientifically skilled, we did not develop the terraforming process as your company did. The ancestors seeking a place to colonize had to hunt a long time and a great distance to find this world. So gradually the commerce between the two stopped and we developed our own culture and characteristics. Eventually our forebears were forgotten as surely as if our own memories had been wiped, which is, now that I think of it, not unlikely.

Puk said, *Originally, our rescuers thought they could bring us back to their world to live, but in their absence, the overpopulation had escalated until the planet was so crowded as to be almost uninhabitable. While we were allowed to stay there for a brief time, we were soon banished, along with our rescuers. We were very sad to have caused them trouble but decided, since we were banished and would die in space sooner or later, to return here to die. In spite of the impossibility of the living conditions when we left, we longed to be here. You see, there has always been something about this world . . .*

Yes, there is, Ronan said. *It's alive. But Grandpa and the other scientists thought that was some kind of odd result of the terraforming.*

The life force is more evident now, Mraka conceded, *but there was always something, and rather than start out on a new place alone, we decided to return here and die on our world and join the rest of our people. We found the world changed. No cities or towns at that time, and only a little animal life, but many alien plants and this great sea covering the rest of the city where our people once lived.*

I bet you were surprised! Ronan said.

And pleased until we realized that another species was responsible for reviving our world, populating it with their chosen flora and later fauna including their dominant life-form.

Us.

Yes. But we saw quickly that your people did not live in the sea, only on the icy landmasses. So we resettled near our old city and found we were able to sustain ourselves on the animals and plants that now occupy the sea. Those near the volcanic vents may have begun differently when you introduced them, but they have become much like those we knew in our former home.

So you guys aren't aliens any more than we are, Ronan concluded. *That's brilliant! My da will wish he'd been conscious when he was here and got to keep his memory. He would so like to meet you. Or remember meeting you anyway.*

Your da? Mraka asked.

My father, male parent. The first seal you rescued.

He went straight to the doctors. I never spoke to him. Did you, Puk? Not I.

Ronan was trying to decide how to ask his next question when his head was filled with a summons. *Seal-boy, where are you? You must come to me in the observation tower at once.*

Kushtaka wants you, Puk told Ronan.

So I heard. But I'm not sure I can find my way back there. I've only been there once.

I'll take you, Mraka told him. *Our shift is nearly done anyway. Come.* She walked out of the room but then began swimming upward. Ronan, still puzzled by the way people moved inside the city, followed her. As if catching his question she replied, *Our air is so dense and moist here that it is as if it were water. We swim in it and it can sustain us, though not fish without the use of real water.*

So what are you really? Ronan asked, puzzling meanwhile that the air was evidently sufficient to keep him in seal form, although it was not actual water. That was a new experience. *Deep sea otters or the other form?*

I might ask you the same question. Are you a seal or a boy?
Both.

We are both as well. The deep sea otter form was convenient for gaining the cooperation of the sea otters, but it is a true alternative form and one we take more often than our original one these days. Our other form was better suited for the planet's first life.

When they reached the observation tower, Mraka waved a paw over the entrance, then deserted Ronan. *Hope it works out well for you, fish juggler. Visit us again.*

He braced himself to face Kushtaka again, glad that all of her people weren't against him too. Aunty Sinead would have called his conversation with Mraka and Puk "puttin' on the blarney," since he had set out to charm them into helping him and giving him information. But there was nothing wrong with making friends. He liked them, though he found it easier to like these people when they were otters than when they were in their jellyfish/octopus form.

He almost swam into Kushtaka's embrace as he entered the observation room. Not that she was ready to hug him. She was in otter form, and swung her paw in an arc, indicating what lay just outside the city's force field. *We seem to be under surveillance ourselves,* she told him.

Perhaps a hundred seals looked into the city as if it were one of those snow globes Aunty Aisling had made him and Murel when they were kids. The seals looked huge from here—probably just because the surveillance devices were so near to them the perspective was skewed.

Friends of yours? Kushtaka asked.

CHAPTER 22

ARMION HAD EXPECTED there might be repercussions from her encounter with Colonel Cally and the *Custer*. The man was too arrogant and too negligent to allow her challenge to his authority to go unavenged. She was rather surprised when she saw the reinforcements he had acquired.

She met them in the transit lounge just outside the docking bay. She did not want them in the main lounge frightening the children.

Besides Cally, there were a couple of junior officers, a squad of Corps personnel in combat gear, and a familiar but not friendly looking man in the robes of a Federation councilman. Beside him was a woman clad in similar robes. She was totally unfamiliar to Marmion. Troubling. She had been neglecting her duties on the council as well as her business lately. To her cost, it now seemed.

"Greetings, ladies and gentlemen," Marmion said, arching her brow in an expression she knew gave her an air of skeptical superiority. "I understand you are under the impression that I have somehow been naughty?" She used the coquettish word deliberately, to indicate that she thought the incident in question, or at least her culpability in it, was as petty as the word implied.

"Madame de Revers Algemeine, you are under arrest for the kidnapping of Intergal company personnel and the theft of Intergal company property. You and everyone aboard this vessel are taken into custody and this vessel confiscated as evidence." Cally recited the charges with relish and nodded to the soldiers, pointing down the corridor. They marched away, their boots thudding a double-time tattoo on her faux Aubusson strip carpeting.

"What foolishness!" Marmie said, pointedly failing to show alarm at the armed nature of the invasion. She waved a hand dismissively. "In case poor Colonel Cally's mind was unhinged by the trauma of seeing the meteor showers destroy the homes of the Intergal company personnel in question, he will recall that he gave up searching for survivors long before we located these people, homeless and soon to starve to death in that desolate, desolate place." She gave a delicate shudder. "No, no, gentlemen, this will not suffice. We kidnapped no one. We simply provided relief from a disaster that overtook them while we were there. We then issued an invitation from another far more hospitable world. They chose to come, of course. They are not idiots." Her tone said, *Unlike the people I am now addressing.*

"Madame, you know very well that once these people have stayed on this world for any length of time, they will become unable to leave it and thus ineligible for recruitment into the career opportunities with Intergal for which they were destined. There was a contract between their leaders and the company," Cally said.

"Slavery is illegal, Colonel, and even if it were not, the dead make very poor servants or manual laborers, which I believe constitute the main career opportunities open to the personnel in question."

"You also stole livestock belonging to Intergal."

"I allowed the refugees to bring their sacred animals with them and the few possessions they still retained. But perhaps you are so ill-informed about what actually transpired because you and your vessel, after the most cursory search, abandoned your feeble efforts and took off for what you no doubt considered more urgent duties." There. She had done it. She had totally lost her temper. She felt her cheeks flaming, her eyes blazing, her voice searing the very skin off the stupid man. She was giving Petaybee's volcano quite a lot of competition at the moment. She knew better. Much as she loathed stupidity, slackness, and cowardice, she of all people knew the value of diplomacy even in dealing with idiots. Losing one's temper gave the advantage to one's adversary. She took a deep breath and said, "It is useless to discuss this matter. You must take it up with my attorneys."

The man in Federation robes spoke. "You are entitled to contact them from the incarceration colony where you will be held, Madame. Under the authority vested in me as a deputized representative of the Federation, I, Jorge Hedgerow, declare you to be under arrest and your properties and assets frozen until you can be bound over for trial. Unfortunately for you, I fear there is quite a full docket these days." The man's supercilious smirk was aggravating. Nevertheless, in the absence of her own allies she knew she would have to comply in order to avoid violence and possible injury to her passengers or crew. She tried once more to reason with the officious intruders on behalf of the passengers staying on the *Piaf*.

"Some of the refugee families were involved in an accident since they arrived. They are no longer on the *Piaf*. All we have aboard here are the children and the old ones, not workers. You will want to either leave the children here with their parents or collect the families to come with us."

"And give you a chance to rally your henchmen?" Hedgerow asked. "I think not, Madame. If the people want to be reunited with their children, they can apply to Intergal for transport to the holding area."

Marmie widened her eyes innocently. "Henchmen? My employees are devoted, it is true, but hardly henchmen. As to whether you gather the families in question now or later, that is of course up to your discretion. As a businesswoman, I naturally point out that it is more cost effective to do it now rather than later." Also, of course, while she remained in custody she would be unable to ensure her passengers' safety or well-being. Given Cally's prior depth of concern for them, having the families together, preferably on Petaybee, was the best way to protect the children, quite young mothers, and elders, all so vulnerable to abuse or neglect.

The gilt com unit in the replica Louis XIV board gave her personal signal. She started toward it but one of Cally's minions blocked her way. She half turned to Hedgerow. "My crew will want a final order from me to surrender peacefully or there could be unnecessary injury or loss of life, and not only to *my* employees."

Cally gave a curt nod and the minion stepped aside. First Officer Robineau said from the com screen, "Madame, there are two armed soldiers demanding access to the bridge. Your orders?"

"By all means show them in, Adrienne, and stand down," she said, using her officer's first name as if she were an innocuous housekeeper instead of a highly trained navigator and engineer. She could not beat the intruders at this point but if her crew gave the appearance of joining them insofar as to offer them hospitality instead of resistance, everyone might survive this situation. If open resistance was futile, killing them with kindness might yield intelligence advantages at the very least. And Adrienne Robineau was quite an attractive woman highly adept at social interchange. "Offer them wine or tea perhaps since they are still on duty, and some of the excellent croissants from the galley. They will be with us for the rest of the voyage."

"*Oui*, Madame. It shall be as you say." Marmie smiled to herself at her officer's quick grasp of the situation. Adrienne, despite her French heritage and name, had no personal ties with La France Nouveau at all. And yet her speech already reflected a strong trace of Marmion's own accent. "And Adrienne?"

"*Oui*, Madame?"

"Pass along to the others that our—guests—are to be accorded courtesy and cooperation from all crew members. I do not wish to entertain further interruptions while I am in conference with their superiors."

"*Oui*, Madame."

"The conference is at an end," Cally said. "We will now depart for Gwinnet Incarceration Colony, where you and your crew will be—accommodated—pending your trial."

IT WAS A long swim and Murel was weary. She wanted to go ashore, dry off, fly home with Mum, Da, and Ro, and sleep in her own bed, maybe after a steaming hot chocolate and a biccy or two. She and Ro could dream together as they sometimes did and share what they'd done while they were apart. He was okay. She was certain he was okay. She'd know if he weren't.

Sky brushed against her consolingly. *Deep sea otters will not harm Ronan, Murel. Seals—bad seals, not river seals—sometimes eat otters, but otters do not eat seals.*

As if mentioning otter-eating seals had somehow alerted the species, she received another message. *Do not worry, half cousin. Our relatives have surrounded the strange new thing in their fjord and are keeping a close eye on it. No harm will come to your sibling with them watching.*

But it was such a long swim. She wished she could have trusted the orcas enough to beg a ride with one of the powerful creatures for her and Sky. But in doing so she'd bring death to the very seals helping her locate Ronan. Perfect Fjord was another day's swim at least, and she didn't see how she could make it without rest. Sky wasn't made for this sort of swimming either. He normally frolicked in freshwater. Long-distance saltwater swimming was completely foreign to him, and he had been through as much as she had.

Sky, you can go ashore if you want to, she said. *You are not a sea otter, after all.*

I am a sky otter, he told her. *And a space otter and an underground otter as well. I can swim in the sea, so although my face is not pale and round, I am also a sea otter.*

In his own way, Sky was as much a shape shifter as selkies or the Honus. He simply didn't bother changing his physical form when he changed his mind about who he was. Her former biology teacher, Dr. Mabo, had an unhealthy fascination with shape shifters—unhealthy for the shape shifters at least. But she would never understand one like Sky, no matter how many otters she tormented.

The farther north they swam, the closer and more wintry the shoreline grew. The ice reached out in broad flat plains from the land. When pieces broke off and upended, they formed the icebergs that seemed to float like castles above the water. Beneath the water they hung in the depths like upside-down mountains. In places along the shore, cobalt cracked glaciers rose high above the ice floe. The sky grew duller and grayer until time for sunset, when it blazed with volcanic-ash-filtered light before dying altogether. The full moon rose, and for many many kilometers they saw little in the blackness of the sea but moon and ice, ice and moon.

Murel used her sonar to keep them off the ice, singing to herself in the night, hoping to hear the other seals soon, the ones who were the relatives of Pork and her herd. Apparently Pork and the others had lost interest in her problems. Probably they were keeping busy evading sharks and the killer whales.

Before long we should be close enough that I can reach Ro, she told Sky, *if our thought-talk can go through the alien city's shield—and I guess it can, since we talked the alien otters into letting Da go.*

For once, Sky did not answer.

She turned her head to the side where he had been swimming and saw only water. She looked all around her. No otter. She dived and surfaced and swam back to the last iceberg. *Sky!* she called. *Sky?* And her sonar returned an otter-shaped image to her, just beneath the surface of the water, not swimming but slowly sinking.

• • •

"The Honu says Murel went to find Ronan," Ke-ola told Yana, nodding at the smallest of the turtles swimming along beside the fishing boat that had picked him up. "She says bring the copter up to Perfect Fjord, but only her papa should swim out to find them. Everyone else should wait on shore in case they're needed."

"Anybody got an ulu?" Yana asked, referring to the semicircular knife women traditionally used in cleaning and dressing animal skins. "I'm going to skin my daughter alive when we catch up with her. Why didn't she *wait* for the copter if she wants us to use it?"

"She needed to be a seal to find Ro," Ke-ola said reasonably.

"Sean is in seal form too. Why didn't she get him?"

Ke-ola consulted with the Honu again.

"He was busy, missus," the boy replied. "Murel needed to go quick."

Sean, swimming along beside them, raised his sleek gray-brown head from the water to look first at the Honu, then Ke-ola, then Yana. He lowered his head as if to roll into a dive. "No! Don't you go swimming off too, Sean," Yana called. "We've got multiple crises and I need to keep track of one member of this family at least. Hop in the boat and change. I have a lot to tell you."

Hopping into the boat was easier to say than do for him, but Ke-ola and the fisherman rescuer cast a fish net and he swam into it and allowed himself to be hauled aboard.

Yana had sent the copter back with Puna, Keoki, Pet Chan, and Raj Norman. After what happened to the *Piaf,* the Kanakas needed to be with their wounded and what was left of their families, and Pet, Raj, and Johnny needed to strategize while she and Sean sorted out how to retrieve their kids as well as the others.

"The *Piaf,* its passengers, and crew, including Marmie, have been hauled off to some Federation Incarceration Colony," Yana told Sean once he was in the boat. "Intergal had Marmie arrested for kidnapping Ke-ola's people and 'stealing' the Honus and the sharks.

Johnny said once the ship's crew knew what was going on, Com Officer Guthe made sure the channel was open so Johnny could hear what happened on the bridge."

"I don't see what we can do about that at the moment," Sean said, pulling his dry suit on over his lean, muscular body, which was momentarily covered with goose pimples. "We can hardly go after them, and with communications as they are, contacting Whit Fiske or one of our other friends who might be able to help Marmie is going to be difficult, to say the least."

They sat together in the boat, Yana impatiently scanning the sky for the copter while Sean wished he were swimming after the kids, even knowing that he would never reach them before the copter could fly him to the fjord.

At last they heard the deep drumming of the rotors again, and the two of them, as well as Ke-ola and Sinead, climbed up the rope ladder to be ferried to the fjord. Rick O'Shay had come alone, with bundles of survival gear and warm clothing, plus collapsible kayaks for the strictly human among them. "Reckoned it being a seagoing matter, you'd need boats," Rick said. "Seamus thought these ones would work for you in a pinch."

The sea looked so cold from the copter, all ice and rolling steel, turning briefly salmon in the volcanic sunset before darkening to black. Yana helped Ke-ola zip into snow pants, mukluks, and a parka, but the boy was still shivering. He sat by the copter door when he was dressed and watched the moonlit icebergs and the black sea rolling beneath the copter's pontoons as the aircraft thudded its way northward toward the fjord.

"What's that down there?" he asked through the headset they all wore to keep in touch with Rick.

"Where?" Yana asked.

"A dark patch on that iceberg down there. Looks like a seal."

CHAPTER 23

SKY? SKY! OTTERS *don't drown, Sky. You can't drown,* Murel thought forlornly as she nosed the half-frozen little body to the surface and kept him bobbing there while she steered him toward an iceberg to try to revive him. It was almost certainly hopeless, though, and she knew it. Even if she got him breathing again, he couldn't survive this cold. She should never have let him come.

Why had everything turned so horrible? All they had been trying to do was find a home for Ke-ola and his people, and all of a sudden everybody was drowning and getting eaten, and maybe worse, it seemed like everybody out here was trying to eat everybody else. She guessed that was what "dog eat dog" meant, not that she'd ever seen dogs eat other dogs. All poor little Sky ever ate was fish of one kind or another. He should never have come. He should have let her know he was too cold and too tired to make it.

She nosed him up onto an ice ledge and after three tries dragged herself onto it too. The sea pounded them so relentlessly that even though she was not still in the water, she could not change, and that was all to the good, she thought. If she changed, she'd have that in-stant before she put on the dry suit when she'd be freezing—maybe shiver her way back into the water. Even if no harm came to her, she'd be no good to Sky.

In seal form, though, she was warm enough, her body well-insulated and furred. Awkwardly, she nosed Sky's inert form into a ball and then curled her own around him, taking the brunt of the sea's beating with her own back. She tried to preserve what little warmth remained in the otter's body with hers while infusing him with her own heat and life force.

I NEVER SAW *those seals before in my life,* Ronan told Kushtaka.

Your sister is not there, or your father?

No, neither one of them. This lot could be keeping an eye on us for them, though.

Tell them to go away, Kushtaka said.

If Ronan had been in human form he'd have shrugged. What dif-ference would it make if a herd of seals saw the city and knew he was inside? Still, he didn't want to antagonize Kushtaka.

Hey there, you seals, what are you lookin' at? he called. *Haven't you ever seen the den of the deep sea otters before?*

Who's that? A seal thought penetrated the city's barrier.

I dunno. I don't see anybody, do you? another seal answered. *Other than the big otters?*

Nobody worth seeing, no, the first seal replied. *You lads see who was talking?*

He could be inside one of those tall things, a third suggested. Ronan was pretty sure he knew where the thoughts were coming from. Three of the seals were crowded close together, studying the city with more intensity than the others. *You there that did the talk-ing. Are you a part-time seal? Because there's a part-time female seal looking for you if you are.*

Yes, it's me, Ronan told them. *Now go tell my sister I'm fine and stay away from here, will you? You're making the natives restless, and when they get restless, they make whirlpools big enough to drown you all.*

Right, fine, we'll do that. Where is your sister?

Because the twins' childhood had been somewhat sheltered, confined to freshwater prior to their being sent offplanet to school, Ronan had never met wild seals before. He was not impressed with their brilliance. *How should I know?* he asked. *I'm stuck in here.*

We could get you out, the most enterprising among them suggested.

No, you can't, Ronan said.

No, we can't, one of the others corrected the first seal. *Shell's too hard. Claw it. You'll see. It's like it's iced over, only the ice is thicker than it looks.*

The scratching of seal claws against the outside was seen but not heard.

Tell them to stop that, Kushtaka demanded.

Stop that, Ronan told them. Then asked her, *Why don't you tell them yourself?*

I did, she said. *They acted as though they didn't hear. You're the one they came for. Get rid of them.*

The seals stopped scratching anyway. *Too hard to scratch. We'll just be swimming away then, all right?*

Yes, go tell Murel and Da I'm fine.

And don't bring them back here or we will be forced to take extreme measures, Kushtaka threatened, but all that was visible by then was seal butts and the backs of flippers.

THE ICEBERG PITCHED and rolled but it kept Murel and Sky from the worst violence of the waves and let them rest like babies in a particularly active cradle. Murel heard seals calling her and raised her head.

Cold bit her nose and stung her eyes, but beneath her it was warm, the ice slightly melted. She had lifted Sky in her front flippers so he wasn't lying entirely on the ice. He was very still but she felt him breathing. Around the curl of his body a shimmer of water overlaid the ice. He was generating his own body heat now.

Here, she answered the seal's call. *I'm here. On an iceberg.*

Okay, got a fix on your position. The seal voice was not Sorka's or Pork's or that of any of the herd she'd dealt with before. So it seemed the Perfect Fjord branch of the family was seeking her out. Above her a pale strip of lime green arced across the night sky. As she watched, it began to wiggle and swirl, other subtle colors blooming at its sides and tips. Those colors began jigging as well, dipping, swishing in broad swaths against the darkness. There was a bright moon but it was boring compared to the lights.

She had missed the aurora without even being aware of it. She and Ronan had been at school on Versailles Station for the best part of three years. It had been interesting in a way, and Marmie saw to it that they had far more than they'd ever been used to. They'd only been back to Petaybee a short time before they'd gone back into space to find Ke-ola's people.

Now, despite the warm waters of the volcano, winter was here. The aurora proved it. And winter was the longest season, the most familiar because she'd known Petaybee wearing winter landscape most of the time. It was the time she loved the best. The lights were one of the reasons why. She knew they were caused by sunspots or electromagnetic fluctuations or some such, but they were still as beautiful and magical as when she thought they were the multicolored fringed skirts of a lady named Aurora fancy-dancing across the sky.

Mesmerized by the flying colors, she didn't see the seals approaching until they ringed the iceberg.

Stopped for a snack, did you? The seal facing her raised himself on his flippers to peer over her ledge at Sky. *Can we have a bite? We've swum a long way to tell you what you want to know and that looks delicious.*

That's not a snack. It's my friend, Murel replied. *He got too tired and we had to rest. And he's not delicious. He's a freshwater otter and everyone knows they're poisonous.*

What's a friend?

Sky had come up with a good definition for his fellow otters, "a family member who is not an otter." Da had overheard it and repeated it, awed at the cultural development of otter-kind, he said.

A friend is a family member who is not a seal, she said, changing the species to fit the situation.

Not all seals are family members, the hungry seal replied. *Part-time seals are not family members so their friends aren't family members either. He may be poisonous to part-time seals but he smells delicious to me. We found what you wanted. We spoke to your sibling. We'll take you there if you share your friend.*

He's not to eat, she repeated. *He's not dead. He's just resting.*

We are resting too, the seal said, making himself comfortable, finding another lower ledge to rest his lower half against. The other seals barked in agreement. *And we don't care that it's not dead. We like live food best. But we can wait. We'll be right here until you get hungry. You will get hungry, you know. If you don't want to eat him, you will need to get back in the water and catch something you can eat soon. Then we'll eat him and then we'll take you to your brother.*

Murel looked into the big brown eyes, the cute whiskers, the face like her own and her brother's and her father's. The seal was threatening her. He wanted to eat Sky and he meant to do it. A silly phrase popped into her mind, as silliness was apt to do at inappropriate moments. She wanted to call out to Ro, "Help, I'm under sealge." But she didn't know how to reach Ro and they did. The Perfect Fjord herd's demand was completely out of the question, of course. They were evil seals. Who would have thought there were evil seals?

I've already had lots to eat, she lied. *You'll get tired of this pretty soon. Go catch some fish and leave us alone.*

Don't you want to know where your sibling is?

Sure, but I'll find him myself if that's the way you're going to be.

Friends don't eat friends or let anybody else eat them either. Unbidden, the image of Jeel's blood rising around the ring of sharks came back to her. *Not if they can help it,* she added guiltily.

Maybe you can't help it, the seal said menacingly. *Maybe you won't be able to stay on the iceberg. Maybe the iceberg won't stay under you.*

What do you mean?

You're new to these parts, aren't you? The stories about you say you're used to freshwater, not the sea. But you have to know about ice.

Of course I do. What about it?

The seal slid up to her ledge, barely touching it with his nose and front claws, but pulling himself up and back. At his bark, three others along the ledge began doing the same thing.

The reassuring sheen of water beneath her and Sky slid out from under them and joined the sea.

It melts, the lead seal said. *That's what.*

THE COPTER SET down on the shore closest to the iceberg. "Sure you don't want to go on to the fjord?" Rick asked. "It's not far now."

Sean said, "No, we need to see why she's on the iceberg, if that's her."

"I'm about out of fuel or I'd wait," Rick said.

"That's okay. You may be needed there anyway." Sean turned to Yana. "You may as well go back with him, love."

"They're my kids, Sean, and I'm not some wimpy little housewife, you know."

"We don't actually have any of those on Petaybee," Sinead said thoughtfully. "But you are the co-governor, Yana, and the newcomers are going to be pretty upset, having the so-called authorities flying off with their kids. Not to mention Marmie."

Yana wanted to mutter something about the shape-shifting Shongilis sticking together and ganging up on her, but that was juvenile and Sinead was right. "Very well. You natives sort it out while Ke-ola and I go and try to sort the rest of it out."

"I should stay, missus," Ke-ola told her. "The warden." He nodded at Sinead. "She's good in the woods but maybe not so good in the water, and she's strong but she's not as big as me. Dr. Shongili can't lift stuff while he's a seal. He can use a big fella like me to help if Ro and Murel need to get hauled into a boat or something. Besides, the warden almost drowned today. I'm fine."

Yana was surprised when Sinead said, "Thanks, Ke-ola. Right on all counts. I'd best go back to Kilcoole with Yana and see what I can do to help. Besides, Aisling will need to fuss over me a bit and make sure I'm okay."

So the survival gear—enough for Ke-ola as well as for Sean and the kids in human form—was dropped off with the menfolk. As the copter lifted up again, Sean was stripping down and Ke-ola setting up the boat. Night fell while they weren't looking, and a dazzling aurora accompanied them all the way back to Kilcoole.

CHAPTER 24

ERY WELL, THEY'RE gone now, Kushtaka, are you happy? Ronan couldn't keep the resentment out of his thoughts.

She ignored him, talking to others of her own species, whatever it was, in their own tongue. He didn't understand all of it—part of it seemed to be technical jargon of some sort, but the gist of it was that it was safe now and they could go.

The water around the dome filled with deep sea otters bearing something unidentifiable in their paws. They scattered, some remaining in sight, others disappearing among the fish and seaweed, the smoking black volcanic chimneys, and rocks. Some dived toward the bottom.

Setting the sursurvus, Kushtaka explained. *We've recalibrated them to cover a broader area. We want to be prepared if the sharks return.*

That won't be your only large predator this far north, he told her.

Somewhere beneath us lies what is left of the second greatest city of our civilization, she told him. *I've visited the ruins many times.*

She didn't like him knowing more about the place than she did.

He didn't want to get Puk and Mraka in trouble by letting on that they'd told him something of their species' history on Petaybee.

Oh, then you know about the bears, he replied in an offhand way. *Bears?*

You know, big white jobs, dive like us, swim like us, but faster, meaner, and eat anything.

Bears live on land, she said, as if he was trying to fool her. *We've seen them when we venture close to shore.*

Normal bears do, he answered. *Black bears, brown bears, grizz. None of them mind a bit of a swim, usually in freshwater, but the white bears are almost as at home in the water as seals like me or otters like you folks. Or the regular kind of sea otters anyway.*

It sounds most improbable, she said.

I thought the same when the sea otters told me about your people, he replied, *and yet, here you are. The bears are real too. Keep watching and you'll see one before long I imagine.*

Is this something else your people have put into these waters to endanger us? she demanded.

That was so unfair it made Ronan forget his manners. *That's bollocks,* he told her. *I'm sorry for your loss. My sister and I were the only ones who even knew you were here, you've been that secretive, so how could anyone else know the sharks endangered you? Even though we tried to warn you about them, you're blaming us for trying to help you. I would think instead of blaming children no older than your own, Kushtaka, that you as leader of these folk would be thinking more along the lines of telling them what was dangerous to them and planning ways for them to fight or escape it.*

When we were the dominant species on this planet, there never were such creatures, she said haughtily.

Maybe not, but there certainly was something because Petaybee didn't survive long enough for you to keep living here, did it? He hoped Mraka and Puk would forgive him, but he wasn't going to let her keep treating him like a murderer for something that wasn't his fault. It wasn't anyone else's fault either, really, except maybe her stupid son's for not being more careful, or hers for not keeping a better eye on him.

Looking at her closely, feeling what she was feeling instead of thinking, Ronan realized that was what bothered her. Jeel's death *was* her fault, and she wanted to blame someone else, however unreasonably, for her own lapse. Would Mum act that way if he or Murel did something dumb that got one of them killed by something introduced by someone else? He thought about it. Probably not. His mum, as a former Corps officer, would claim full responsibility as her own lapse, put his picture on the shelf by the stove, then hunt down whatever had killed him and obliterate it.

Of course, if those who had introduced the danger gave Mum any further grief, they would be in danger of obliteration too. He looked at Kushtaka again, wondering what, if any, means of obliteration she had at her disposal.

She returned her attention to the activities beyond the dome, but seemed to be deep in her own private thoughts. Since she didn't dismiss him or have him carried away by the flippers again—that was an experience to be avoided at all costs!—he watched with her as, one by one, the surveillance units were placed and new areas of the surrounding ocean were revealed. Most of them were dark and cold and wet, no big surprise there.

But after one placement, what showed on the screen was two of the big otters—probably the ones who had set up the equipment— surfacing, looking startled, diving again and swimming hard before jumping out of the water and splashing around, seeming to try to draw attention to themselves.

Ronan was sure he recognized them too, since he had just spent quite a lot of time with them. Puk and Mraka were either scared or they were up to something.

COMMUNICATION WAS DIFFICULT without the Honu to keep him in mental touch with Sean, as Ke-ola now thought of his friends' fa-

ther. It was hard to think of a seal as Dr. Shongili in furry trunks. To
try to tell what he was to do next, Ke-ola had to watch the seal-man
as well as he could in the moon and aurora-lit darkness.

The iceberg where they had seen the seal who might be Murel
was three or four kilometers offshore, and before they reached it
they had to slide out onto the thin ice. Some of it was left over from
past years, the permanent ice pack that rimmed the northernmost
shores of the northern continent. Some was fresh ice, newly formed
for the winter that was only beginning in Kilcoole. Ke-ola, being
large and heavy, was afraid he would fall through before he found a
clear enough spot so he could hop into the boat and paddle out.

Sean, in spite of his worry over Murel, was thinking about him
too, Ke-ola saw. Seals knew where the thin ice was, and Sean solved
the problem by clawing a hole in it with his front flippers and en-
larging it all the way out to the open—or more open—sea.

Ke-ola widened the opening with his paddle, making a place big
enough for the emergency boat, then climbed in, kneeling in the
center of the boat and breaking the ice with the paddle as he used
it to push away from the jagged edges and into the open sea.

Once there, he spared a glance for the colored lights dancing
overhead, reflected in the rolling water. His winter suit was warm,
if bulky. The boat was neither a kayak nor a canoe but a semirigid
inflatable made of a pierce-proof synthetic fiber, the shape somewhere between that of an Irish fishing dory and a raft. It had a compact but powerful motor unit as well as the paddles. He tried the
motor, and to his relief, it immediately roared to life.

Across the color-sheened waves he heard the barking of seals.
More than one, so it was not just Sean, or even Sean and Murel. Besides, he saw Sean's head bobbing ahead of him as the selkie swam,
his fur shining pink, then green or orange. Ke-ola had a torch in his
snow pants pocket, but the boat had no running lights.

The rhythm of paddling came naturally to Ke-ola, even though
Halau had all of its water underground and no seas underground
that they had ever located. But all of the chants and dances he had

learned from Aunty Kimmie Sue had a similar rhythm, one that came to him when he dipped his paddle. He was singing inside himself, and his song and these wild northern waves fit together in a pleasing and calming way.

Other icebergs loomed up ahead of them, but he didn't mistake them for the one with the seal because Sean seemed to know which one that was. The wind was loud enough to mask most sounds, but Ke-ola could still hear the barking of seals once in a while over the dual roar of the sea and wind. The wind was icy, sticking pins and needles in his nose and making his mouth feel lipless and dry. He pulled a scarf across the lower half of his face, tucking it into his hood as Clodagh had once showed him, playing "dress up like a real Petaybean" at a pre-latchkay gathering at her cabin after he first arrived. The scarf had been crocheted by Sinead's partner Aisling in a lacy pattern from the mud-brown undercoat of a musk ox. It was soft and stayed dry inside even when it iced up outside.

The seal barking grew louder and louder. Sounded like an argument to him, and he was pretty sure he could hear Murel. Sean barked too but his was a solo voice. Somewhere close there were a lot more seals, all in a group.

Two more dark heads raised out of the water, otterlike but bigger than Sky's head or that of a regular sea otter. These guys started bouncing up and down on the waves, going "Hah! Hah!" and making chirpy noises that were not quite as loud as the barks. They were waggling their paws, as if they were waving too. Something was definitely disturbing their world and they seemed to be trying to warn someone—the seals?

Sean swam back toward the boat, and a couple of dozen other seals swam in the same direction, heading frantically back for the ice.

Ke-ola strained his eyes to see what was bothering them but the black fins were almost impossible to see until they almost touched the boat, then they were under it and Ke-ola was paddling air until the boat rolled sideways and dumped him in all of his heavy clothing into the frigid sea.

As SOON AS the other seals dived and swam away from her iceberg, Murel, feeling Sky move, looked down at him.

He looked up from busily grooming his fur, his eyes as bright and curious as ever. *Hah!* he said. *Fooled those seals.*

I didn't know otters could play possum, Murel said. But glancing up again, she saw other otters playing at something else. Two of the deep sea otters seemed to be trying to get her attention.

No more seals, she told Sky. *Can you make it now? Shall we go see what they want?*

Otters need sleep sometimes, but when they wake up they can swim very fast, Sky assured her. *Also, otters do not like seals-who-eat-otters.*

Selkies don't like to see those seals either, Sky, she said, making a clear distinction between herself and the attack seals. *Those deep sea otters seem to have scared them away.*

What deep sea otters?

That's funny. They were right over there, she said, diving in. Sky slid into the sea beside her and she sent out her sonar signal. The two large otters were not far from them, underwater, though she couldn't see them in the glacial flour clouding the northern sea so close to land. However, she also sensed something else: a large group of large something elses.

CHAPTER 25

EXCUSE ME, SEAN heard the whale tell the rapidly sinking Ke-ola, *you looked just like a shark from that angle.*

Allow me, Sean said, diving after Ke-ola and catching his parka hood in his teeth.

You again, the orca said grumpily. *I suppose you don't want us to eat any of this new herd of seals either.*

You're on your own with that, as long as none of them are my kids or their otter friend, Sean told them. *Ask before you bite, though. Murel is out here somewhere. She was on an iceberg but I don't hear her now.*

WHEN SHE SENSED the large group of finned creatures approaching, Murel first feared the sharks were coming. Then she knew it couldn't be the sharks. They were unaccustomed to water this frigid. Maybe later Petaybee would change them so they could live in more of the sea, but they were new here. They would have returned to the volcano-warmed waters. That left the orcas. They

were being helpful again. Surprising, considering their pointed re-
marks about being used to fetch and carry for her. Nevertheless,
this time they scared off her menacing relatives. She owed the orcas
yet again.

It is good whales want to eat the otter-eating seals instead of us, Sky
said, clarifying the situation. He was right. The orcas weren't doing
her another favor—they were feeding. No sense getting carried
away with gratitude.

Right you are, she replied. *Let's follow those deep sea otters and see
if they take us back to Ronan.*

She broadcast her sonar signal and picked up the retreating creatures. They did not seem to be in a hurry. Sky was refreshed enough
to catch fish and frolic beside her. Sooner than she had dared hope,
they entered Perfect Fjord. Along the bottom was an area of the undersea chimneys and plant life similar to that near the big volcano.
Black chimneys, sulfurous waters, red-mouthed vents. Over a glowing rift in the sea floor lay the city of the deep sea otters.

To her surprise, two of the city's inhabitants—and she supposed
it had to be the same two she had been following—lingered outside
the shield until they saw her.

Hah! one of them said. *You got away. That is good. That will show
those seals not to bother our little cousins the river otters.*

Sky otters, Sky corrected.

Of course. Come. The other seal is waiting.

Can you bring him out here? Murel asked, suddenly scared.
Kushtaka must have been very angry to whisk her city away the way
she did and to keep Ronan.

But the deep sea otters didn't reply, just rubbed their paws across
the shield and entered. Sky followed closely behind them, and
there was nothing for Murel to do but follow. As they swam toward
the ground level, Ronan and Kushtaka swam up to meet them,
while Tikka came from another direction.

Kushtaka said, *Good, you're back. It took you long enough.*

Tikka started toward Murel too but Sky swam up to the youngster and climbed onto her shoulder, chirruping and purring like a happy cat, though his were actual otter noises, and they had the charming and distracting effect on the child he had surely intended.

I tried, Murel told Kushtaka before Jeel's mother could say anything. Misery swept over her again as Jeel's death came back to her. *I know I said the sharks would listen to me and I thought they would, but they didn't.*

Ronan swam between his sister and Kushtaka. *So what?* he demanded of the elder. *If Murel and I hadn't said we could stop the sharks, what would you have done? Gone out yourself or sent some of your other people out there to get eaten too? At least she tried. You want to blame someone because Jeel got killed doing something he wasn't supposed to, but it's not fair to blame us.*

And yet you brought the monsters to this sea, Kushtaka said.

Maybe so, but everything got brought here by someone at some time, as you should know, Kushtaka, Ronan replied. *I heard how even your people came from someplace else, and they must have messed up too, because while you were living on Petaybee, it died. You had to leave, and while you were gone, our people came and revived the world so it survived for you to return to. We did you a big favor and you're quibbling about a few sharks. I know, I know, they killed your kid. They'd have killed us too at one point. Killing is what they do.*

Killing is what a lot of things in the water do, Murel said, thinking of the seals and the whales as well as the sharks. *It's how things work. You hide from people as if we're the worst things on the planet. But all most of the animals are interested in is eating other animals. If you can't deal with it, then you'd better go back where you came from.*

Ronan interrupted her defensive tirade, directing a private thought at her. *Actually, sis, they've been here longer than we have and are as much Petaybean as we are.*

Is that so? Well, they don't act very Petaybean to me. They're snooty, for one thing.

Kushtaka, waiting until they ran out of things to say, answered their preemptive tirades, surprising them both then by continuing, in a softer tone, *I am not glad you returned in order to punish or blame you, Murel. I am glad you returned because I wanted to thank you for trying to save my child. I was angry, but all that you say is true. I had intended to keep your brother with us so that your parents would endure something of what I endured, but that would help no one. But it is good that you returned so both of you can have your memories wiped and we can send you back to your people before we leave this planet to search for a new one, with fewer predators.*

With an apologetic look at Puk and Mraka, who floated nearby taking in the scene, Ronan told Kushtaka, *But all of this mistrust and wiping people's memories, that's part of the problem. You saved our father's life. He wouldn't have wanted any harm to come to you if he'd remembered about you. He and Mum both try to make everything better for everyone. If you hadn't erased his memory, Da would have taken you into consideration before releasing the sharks and figured out a way to protect you. You swore Murel and me to secrecy, so all we could do was try to warn you.*

Perhaps, Kushtaka said, *but nevertheless, your memories must be wiped. No one must know about our colony.*

Sorry, Murel said, *I'm afraid it's a little late for that.*

WITH THE HELP of one of the orcas, Sean got Ke-ola back to the ice, though he had to drag him through the water until the ice would support him. Then, with a whale supporting the boy from beneath the ice, Sean changed into his dry suit and pulled Ke-ola the rest of the way up. He retrieved the extra dry clothing from the survival cache farther back on shore and helped the cold-numbed boy strip off his clothing. Ke-ola could never have done this alone. His hands were like clubs. Sean feared the newcomer to Petaybee might lose fingers or even his hands to frostbite if he was not able to warm up quickly enough.

Sean wrapped the thermal blanket around the boy while he redressed him in warm clothes, then helped him the rest of the way to the dropoff point, the closest place where it might be safe to start the heater. Because of the warmer currents from the volcanic activity, even this far north, the ice was thinner than usual. When it was six feet thick, it didn't hurt if you built any sort of campfire on it, but now it was only three feet in the thickest spots.

The stowed gear included a heat generator powered from a very small canned flame easily ignited with a mechanical clicker. Once this was going, Sean was able to make some snow tea with herbs that had a restorative effect on hypothermia victims. He instructed Ke-ola to stick his bare hands between his dry pants and his bare stomach, since his trunk would be the warmest part of his body. Then he put the teacup—actually a heat-proof fiber tea bag—to Ke-ola's mouth and had the boy swallow.

The lad's teeth were chattering so loudly that it wasn't until he swallowed that Sean actually heard the awful din the seals were making. He looked up and saw seals rapidly advancing until they were only about twenty meters from the fire, with still more back down on the beach. There was a great herd of them and they were very upset indeed.

Sean picked up the mobile, hoping it would work, but found he couldn't hear himself speak much less anyone answer over the barking of the seals.

"Shut up, you lot!" he hollered aloud, but with no noticeable effect.

Those closest to the campsite moved in, flopping forward on their flippers and barking their heads off.

You, the part-time seal with two legs, make them go away! the foremost seal demanded.

Make who go away?

Them! Those black-and-white seal-eating bullies you're so friendly with. We noticed they don't eat you.

He told them they could eat us, another seal said accusingly. *I heard him! He doesn't care. Fine kinsman he's turned out to be, loos-*

ing monsters on his poor little cousins just because we're full-time
seals, not changeable like him.

Sean sighed and keyed the mobile off. He scanned the horizon
and saw the orcas at play just offshore, sounding and blowing and
generally having a good time. *I can't see why you have your flippers in*
such a twist, he told the seals. *It's not as if the orcas can come ashore.*

No, and it's not as if we can catch our suppers with them out there.
And there are a lot of us to feed here, in case you hadn't noticed.

Almost had us that fat little otter if that stupid lass of yours hadn't
been so selfish, another seal said accusingly.

We'd have had him too if those finny fiends hadn't showed up, a
third seal added.

Murel? You saw Murel and Sky? You tried to eat Sky?

He's an otter, part-time. Get over it, the first seal said. *Seals eat ot-*
ters. Seals try to escape orcas, except for yourself, of course, and your
pesky pups, and you're all just plain peculiar.

Rude too, another seal added. *No idea of fair play in your family.*
We guide the seal-lass here, keep an eye on the underwater otter den
where your laddie is, and she won't even share her so-called friend.
Then here you come siccing killer whales on us. I don't know how you
come to be a seal but we never had the likes of you on my side of the
family.

Sean took a deep breath and reminded himself that calm and
clear communication was necessary here. This herd of seals might
contain or even be led by a few of the most annoying members of
the species he'd encountered so far, but they were, to some extent,
his people. He owed them his attention and patience as much as he
did the people of Kilcoole. Especially if they knew where Murel and
Ronan were. He could scarcely blame them for being angry that he
had turned to their predators for help. He supposed he had been
callous about the cost to them, but he'd been angry. It wasn't good
for a biologist to be so intimately involved with his subjects. He'd
lost his perspective because of his concern for his kids, but these
fellows evidently had been trying to help his family, except for Sky,

who was not a seal. Of course, it was perfectly true that seals often ate otters—sea otters anyway. So he cleared his mind and made his thoughts soothing and logical. *Let me get this straight. You know where my son is and led my daughter to him but in exchange you wanted to eat our otter friend? Is that about right?*

The seals conferred and all agreed that it was.

So where is he? Did she go after him? Sean asked.

How should we know? the first seal asked. *We were too busy avoiding massive jaws to pay much attention to seals and otters who don't have to worry about killer whales.*

You found the underwater city Murel mentioned, though? Sean asked in a way that showed he was impressed. *And Ronan was definitely in it?*

Definitely. He definitely told us to go away. Rude again.

I'm sorry about that. Pups. No manners. They've picked up some bad habits at school offplanet.

At least they didn't tell those killers to go ahead and eat us, the second seal complained. *Traitor to your kind, you are, even if you are only part-time.*

Sean sighed. *I never told them to eat you. I told them not to eat my children or their friend.*

You could have said us too. They listen to you. Don't think it escaped our notice that one of them helped you with the big two-leg pup there.

Very well, I'll tell them. Then will you take me to the place where you spoke with my son?

They agreed, or at least three of them did, so once he reassured himself that Ke-ola was warming up nicely, he went back to the ice and addressed himself to the whales.

You orcas are going to be dead bored hanging about this place, Sean told them.

Bitfin answered, no doubt feeling he and Sean had a personal connection since Sean's daughter had bit off part of his fin. Like being involuntary blood brothers by proxy? Sean wondered. He was a biologist, but he had yet to understand all of the ins and outs of marine life behavior and attitudes. But then, he could say the same of human behavior and attitudes. *We'll be grand once your furry friends get hungry enough to come back in the water and feed us,* Bitfin told him.

Not that likely to happen, mate, Sean replied.

And that would be why?

Because they're just hanging around here to talk to me, then they'll be heading for that saltwater lagoon fed by the hot springs. It's always open, connects by a narrow underground channel to the sea itself, and is teeming with tasty fish. There are so many that the people living hereabouts can't catch them fast enough to keep them from overcrowding the lagoon, so they'll be happy for these fellows to thin the population.

You're full of bubbles, seal-man, Bitfin told him, and turned to his pod. *Any of you ever heard of a warm water lagoon with fish?*

Sean shrugged and seemed to study the gray-and-white snowflake pattern knitted into the top of the mittens he now wore, along with other winter clothing, atop his dry suit. *Ah, but then you're not from around these parts ordinarily, are you? Usually swim a bit farther south, right? And both the channel and lagoon in question are far too shallow for your great selves, so why would you hear of a place that's of no use to you? Doesn't matter, does it, when you can swim wherever you want in Petaybee's great sea? I only mention it so you'll be aware that the seals—we seals—have another way out. Pity for you to waste your time here with those other pods gathering to mate. It's highly disappointed they'll have such great handsome beasts as yourselves lacking for the mating.*

Mating?

Oh, aye, saw it on the copter's radar, which covers more area than my sonar or even yours. A superpod is forming up south of the volcano, about halfway between the cone and the southern landmass. Looked like twenty or thirty pods headed that way.

Now it's you thinking we've bubbles for brains, to believe that sort of tale. The senior whale had taken an interest in the conversation. *Even a seal-man should know that we pods have our ways of keeping in touch. We've sweethearts in those southern pods. They'd have let us know about the party.*

Yes, they would have, and I feel badly about that, which is why I'm telling you now, Sean said. *You were busy helping my folk recently, weren't you? Not exactly alert for distant signals? Not been your usual relaxed sort of lifestyle lately, has it? The pods were still at some distance from your feeding grounds too, so you mightn't have heard them anyway, but I reckon if you swim hard and fast you can meet up with the others just before the fun starts.*

Black tails waggled back and forth in the air and water as the pod consulted. Sean wasn't sure if the waggling indicated indecision on their part or derision. He also had no idea what had possessed him to come up with such a load of blarney, and him usually so partial to the truth. It had just come to him all of a sudden. He stifled his amazement at his own invention lest the pod pick up on it. He whistled a bit and tried to look unconcerned as he waited.

Bitfin separated from the pod and swam south, then suddenly leaped in the air, making a perfect arc in the water. *There it is! The invitation! They are calling us, brothers and sisters, just like seal-man said. Do you hear it now?* Another whale also left the pod, leaped, and confirmed Bitfin's impression, and then it was twos and threes, and finally the whole pod, and away they went.

The power of suggestion was a wonderful thing, wasn't it? Sean wondered to himself. Then he realized that his own hearing, less acute as a man than as a seal, seemed to be picking up distant whale song, though of course he couldn't be sure.

The last black fin disappeared from view, which wasn't very far in the dark waters and at night, despite the full moon. The aurora had faded to a wash of pale green diluted by the vastness of the sky. Sean turned back to give the seals the all clear and saw not a thing but Ke-ola warming himself by the heater.

"Where'd the little buggers go?" Sean asked. After that great load of codswallop he'd dispensed on their behalf, he at least expected them to be there to answer his questions.

Ke-ola shrugged and took a hand out of his clothing long enough to point inland. "While you were down there starin' at the whales, the seals suddenly scooted off in that direction."

"I'll go have a look. Are you warmed up enough yet? Want to come along?"

"Bettah I start movin' my feet before they fall off," Ke-ola said, nodding.

They had pulled out of the water at the extreme point of the fjord, which was the only relatively low flat area. The rest of the shoreline was steeply ridged with glaciers. Looking back from their camp across the snowy expanse leading inland, the terrain appeared to be an unbroken level expanse. However, before they had walked another two hundred yards, the ground fell away into a steep dish filled with steamy water and seals.

Sean touched his mitten to the back of his parka hood, as if to scratch his head. "I could have sworn I was lying about this," he told Ke-ola.

Ke-ola shook his head. "Man, I know this wasn't here when we flew in here. I'd have noticed this kinda thing."

The lagoon was sizable and clear, with a shimmer of steam rising from the surface. The seals were having a wonderful time catching fish and tossing them back and forth in the air.

"I didn't see it either," Sean admitted.

"Then how'd you know it was here?"

Sean thought about that. "Scientific intuition?" he asked lamely, the two terms being mutually contradictory as far as offworld science was concerned.

Ke-ola had had enough science classes to guffaw at this, so Sean felt he had to provide some basis for his remark. "What I mean to say is, with all the renewed volcanic activity in the sea, warming has been occurring all over, and we know that. So it isn't unlikely that this sort of lagoon might have sprung up, or perhaps melted down.

Of course, it could be the result of a glacial rift. They're always shifting and changing their topography. Knowing that, I postulated something of the sort to the whales. It's just a coincidence that there actually is such a place here."

"Yeah, man, but if it wasn't here before and then the minute you said it was, there it was, that's kinda weird, don't you think?"

Sean had to agree. His explanation had sounded flimsy even to him. So, abandoning science for the moment, he clapped Ke-ola on the back, saying, "Boyo, when you live as long as I have on a planet that has a mind of its own, you learn that weird things happen. Could be Petaybee knew about the whales wanting to mate and it let me know. Could also be that Petaybee was about to open up this lagoon and somehow communicated *that* to me too. Or it could be, once I made up the lie and the words were out of my mouth, Petaybee thought to itself, 'Good idea!' and made it happen. Whatever the case is, time to stop wondering about it and collect the seals' share of the bargain."

Before he did that, though, he took the mobile from his pocket to contact Yana.

She didn't answer, but Sinead did. "How're the kids?" she asked before he spoke.

"Don't have them yet but I think we will soon. The thing is, Ke-ola needs to get back. He took a dunking. Warmed him up as well as we could out here but he should be where it's warm."

"I know the copter's low on fuel, and I'm not sure how much is left at the supply depot but I'll check."

"Rick was planning to come back for us so he must reckon it's possible," Sean said.

"I'll alert the folk at Perfect anyway and have them snocle or send out dog teams for you. They can take Ke-ola to shelter."

"Good," Sean said. "He seems okay now but I need to leave him here, so tell them to come as quickly as they can, will you? He's still a cheechako and feels the cold more than we do. I've yet to find the twins, and I'll need to go back in the water for that."

"Will do. Ah, it's started to snow. Doubt it will accumulate enough at this point to let us use our own dogs or snocles but it's a start. There's always the curly coats if all else fails. Slainté, Sean," she said, using the old Gaelic toast to health, which on Petaybee was also a greeting and a farewell.

"Slainté, sis. See you soon I hope."

"Sure you will," she said.

CHAPTER 26

COMMUNICATIONS OFFICER STEVEN Guthe kept a channel open to Petaybee for as long as possible. Guthe was an easygoing fellow who saw humor in most situations and something to like in most people. He was not Irish but might as well have been, with his gift of gab and love of music and good times. He was adept, when he needed to be, at seeming mild as milk while stubbornly following his own agenda.

He drew the Corps specialist sent to oversee his station into conversations that would let Marmie's dirtside associates know as much as possible about what was happening. He kept alert for an opportunity to notify one of her influential offplanet friends of the situation as well.

"So, Specialist Messer, you know much about this place we're going to?"

"Gwinett? I know a lot about it. All of it bad. That lady must have pissed off a lot of people in high places."

Guthe grinned and nodded. "Well, yeah, she does that with some people, I guess. But she's a very good lady. I'd hate to see anything happen to her, no matter what they're saying she did."

"Don't worry, buddy, you'll be in the same place so you'll be able to keep an eye on her. The whole crew is going down with her."

Guthe clucked his tongue. "My my. Well, I hope the same thing doesn't happen to you folks just for being part of all this when she's released. Because she may have a few enemies but she's got powerful friends as well. People on Petaybee will notice we're AWOL sooner or later."

Messer raised brows so blond they were almost invisible against his freckled skin. In fact, you could see the freckles right through his eyebrows. "Maybe so, but they won't have long to wonder. Some of our contractees and the livestock are still down there, being detained by your accomplices. Colonel wanted to round her up first before she can pull any strings for that ice ball down there. Troops are on the way to reclaim what belongs to the company and arrest everyone responsible, directly or indirectly, for their removal. Sounds like a planetwide conspiracy to me. Turns out the two kids with your boss belong to the Shongilis, who got themselves named governors of the planet. They've been a pain in the company's arse trying to hog the whole planet for themselves and a handful of other people. Your boss lady has interceded with the Federation for them but she won't be able to save them this time. I wouldn't count on her or any of you ever being released either, pal. People who go to Gwinett under this kind of circumstance usually have a way of disappearing."

"I thought Gwinett was just a holding place pending a Federation hearing and maybe trial if they decide to take the charges in question seriously," Guthe said, sounding surprised, though he had actually heard a thing or two about Gwinett in the past. Prisoners tortured to death before they even got to their cells. Sick prisoners left in filth where they died. Prisoners with open wounds made to clean cesspits or other jobs that would result in infection, amputation, death. Routine beatings by guards. It was all coming back to him now. Madame surely wouldn't have to worry about that kind of thing, though. They wouldn't dare treat her that way, would they?

As if reading his thoughts, the soldier said, "The bigger they are, the harder they fall. You can see how it might be real profitable for some folks to watch Mrs. Algemeine fall such a long way she never came up again. And it will be a big relief to the company bigwigs and some of our esteemed Federation Council members to have the Shongilis out of the way as well."

Guthe gave a low whistle, realizing that out of the mouths of grunts came good insight into bad motives. "But they won't make the injured people, young mamas, and little kids stay there, will they?"

"Not to worry. The injured ones probably won't survive the first week. There's a special island for orphans, where we can keep an eye on them. As for the young mamas . . ." He waggled his thin blond eyebrows in a suggestive way that made Guthe suddenly like him even less than he was originally inclined. "We can always find something useful for them to do."

RICK HAD ALERTED Yana as soon as he received the *Piaf*'s transmission on the copter's com. He fed it to the earphones she wore during the journey back to Kilcoole. Yana listened to each grim word but the burst was fairly brief. Within a few minutes the interference surrounding Petaybee from the volcanic activity scrambled the signal beyond all possibility of deciphering it.

Frag it all, the PTBs never stopped their harassment, did they? For a long period, Petaybee's autonomy had been respected and they had been allowed to guide Petaybee's affairs according to Federation guidelines. This was largely thanks to Marmie's influence. So when Marmie offended Cally by showing him up for the incompetent coward he was, the colonel had evidently interested some of her powerful enemies in trumped-up charges that would remove her and them from stewardship of the planet. By now it was well known that you couldn't take a Petaybean off Petaybee without killing them. That was no doubt fine with their enemies.

As she listened to the rest of the transmission, her teeth clenched angrily hearing the frightened, indignant questions of the young mothers and the crying of the children who sensed something was wrong. There were several bursts where the voice of First Officer Robineau asked after the comfort of her captors.

Later, as if accentuating the difference in priorities between the *Piaf*'s crew and their captors, Robineau's voice rose amid the wails of the children. She announced that the ship's cat, Zuzu, wanted to meet them. The wailing gradually turned to snuffles and then giggles and delighted squeals while the cat entertained the frightened kids. Meanwhile, Robineau talked in a low voice with the mothers. Her voice was lost in static before Yana could tell what she was saying, but she had heard enough.

It had been snowing heavily as the copter flew across the landscape, and Kilcoole was already thickly overlaid with drifts and folds of glistening snow by the time they landed.

Yana and Sinead stopped long enough to strap on snowshoes before hurrying to the village's small but modern hospital and clinic. There, Clodagh and her assistant, Deirdre, dispensed soothing teas and herbal remedies. From the time they first arrived, the facility's physicians had accepted the help of Petaybee's native healers. It was a direct conduit to the planet's own powerful healing properties. Though it had been mere hours since the injured were delivered, they seemed to have made considerable recovery already. However, everyone was perplexed by the *Piaf*'s sudden departure. They didn't know enough yet to be furious or frightened.

Yana hung her parka on the rack inside the hospital's mud room before going to find Clodagh to tell her about the transmission. She heard the mobile signal buzzing behind her but it wasn't until Sinead touched her on the shoulder that the nature of the sound actually registered.

"Yana, Sean just called. He and Ke-ola are back where we left them. Ke-ola took a spill before they could reach Murel so now Sean's got to go hunt for her again. Meanwhile, I called Perfect and they're sending out a snocle for Ke-ola and others to wait for Sean and the kids. I checked with Rick and Johnny, but the soldiers who took the *Piaf* emptied the fuel station before they left and we've not even enough to make a round-trip as far as the snowline in the copter."

"But there's enough to get me there, right?" Yana asked, pulling on her mukluks. "There was enough fuel left in the tank when we returned for that, at least."

"Yes, but how will you get the copter back?"

"We won't. We'll hide it when we go to ground ourselves, along with Clodagh and her patients and anyone else the PTBs are targeting with their witch hunt. I've warned Clodagh, and Deirdre has gone out into the village to organize the evacuation to the caves."

Sinead grinned wryly. "These pests must be new to our fair planet. They don't seem to have any idea what they're messing with when they mess with Petaybee. It will be interesting to see what happens if they try to take our people out of the caves."

"Let's hope it doesn't come to that," Yana said. "I just wish there was some way we could help the people on the *Piaf*. For now, I need to join Sean and the kids."

"I'm going to find Aisling," Sinead said. They both strapped their snowshoes on again. When they opened the clinic door, they were met by the rest of Kilcoole, people, track cats, dog teams, and curly coats, all laden with blankets and packs of provisions to sustain themselves and the hospital's staff and patients.

FROM WHAT THE seals had told him, Sean felt certain the kids were all right, or at least had been. The seals also claimed that the strange underwater city was not far. That was what he clung to as he battled the seas, though it could have been within a few lengths of him and he would not have known it. With the whales gone, the

seals saw no reason to stay close to the lagoon or to be overly helpful. They also had no reason to struggle with the water as he was
doing. The seas had roughened considerably since Ke-ola fell into
the water, and now the waves towered higher than the tallest icebergs and plummeted so low they threatened to sweep the seaweed
from the ocean floor.

Sean could hardly blame the seals. Though creatures would go
here and there for food, mating, giving birth, most of them most of
the time would quite literally "go with the flow." The ocean was bigger than all of them and had a mind of its own that seemed distinc-
tive even from the larger consciousness of the planet.

After Sean had been swimming what seemed an endless time,
he spun around on the crest of a wave to judge his distance from
shore. It looked as though he hadn't moved from the place where he
put in.

Mountainous waves tossed him back and forth while the field of
icebergs tumbled around him, threatening to grind him between
their jagged edges and battering him as they crashed past.

He tried to search for the kids using sonar, but the icebergs and
the violence of the waves created constant interference. He called
and called to them both with his seal voice and his thought-voice,
but he couldn't hear himself think, much less expect them to do so.

OF COURSE YOU *can go home,* Kushtaka assured the twins, *but you
can't go out in that.*

But we're not far from shore, Murel assured her, *and we're sea creatures. Or s'posed to be. We can swim in rough seas, right, Ro?*

It is awfully rough out there, sis, he replied dubiously. Kushtaka
had dissolved the walls of the sursurvu to ensure that all surveillance devices were in place and all of her people were safely back
inside the city. Kushtaka, the twins, Tikka and Sky, Mraka and Puk,
surveyed the fitful seas topside while all around them business
went on as calmly and matter-of-factly as usual.

But I didn't tell Mum and Da that I was coming here, Murel said. *They'll be so worried.*

Yes, but without justification at this point, whereas if you go out in that, all of their fears may be realized, Kushtaka told her.

Murel and Ronan stood there with the others watching as the waves scooped so low that the dome momentarily was all but exposed to the night sky. Kushtaka switched from one view to another, surveying the area where devices were recently planted, scrolling over the roaring seas.

The field of icebergs of which Murel's haven had been the handiest specimen now danced like oversized snowflakes on the pitching seas.

Kushtaka focused on that section, watching the icy structures crash together, spin apart, rise like white stars, and fall like comets.

And amid all of these was a lone seal, trying to swim but rolling over and over like a log.

Da! the twins cried together.

You can't be sure it is your father, Kushtaka said.

They were sure, however, and now that they could see him, they felt him calling them. Why else would he be out there? A regular seal would have had his herd and sense enough to be on land this close to shore.

Bring him in, Kushtaka. He'll get killed out there, Murel pleaded.

He's too far, she said. *The beam can't reach him.*

And so they watched him struggle, disappearing and reappearing until he finally failed to reappear at all.

They huddled together and Kushtaka watched them closely. If she still wanted revenge on them for Jeel, this was a good one.

But she looked as distressed as if seeing them lose sight of their father was like her losing Jeel all over again.

Kushtaka, let me, Mraka said, stepping in front of the leader and raising a paw. The scene shifted and she somehow caused it to pan back and forth, then shifted it again, panned again, a third time, the same procedure, calmly, as if it were a routine she performed every day. Then, *Ah, there he is. A bit the worse for wear but closer. I think we have him now. Puk?*

They looked around but Puk was no longer there, though they heard his thought, *I know.*

Da was still trying to swim but he could barely move and mostly just washed back and forth, up and down, with every massive movement of the sea. They felt him calling again, and they called back, *Hold on, Da. Help is coming. We're here. We're safe. It's okay.*

Da's head, which had been drooping wearily, lifted in alarm as the horizontal whirlpool beam drilled toward him. They saw his mouth open to bark before the beam grabbed him and pulled him down.

CHAPTER 27

THE COPTER WAS deserted when Yana reached it. Rick would be looking for Johnny and Pet, she thought. She wasn't sure whether she hoped they were with Marmie on the *Piaf* or would be relieved to find they were still assisting with the refugees.

The snow became a blizzard and then a whiteout, and she had to fly by instrument all the way to Perfect. Her gas gauge ran dangerously low by the time she judged herself close enough to safely set down. She kept transmitting that she was on her way but in return received only a signal as snowy as the weather.

She did manage to land the copter blade side up, however, which was no mean feat. She and the copter were encased within a directionless cocoon of white sky, snow-blanketed landscape, and, most dangerously, sheets and sheets of snow blown hard against her windshield.

She shouldered a survival pack of warm clothing, blankets, rations, and fuel and strapped on her snowshoes again. How was she going to find Perfect in this weather? She could walk in circles within a few feet of the copter and never know the difference.

Her good sense was still warring with her need to find Sean and the kids when a team of harnessed dogs punched through the whiteness. An ice-encrusted figure ran a mitten along the harness until she reached the copter, then peered up at Yana and beckoned.

Yana jerked open the copter's door and jumped the short distance into the snow piling up around it. Her snowshoes sank from the jump, but with the help of the newcomer, she pulled her feet up one by one onto the top layer of snow. Following her rescuer back to the sled, she allowed herself to be strapped in and driven a short distance to a place she could barely see until the newcomer opened the door to a small, blessedly warm cabin. Another parka-clad figure met them at the door, and a man yelled against the wind, following them inside, snow piling up behind them, "You warm up and make our guests comfortable, will you, Charlene, while I tend to the dogs?"

Yana's driver nodded exaggeratedly so the man could see the gesture even with the parka's hood up.

When the man had closed the door behind him, the woman's parka hood went back and a woman with icicles on her eyelashes, brows, and the fringe of hair around her face smiled a welcome. "Hi, Yana. It's me, Charlene. We met at your twins' last birthday latchkay, but I can't expect you to remember. You were that busy!"

Yana remembered her; Charlene Flood, before her recent marriage. Pretty woman, she showed her Eskimo/Tlingit heritage in her round face, high cheekbones, and almond eyes, but talked faster than an Irish fiddle tune. "Oh, sure. Charlene, hi. I don't think I'd have made it if you hadn't come to get me. Whew!"

"Winter isn't messing about this year, is it?" Charlene asked. "We saw you land. Fortunately, we hadn't unhitched the dogs yet from picking up the new lad Sean called about or I doubt I'd have still been able to spot you by the time I got there."

They peeled off mittens, hats, scarves, and coats and hung them on hooks inside the door.

"Did Sean come too?" Yana asked, doubting that could be so but hoping. "And how about my kids?"

"I'm afraid not. Cold as he was, it was all we could do to get the young lad to come with us. He's warming his nose over a cuppa now. You look like you could use one too."

Ke-ola sat at the family table near the stove. He wouldn't look up until Yana sat down opposite him.

"I'm sorry, missus—I mean, Colonel," he said miserably. "I was useless. I c-couldn't help anyone at all, not Murel or even Sean."

She took a deep breath of nonfrozen air fragrant with the balsam-scented warmth from the fire and said, as if she hadn't another care in the world, "Oh, yes. I know that feeling. They have a way of making you feel like a total waste of space sometimes, don't they?"

"Not you, surely, ma'am!" he said, his lashes dripping water from melted snow or maybe tears when he widened his eyes at her. He was such a big fellow it was hard to remember he was only a little older than Murel and Ronan.

"I'll tell you something, Ke-ola," she said. Charlene poured a cup of tea for both Yana and herself and sat down with them. A track cat slightly smaller than Nanook nudged her knee and curled up under the table, warming all of their feet with its tiger-sized body. "After all those years I spent in the Company Corps and all the action I saw, I never thought when I moved here and finally married I'd settle down to be not only the little woman but the little human in my family. Not that Sean and the kids aren't human too, at least most of the time when I'm with them, but you know what I mean."

She tried to sound reassuring while wondering how the evacuation was going. There was no sense mentioning the latest emergency until Charlene's husband returned anyway. The fact that Perfect Village had had no part in the relocation would not necessarily make them exempt from the scrutiny of the corrupt PTBs who had arrested Marmie and meant to arrest her own family and apparently most of Kilcoole besides. But even if a ship was landing at this very moment, it wasn't any more likely to be able to find the village in this blizzard than she would have been if Charlene hadn't fetched her.

As they sat and watched the snow pile up to the windowsill, then halfway up the pane, she felt the big Kanaka lad relax beside her.

She, on the other hand, grew increasingly tense and wondered all the while what she would do if her family didn't come back. Handle the crisis, certainly. Without Sean and the kids, she didn't care whether or not she died offworld, if she saved the world and her friends in the process.

If Johnny, Pet, and the warlike Raj had not been taken, she could put them to good use. Her skills might be a little rusty, but she thought with four of them they could hijack any ship sent to arrest more people. First they would set traps for the would-be arresting troops. Petaybeans were used to setting traps and, she thought, would make excellent guerrilla fighters—especially when aided and abetted by the planet. Then she, Johnny, Pet, and Raj should be able to hijack the invaders' ship. Once they were away from Petaybee's communication problems, it shouldn't take them long to find allies among the Federation to secure the release of Marmie and the *Piaf*'s human cargo.

The same allies could stop the invaders from harassing the Petaybeans, although she wondered who might be harassing whom by then. Maybe they could go into space and complete their mission in a short enough time that she wouldn't sicken and die. Other Petaybeans had done so in the past, but they were native born and she was not.

Clodagh said that wouldn't make any difference, but Yana thought that under the circumstances, it was worth the risk.

She wasn't sure she could bear to live on Petaybee without Sean and her kids anyway. Without them, it would be as cold and bleak as the snowstorm. She looked up at the window, expecting to see it completely covered. Instead she could see the sky again, still white but without snow blowing out of it. There was even a snowball of a sun.

The door banged and Charlene's husband called out, "Hey, look what I just found!"

Something wet and brown squirmed out of his arms and ran to Yana and back to the door again.

"It's Sky!" she cried, leaping up so fast her tea sloshed the table. "This is the kids' otter friend. They must be back."

"I had a feeling it was something like that," Charlene's husband said, and added to his wife, "I tried to unhitch the dogs and they started going nuts. Turns out this little guy was slogging through the drifts toward the house. I thought he was about frozen but he looks fine now."

"Hitch mine up too!" Charlene said. "We'll get Sean into one basket and the kids into the other."

"I'm coming," Yana said, even though she feared she might slow them down. "We have to take extra clothes and blankets too."

"I'll get the neighbors to bring their sled," Charlene said.

"I want to come," Ke-ola told them.

"Okay, I'll get two neighbors then," Charlene said.

"They won't be far," Ke-ola told Yana, his eyes shining now with joy. "I'll bet Sean's taken them to the new seal lagoon.

"The new *what?*" Yana asked.

WITH THE SKY clear, the temperature dropped sharply, so the new snow packed well. They took turns breaking trail and the horizon looked a long way away to Yana as they crested a hill she could have sworn was part of a snowy plain.

Sky jumped down from his perch on her shoulder and disappeared over the hill in his undulating run.

The sleds stopped. Ke-ola and Yana unstrapped themselves and she followed the boy. The lead dogs looked down their noses into a steamy lagoon where three seals swam in circles. The rescuers brought the clothing and blankets from the sleds and they all carried the supplies down the hill. Yana nodded to Charlene and she called the villagers to return to their sleds.

One by one the seals rose from the steaming water and shook themselves off, making the change which was by now as familiar to Yana as seeing them rising from their bedclothes in the morning or taking off their winter clothing when they came into the house. "Where have you lot been?" she asked as she hugged them. "Quite a lot has happened while you've been away."

CHAPTER 28

Back at Charlene's, everyone crowded around her tiny table, sitting on whatever could be used as a chair: upended logs, toolboxes, and a stool made from a single whale vertebra. The conversation was far from cheerful.

Their coats and pants hung steaming beside the stove, drying. Their boots were on the stone hearth and their mittens on a line Charlene had rigged around the chimney. Charlene and her husband, Dan, were outside unhitching and feeding their dogs and helping the neighbors with the other teams. It was snowing again, and through the cabin's window, already halfway snowed in, the people out there were hard to make out, little more than shadows moving clumsily within the heavily layered draperies of falling snow.

Mum tried the mobile but shook her head in frustration as she pocketed it again. "I hope Sinead and the others haven't started from Kilcoole to pick us up in *this*."

"If they have, they'll be grand, love, sure they will," Da reassured her. "A whiteout is no big thing to Sinead and her team, or the others, for that matter."

"Any more news about Madame's ship and the kids?" Ke-ola asked.

"What about them?" Murel and Ronan said, startled by the question and alarmed by the looks passing from Mum to Ke-ola and Da.

Mum swallowed a gulp of tea. "While we were out at the volcano and the copter with Rick, Johnny, and Pet, and Raj was coming back to help the uninjured survivors back to base, Marmie and her crew were arrested and the *Piaf* was impounded with all passengers aboard."

"They can't do that!" Murel exclaimed. "That's against Federation law."

"Which statute?" Ke-ola asked anxiously.

"I dunno! I can't remember everything," Murel said impatiently. "But it just is. It has to be."

"It's against common decency and common sense," Da agreed. "But that doesn't always have a great deal to do with the law."

Mum sighed. "We've had no luck trying to raise other ships or any of Marmie's allies because of the interference, but the crew was able to keep the channels open for us until the ship got out of range of the clear signals we *can* receive. It's looking pretty grim. They're apparently being hauled off—secretly from what we can tell—to Gwinett Incarceration Colony."

"On what charges?" Ronan demanded indignantly.

"Kidnapping the Kanakas and stealing the turtles and sharks."

"I wish we could give them the sharks back," Murel muttered. "In fact, I'd like to see the punters swim in and get them."

"Gwinett?" Ke-ola looked stricken. "That's a terrible place. They're taking the kids there too?"

Mum nodded. "From what I can gather. And you're right, Ke-ola: it's bloody brutal there. I hate to think of Marmie there, much less the kiddies. But we can't do a blessed thing about it, and furthermore, I'm afraid that's not all there is to it." She told them about the transmission she'd overheard.

Da grunted. "Arrest us all so they can take over Petaybee? Must be a new generation of bullies who haven't heard how well *that* works." He looked at the window. There wasn't much of it left uncovered by snow. "In fact, I'd say offhand that Petaybee may be taking evasive action right now."

"If only we could hail another ship," Mum said, "then Pet, Johnny, and Raj could hunt up some of the other powerful people in the Federation and even in Intergal—those who are friends of Marmie's and would put a stop to this nonsense soonest."

"Nonsense it is too, Mum," Murel agreed. "You said it was that Colonel Cally and his lot that brought charges. Mum, they were going to just abandon Ke-ola's people and not even check to see if they'd survived the meteors—just leave them there for more of the same. If we hadn't been there, they'd be starving while waiting for the next meteor shower to squash them."

Ke-ola said, "It's our fault you're all in trouble."

Da snorted. "Nonsense, lad. Petaybee would have been a giant strip mine and ourselves more or less slaves if Yana and Marmie hadn't drummed up influential people with consciences enough to prevent tossers like the one's Cally brought in from winning. Your folks are only an excuse for them to try their same old tricks again. But the fact is, they'll find it's very hard to invade us in the winter, and very hard to lay siege to people who are more or less under it two-thirds of the year anyway. We've not allowed them to map us completely, and Petaybee has very tricky terrain. Even if they did have a map, this world is capable of changing things around just to confuse them."

"But Breakup will come eventually," Murel argued. "And meanwhile, Marmie and the others will be in their awful prison. We have to do something."

"*Have* to," Ronan agreed.

"We will," Mum said. "But we must each do our part, and right now for you that means returning to the cave and staying where I can keep an eye on you."

"Oh, *Mum*," Murel and Ronan said together. As if they hadn't already been into space twice and solved all kinds of problems.

"Kids, there's nothing else you can do for now. Our communications are still inadequate to reach even as far as Marmie's spaceship. We'll just have to wait until one of our other friends arrives and get them to help Marmie and us. We've no other choice. With the *Piaf* gone, there's no craft to carry our message."

"There is one," Ronan said.

"OUT OF THE question," Mother said.

"Too dangerous," Father said. "From what you kids tell us, the deep sea other people are just this side of hostile, though they were perfectly pleasant to me when I came to get you. Perhaps we can persuade them to take *me*."

"You can't, Da," Murel told him. "You'd have to take human form to tell anybody about Marmie and you'd have to leave the city also. You know you wouldn't be able to live offworld for long, and there's no telling how long it would take."

"Don't tell me what I can and can't do, lass," Da said with uncharacteristic gruffness. But Murel knew he was only being gruff because he hated that what she said was true.

"I will go," Ke-ola said. "It's because of me Madame is in trouble, her trying to help my people."

"I don't think someone who's human all the time can live in their environment, Ke-ola," Da told him.

"The Honu should go, then. The children will be afraid. The Honu will calm them."

"We may never even see the children," Murel said. "All we have to do really is make sure Marmie's people know she needs all of her lawyers and every friend in high places she's got to get her and everyone else free and off our backs."

"None of you are going and that's final," Mum told them. "You twins are at the top of the Most Wanted list. If you stay here, they'll never find you and you can help the rest of us hide by keeping us informed of intelligence the animals might gather."

AWAKENING IN THE sulfur-smelling darkness, Murel knew she was not back in the cabin in Kilcoole. Then she remembered: they were in the communion cave where the village had taken refuge. The cave was too small for everyone to live in, but the white Nakatira cubes were invisible in the snow—and there was plenty of snow now.

Murel heard the waterfall outside the cave and, beyond it, voices: her mother's and others', not Da's.

It's Pet, Ro told her, reaching between their cots for her hand. *And Johnny and that Raj guy.*

What are they saying?

Dunno. Can't hear for the waterfall. Let's see what they're doing.

They crept out of their sleeping bags and over the bodies of other people and animals sleeping nearby, then walked down the path from the communion cave to the one under the waterfall, stopping just outside it.

"Let us handle it, Yana," Johnny was saying. "You stay here and take care of your family and the planet. It's my ship that was taken."

"And my boss," Pet said.

"And we'll be using my firepower," Raj said.

"Right. And it's my family and my home that's being threatened, folks. Besides, the Federation will want to talk to me. Better to do it offplanet where nobody else is going to be exposed."

Johnny laughed. "You just don't like hiding. What does Sean think of his co-governor as a hijacker anyway?"

"He doesn't know. And we haven't hijacked anything yet. They haven't sent the ship. Maybe they won't. Maybe Marmie's friends found out what they were up to and were all over them before they got her to Gwinett. If the next ship that comes is friendly, we can ask them nicely to help. If not, we go with my plan. Agreed?"

"Agreed," they said.

The twins crept back to their sleeping bags, where Sky slept between them. Murel stroked his fur and cried a little. Adventures away from home were one thing, but having to leave your home to hide because it was under attack was far more worrying. Mostly she was worried about Mum doing something foolish while forbidding everyone else to take action that she thought was foolish, even when she didn't understand what was involved.

She finally fell asleep, awakening only when Ronan shook her shoulder. Sky was gone, no doubt already fishing for breakfast. Outside the cavern, wan light glanced off the snow sifting into the sulfurous steam of the communion pool.

Murel and Ronan stripped down and dived in.

At the river, Aunt Sinead's partner, their Aunty Aisling, was standing guard. She looked very strange with a hunting rifle instead of a piece of needlework across her lap. She looked up when they swam past her.

"Where might you young rascals be off to this morning?" she asked. "Worrying your poor mum into a head full of gray hairs again, are you?"

They barked that the truth was just the opposite—it was Mum that was worrying them—but Aisling didn't speak seal; she just waved and they swam onward.

Along the way, they spoke to the animals they met on the riverbanks. They told them about the threat to Petaybee and asked them to let Da know about any strange ships in the sky, or any men on the ground, as soon as they saw such things or heard of them from others. All along the length of the river they spread the message.

When they reached the sea, they expected to be met by Sky's relatives and cousins. Instead they saw only Sky, climbing up an icy bank, searching the horizon, then sliding down and climbing up again.

Sky! Murel called.

Hah! There you are, river seals. Good. Sea otter cousins are coming.

Where have they been? Ronan asked.

You will see, Sky said.

And then they did see. Offshore, to the north and just beyond where the sea otter island had been, the water parted in a great whirling path that sucked it down then released it into a wave that swamped both the twins and Sky.

Sea otters began swimming ashore, and then, to the twins' amazement, they were followed by the larger variety of sea otters, the deep sea otters. Mraka, Puk, Kushtaka, and Tikka floated off-shore. Sky joyously dived in to join them.

Come, river seals, he called. *Otters know the wishes of relatives who are not otters. You wished to see the deep sea otters again. Sky otters cannot swim so far again so soon, but sea otter cousins can. Deep sea otters come to see you.*

The twins swam out to the big otters, who were being loaded down with gifts of clams, crabs, and shell-cracking rocks by their sea otter hosts.

Sky dived under Kushtaka and surfaced on her other side, where he took Tikka's paw and pulled her out of the water and over to his slide.

I didn't think you could put your bubble where there was no vol-canic vent, Murel said to Kushtaka.

For a short time we can, when we have gathered full power. There is no vent here, but also there are no sharks.

Before Murel could make another remark, Kushtaka said, *The ot-ters say that new trouble threatens our world. Why?*

Murel and Ronan began to explain. Despite the mistrust that had marked the beginning of their dealings, Kushtaka listened carefully to everything they said, asking questions when she didn't under-stand. When they finished, Murel and Ronan felt they finally had an adult ally who understood the entire problem and was willing and able to help solve it.

Tell Da that Kushtaka says we won't be long, Murel told a sea otter cousin.

And tell him to tell Mum not to do anything rash, Ronan added. Then, with Tikka and Sky sliding down the ice crust and jumping into the sea to join them, the twins followed Kushtaka, Mraka, and Puk back to their undersea bubble.

About the Authors

ANNE MCCAFFREY, the Hugo Award–winning author of the bestselling Dragonriders of Pern novels, is one of science fiction's most popular authors. She lives in a house of her own design, Dragonhold-Underhill, in County Wicklow, Ireland. Visit the author's website at www.annemccaffrey.net.

ELIZABETH ANN SCARBOROUGH, winner of the Nebula Award for her novel *The Healer's War,* is the author of numerous fantasy novels. She has co-authored nine other novels with Anne McCaffrey. She lives on the Olympic Peninsula in Washington State. Visit the author's website at www.eascarborough.com.

About the Type

This book was set in Fairfield, the first typeface from the hand of the distinguished American artist and engraver Rudolph Ruzicka (1883–1978). In its structure Fairfield displays the sober and sane qualities of the master craftsman whose talent has long been dedicated to clarity. It is this trait that accounts for the trim grace and vigor, the spirited design and sensitive balance, of this original typeface.